PATCHWORK
Bride
JILLIAN HART

Steeple
Hill®

Published by Steeple Hill Books™

STEEPLE HILL BOOKS

Steeple
Hill®

PLEASE RECYCLE
THIS PRODUCT IS RECYCLABLE

Recycling programs
for this product may
not exist in your area.

ISBN-13: 978-0-373-82841-8

PATCHWORK BRIDE

www.SteepleHill.com

Printed in U.S.A.

A man's heart plans his way,
but the Lord directs his steps.

—*Proverbs* 16:9

Chapter One

Angel Falls, Montana Territory, April 1884

Lord, what have I gotten myself into?

With the crisp April wind in her hair, Meredith Worthington braced her hands on her hips and glared at the mud-caked fender of their ladies' driving buggy. The vehicle was currently mired in the deep mud in the country road. Totally and impossibly stuck and she didn't know what to do. How would they get home from school?

This had never happened when she was at her finishing school back east. Then again, she never would have been allowed to drive a horse and buggy along the busy city streets. A lady was expected to be driven, not to do anything as garish as handle the reins herself.

"This is a fine mess I've gotten us into," she muttered, sloshing through the mud in her new shoes. "Me and my bright ideas."

"You wanted to drive." Her littlest sister rolled her eyes. "In fact, you insisted on it."

"Don't remind me." Not a request she'd regretted

because she'd been wanting permission to drive for a long while, but why did this happen on her first day? She stared at the axle nearly buried in mud. Who knew the mud puddle would be that deep?

"I bet you miss Boston now." Wilhelmina, Minnie for short, hopped in the shallow mud at the shoulder of the road, making little splashes with her good shoes.

"Miss that place? Hardly. Finishing school was like a very comfortable, very pleasant prison." Meredith puffed at a hunk of hair that had fallen down from her perfect chignon, but the stubborn curl tumbled right back into her eyes. Much better to be home in Montana, even if she had to figure a way out of the very mud her mother had warned her against.

She winced, already hearing the arguments. Her independent ways were not popular with her family. If she didn't get the buggy home and soon, she feared she would not be allowed to drive ever again. And if she couldn't drive, how would she secure employment and get herself to work every day? Her dreams may be as trapped as her buggy.

"A prison? I'm telling Mama you said that."

"You will do no such thing," she informed her sister, who squished around in the ankle-deep mud quite as if she liked it. "If you don't stop playing and help me, we will be stuck here forever."

"Or until it starts to rain." Minnie looked up from making shoe prints in the soupy earth. "It looks like a storm is coming. With enough rain, the mud will thin down and we can get the wheels out."

"Yes, that's exactly what I want to do. Stand here in the mud and rain for hours." She tugged affectionately on Minnie's sunbonnet brim. "Any excuse to stay out of doors, I suppose."

"What? I *like* outside. I don't know how I shall ever survive when Mama sends me away to school." The girl wrinkled her freckled nose at the thought of the expensive and well-respected finishing school where two of their other sisters were currently attending. "Was it really like a prison? Is that why you don't want to go back?"

"No, I just didn't like feeling as if I were a prized filly being prepared for a contest. Everyone was set on getting married, as if that is all a girl can do." Her parents said that an appropriate match was the most important thing a girl could accomplish, and sadly, her mother was bent on finding her a suitable husband.

Forget suitable and appropriate. She wanted true love in her life, the kind that surpassed reason, a riot in the heart and soul, an eternal flame of regard and feeling that outshone all else. *That* would not be easy to find.

The cool wind gusted, reminding her she was about as far away from her dream as a girl could get. She swiped the curl out of her eyes again. Those rain clouds definitely appeared foreboding. She may as well concentrate on the goals she could attain.

She braced her hands on the buggy's muddy wheel well, ignored the muck that squished between her fingers and called out for Sweetie to get up.

"We are never going to budge it. Our horse isn't strong enough. We ought to unhitch Sweetie and ride her home. We can get Papa and Eli, and they can come pull out the buggy." Minnie grinned, proud of herself for solving their problem.

"Do you want to give Mama heart failure?" The girl, she feared, was a lost cause. "Our mother would never recover if her very proper daughters rode the countryside perched on the back of a horse for all to see."

The old gray mare gave another valiant try. The wheels rocked just enough to give a girl hope, but they could not escape the bonds of mud. Exasperated, she blew the lock of hair out of her eyes again. "Minnie! Why aren't you helping? Do you want to stand here all afternoon?"

"Look, I made a smiling face." The girl grinned ear to ear, pleased with the imprint of eyes, nose and a curving mouth her shoes had made. "I don't recognize those horses. Do you reckon that's the new deputy? He looks in charge."

"What are you talking about?"

"The two horse and riders." Minnie pointed down the road.

Riders? Meredith peered over her shoulder, squinting through the weak shafts of disappearing sunlight. Sure enough, two riders ambled close on horseback, but her gaze found and stayed on only one of them. He wore a black Stetson, a black coat, denims and boots. Dark hair tumbled over his high forehead to frame blue eyes. Awareness crashed through her hard enough to wobble her knees. It was like she knew the man, as if she had known him somewhere before.

"Good afternoon, ladies." He tipped his hat, amusement curling up the corners of his mouth. "Looks like you have a problem."

A problem. Meredith opened her mouth, but nothing

happened. No words, not a sound, not even air. Her entire head had gone blank, as if she had forgotten every word in the entire English language. She straightened, the mud sucking at her shoes and clinging to her skirts, and swiped at that curl with one hand.

"Yeah, we're stuck!" Minnie spoke up.

"So I see," he drawled, just short of mocking, as he dismounted, his boots landing with a splatter in the shallow end of the mud hole. "April is going out like a lion. We've been battling hard rains all over the territory."

"Where you are from?" They weren't locals. Angel Falls was a small enough town that she would have seen him before. His was a face she would never forget. Was he passing through or had he come to work on the new railroad grade up north?

"I'm from Virginia." Blue eyes twinkled handsomely as he plunged closer, disregarding the mud sticking to his boots. He gestured to the much older man still mounted behind him. "Braden is from Texas."

"You're both far from home." A strange skitter of sensation traveled down her nape. One of warning, or of something else? It didn't feel comfortable and she took a step back. Something felt out of place. Should she refuse his help?

He stalked closer, impressively strong. Even wearing a coat, he gave an impression of power and confidence. There was no mistaking he was a man who worked hard for his living. He had an edge to him. It was in the day's growth shadowing his granite jaw and the sense of worldliness he carried easily on his wide shoulders.

"I'm Shane Connelly." He tipped his black hat,

revealing more of his face. What struck her most was the chiseled high cheekbones that gave him character. With his dark blue eyes, straight no-nonsense nose and hard slash of a mouth, he could have been a dime-book hero come to life. A down-on-his-luck man of principle who was capable of defeating any bad guy.

There she went, being far too fanciful again. The trouble was that she read too much. Was it her fault that men were better in books than in real life? He was obviously trouble on two feet, and she could well imagine what Mama would say if she were to learn she was accepting such a man's help.

"I'm Minnie." Her little sister spoke up, clearly interested by this turn of events. "Can you get our buggy out?"

"I plan to try." He swaggered over to inspect the front wheels and as he bent, his coat shifted, revealing an inlaid silver belt buckle and a gun.

She gulped. He was armed, a rarity for those riding these peaceful country roads. Proof the man was not as civilized as seemed.

"You managed to get the wheels wedged in good." He straightened, shooting her a breezy grin bracketed by dimples. "It might take some muscle to get this out. Good thing for you Braden and I came along."

"I suppose so." She took a step back, her pulse thudding in her ears as he approached. My, he was certainly tall and imposing. She bumped into the buggy's fender. She wasn't entirely sure she should let them stay. "Thank you for going to the trouble."

"Oh, we don't mind." He went toward her like a predator scenting prey, his Stetson slanted at a jaunty angle, his chiseled jaw rock-solid. He didn't blink. It didn't seem as if he breathed.

"But I do." If she was going to be a woman of independence, then she ought to solve the problem herself. After all, she intended to be driving her own buggy working for the Upriver School District this summer, God willing. She could not depend on a rider happening along to help her then, could she? No. Besides, she didn't like the look of these two strangers. With their trail dust and unshaven jaws, they could be anyone— drifters, thieves, escaped convicts from the territorial prison.

Fine, they did not look *that* disreputable, but there was something amiss about Shane Connelly. "I'm not used to being beholden to strangers."

"Then you might want to keep the buggy wheels up on the grass and out of the mud hole next time."

"And risk turning over in the ditch?" As if she hadn't thought of that for herself. She didn't remember asking for his advice or for the way he bent to inspect the rigging. "I know how to drive."

"I see that." A friendly smile flirted along with his dimples. A hint of kindness, not meant to make her feel chastised or defensive.

She wanted to be defensive for some peculiar reason. "For your information, my cousin was blinded and her parents killed when their buggy overturned. I was trying to be prudent."

"Then the mud was the right decision." Good humor beamed across his granite face, softening the lean planes and hard angles and turning his eyes an arresting midnight blue.

"You have a smear on your face."

"I do?" She gulped, watching as the distance between them began to vanish. He stopped a hand's breadth from her. My, but he was close. As he unfolded a clean handkerchief from his pocket, time screeched to a halt. Something deep within her shouted to turn and flee while she could, but she did not move as the piece of muslin brushed against her cheek.

Should it surprise her that his touch was gentle? She'd never been this close to a man her parents did not know. Her cheek tingled from the dab and scrape of the cloth. He folded his crisp white handkerchief and rubbed again at her cheekbone, close enough that she could smell the rain on his coat. Near enough that she could see the individual stubbles of his unshaven jaw and the threads of gold in his breath-stealing blue eyes.

Should she be noticing such things? Aloof, he tucked the handkerchief into his pocket and took several steps back. Now that he was not so near, the breathless feeling should go away, shouldn't it? Oughtn't her pulse rate return to normal?

"I had best see to your buggy, miss. You need me to carry you over to the grass?" His baritone held a smiling quality as he took another step back, his gaze never leaving her face.

An odd feeling, being peered at like that, as if she were something worthy to be looked at. Vaguely she remembered the buggy and her little sister somewhere nearby watching, cleared her throat and tried to do the same with her cluttered mind. "No, I'm not afraid of a little mud."

"A little? You look like you were in a rolling contest with a pig and won. No offense, miss."

"None taken." Why was she laughing? She looked down helplessly at the drying mud on her light yellow silk overskirt. Mama would definitely get the vapors when she saw this. "I feel as if I should lend a hand. At this point, I cannot get any muddier."

"Don't be too sure." He knuckled back his hat, revealing dark brown hair that was thick, untamed and a little too long for decent fashion. "I was wrong about you. At first look I mistook you for a vain, helpless miss, but you are clearly a country girl."

"Surely I am at heart." There was no way he could know how wrong he was. She worried that no matter how hard she tried to be otherwise, she would always be Robert and Henrietta Worthington's daughter, expected one day to be the perfect wife living an impeccable life of giving parties, raising well-mannered children and upholding the family's fine reputation. She feared her dreams of teaching children would never be realized.

"It'll only take a moment to hitch up." He whistled to his horse.

The wind gusted, batting the troubling lock of hair back into her eyes. She swiped at it, wondering how she must look standing in the mud with her hair a tumble and her skirts spattered enough to hide the intricate shirring and stitching and expensive satin hem. Easy to see how he could mistake her for a country girl, which she truly longed to be. Her friends, Fiona, Earlee and Kate, were country girls and some of the best friends a girl could have. She wanted nothing more than to be like them.

The spotted bay gelding trotted obediently forward, nose outstretched, nickering low in his throat in answer to his master. Shane took a moment to stroke his horse's nose, and Meredith remembered his gentle touch. Another shiver slid down her spine imagining being taken up in his arms. If a girl were to lay her cheek against his broad chest, she might feel safe and sheltered. Maybe even treasured.

There she went, spinning daydreams again.

"Are you coming, Braden?" Shane knelt to squint at the buggy's rigging, his horse nibbling at his hat brim.

The other man didn't answer, only nudged his big black horse forward. This one appeared much older, his face weathered and not a hint of softness on his features. When he rode by Meredith, it was like an arctic wind blowing by, cold and impersonal. Definitely not a friendly man.

The first drops of rain pelted from the sky. They struck the ground like wet bullets, tapped on her bonnet and *plinked* in the enormous puddle at her feet. The prairie stretched around them to the horizon without more than a single barn in sight, one big curtain of rain. With no one else on the road, she suddenly felt vulnerable. A small hand crept into hers—Minnie's.

"Do you reckon they are outlaws?" Her littlest sister's whisper was incredulous, and her big blue eyes widened with excitement.

It was hard to tell the manner of man Shane Connelly was, and even harder to guess at the older man who was hitching the two horses alongside their gray mare. But Shane must have heard Minnie's whisper, for he glanced over the wheel well and let his eyes twinkle at her. Humor danced in those dark blue depths and told her all she needed to know about the man.

"No, I reckon he's a never-do-well with an appalling reputation," Meredith answered wryly.

"True." Shane's gravelly tone deepened as he chuckled. "I am one sorry renegade."

"Are you like Robin Hood?" Minnie boldly asked. "Do you help those down on their luck?"

"I have been known to aid a lovely country miss or two, if the peril is great." When Shane rubbed a hand over his gelding's muzzle, a softness came over him.

A kind man, then. Hard not to like that.

"You've got a pretty horse," Minnie spoke up. "What's his name?"

"This is Hobo. He's an—"

"Appaloosa." The single word tumbled across Meredith's tongue. "He's beautiful."

"You know of the breed?"

"My father has a fondness for Western lore," she answered, her face heating. Was she really blushing? "Perhaps I do, too."

"Perhaps?" He questioned, his dimples deepening.

"Fine. I love everything Western, but it's not ladylike to admit it and my mother would have an apoplexy if she heard me say it."

"Then it's best not to tell her." He winked, and opened his mouth about to say something else when the other man hollered out to him.

"That's enough, Romeo. I've got the horses hitched. Time to push."

"Gotta go." Shane waded to the buggy box and

positioned his hands on one side of the soiled fender. "You two ladies might want to hop onto the grass."

"I told you. I intend to help." She mimicked his stance on the other side of the buggy by bracing her feet and placing her hands. "If this happens again, I want to know what to do."

"I really don't think—" His argument was cut off as a "Git up!" from Braden rang from the front of the buggy.

Horse hooves clamored on sodden, wet earth. The vehicle rocked forward and then back. Another "Git up!" and the buggy rolled forward again. The mud gripped the wheels, refusing to let go.

A little help please, Lord. She prayed and pushed with all her might, fearing there was no way the vehicle would move. She fought visions of their little driving buggy stuck here in the middle of the main road to town for the rest of the rainy season. Folks would have to somehow maneuver around it, muttering about that Worthington girl who had the poor sense to have dropped out of finishing school.

"Harder!" Braden shouted as he tromped through the mud and grabbed the bumper nearest to her. Even Minnie took a position and pushed. The buggy rocked again, almost out, before it sloshed back into the muck.

She hardly noticed because what was she watching? Shane. Out of the corner of her eye, his grimace fascinated her. All her friends, except for Fiona who was engaged, agreed no man ever had been as handsome as Lorenzo, the most gorgeous boy in their class at school. But now she begged to differ. Shane Connelly was stunning, but something beyond his physical good looks made him captivating—some strength of spirit, she suspected, and a steadfast character, she hoped.

The buggy lunged forward, suddenly rolling up out of the muck. Mud flew off the fast-turning wheels and sprayed like slop across her face, cold and wet. Too late, she realized she was the only one standing directly behind one of the wheel wells. Ooze clung to her eyelids and dripped like thick cream frosting down her face. The earthy taste seeped between her lips. The cold weight pressed on her, penetrating her bodice and weighing down her skirt.

"Oh, Meredith," Minnie soothed, shocked. "Your dress is ruined."

Humiliation seeped into her, as cold as the mud. She swiped the yuck from her eyes with her sleeve and only managed to smear it.

"Whoa!" Shane and Braden shouted together from a fair distance away, stopping the horses on the uphill slope of the road. When young Mr. Connelly turned around and spotted her, a wide grin stretched his mouth and he shook his head slowly from side to side. "Something tells me you are a whole peck of trouble, Miss Meredith."

"She is," Minnie spoke up, sounding pleased as punch. "It's her first time driving the buggy alone."

"Minnie, don't tell him that." Really, she looked bad enough without adding "idiotic, inexperienced driver" to the list. That was what she felt like. Out of her element, when she wanted to fit in so badly. Too badly—maybe that was what the Lord was trying to tell her.

"You are a right mess." Shane pulled out the

handkerchief again and wiped the white surface across her eyes. This close, she could see there were green threads, too, in his deep blue irises, to match the gold ones, and something noble within.

There she went, being fanciful again.

"The good news is that your horse and buggy are fine, aside from the mud." He folded the cloth to scrub at her nose and cheeks. His nearness was a funnel cloud, pulling her helplessly toward him. "You, miss, I'm not so sure about. Maybe Braden and I had best see you home."

"No!" That came out a mite defensive, but she could imagine Mama's reaction. "Please, if our mother knew there was a mishap, she wouldn't let me drive again. It's imperative for me to become a better driver."

"You don't sound like a country miss to me." His gaze narrowed, his presence and his sculpted features steeled. "Who are you?"

"Just Meredith." That was who she wanted to be. She needed to be herself, not her father's daughter, not her mother's achievement, but someone real. This man, who rode where he wanted and who did as he liked, would never understand.

"All right, then, Just Meredith." His grin returned, crooked and dimpled. "Let's get you in the buggy and on your way home."

Chapter Two

Just Meredith was beautiful, no doubt about it. Shane glanced over his shoulder to make sure the gray mare pulling the buggy was managing all right. The spring storms had turned the roads to every kind of muck, although judging by the downpour it was hard to call this brand of cold spring.

"Stopping to help those girls made us late for our next job," Braden commented drily as he tucked the much-folded telegram for the riding directions back into his slicker's pocket.

"Helping them was the right thing to do." It wasn't something they hadn't done before in their travels. "We couldn't leave them there."

"I'm not arguin' that. Truth is, this new stint has me worried. Heard the wife is a whole peck of trouble."

"Wife? I thought that we were working for a mister, not a missus."

"Shows what you know about marriage." Braden cracked a rare smile. "I say we give it a trial before we commit. I don't want to get knee-deep into a job, figure out it's more trouble than it's worth and then tear myself up trying to figure if I should run for my sanity or stay and finish the job the right way."

"I see your point." Shane was new at this. Not green, but not experienced either. He'd only had a year of apprenticeship under his belt since he'd hooked up with the best horseman this side of the Mississippi. He'd left everything behind in Virginia—family, reputation, duty—to learn horsemanship the real way. It had been the roughest year of his life and the best one. Finishing his apprenticeship was all that mattered. So why was he thinking about the woman and not the upcoming job?

Another glance over his shoulder told him why. There was something special about her, something extra—like a dash of both sweetness and spirit not often seen. "Just Meredith," she'd called herself in a dulcet voice that made him think of Sunday-school hymns and Christmas carols. And pretty? She put the word to shame with those blond ringlets tumbling down from beneath her plain brown hood and eyes the color of the sea in the rain. She was a rare beauty with creamy skin, delicately cut features and a mouth made for smiling.

He liked country girls the best, he'd learned long ago, not missing the perfectly mannered and prepared debutantes who were part of his world back home. It heartened him to see honesty and goodness in a female. It was far preferable in his opinion to the veils of pretense that filled his growing-up years.

Out west, things were more likely to be what they seemed and the people, too. He liked the image of Just Meredith in her simple but elegant brown coat, pretty yellow dress and sincerity. She made quite a picture holding the reins as the chilly weather battered and blew. With the smears of green in the nearby fields and the world of colors blurred and muted by the rain, she could have been the focus of an impressionist watercolor. A prized painting meant to be cherished.

"You're watching me," she called out above the twists and gusts of the wind. "You think I'm a bad driver and I'm going to get stuck in the mud again."

"No, but I *am* keeping track of the mud holes. I don't see a thing you can get mired down in, at least not yet." He let Hobo fall back alongside the buggy. "You're doing pretty good for it being your first day driving."

"You may be fibbing." The look she threw him from beneath her brown hood was a challenge.

He laughed. He liked the dazzle in those interesting gray-blue eyes. "I'm trying to be encouraging. Keep to the positive. Avoid the fact we nearly had to go in search of a pair of oxen to free your buggy."

"Thanks for not mentioning it." When she grinned, she was like a sunbeam on this dismal day.

"You still don't figure on letting your mama know about this?" He couldn't resist asking, not that it was his business.

"What she doesn't ask about, I won't have to tell her."

"And what if she notices the mud?"

"That's the flaw in my plan. I'm hoping Mama doesn't notice. She could be busy and not even hear us driving up."

"She will be watching, Meredith." The little girl wrinkled her nose. "Nothing gets past Mama. You ought to know that by now."

"That won't stop me from trying." She laughed. At heart she was not a deceitful daughter but one apparently amused by her mother. "If Mama revokes my driving privileges, then I won't learn enough about driving to make it on my own come June."

"Why June?" Call him curious. He couldn't help it. Something tickled in his chest like a cough, but maybe it was interest.

"That's when the summer school term begins." A ringlet bounced down from beneath her hood to spring against her cheek. "I'm studying for the teachers' exams. If I pass, I hope to get one of the smaller county schools just north of here."

"A schoolteacher." A fine ambition. He couldn't say why that pleased him either. He wasn't looking to settle down, not with his long apprenticeship hardly more than half over.

"But Mama doesn't know," the little girl added impishly. She was a bit of trouble, that one. "And no, Meredith, I won't tell on you, but it's likely to kill me."

"I wish you had never overheard me talking with my friends. You can't keep a secret to save your life." Meredith wrapped an arm around her sister's neck and hugged her close, an affectionate gesture. "I'll never forgive you if you blurt it out and ruin my plans."

"It won't be easy." The girl rolled her eyes and huffed out a sigh, as if her life were truly trying indeed.

"It seems you keep a lot of secrets. The mud incident, the teacher's exams." He swiped rain from his eyes. "It won't be as easy to hide an entire job when summer comes."

"Oh, I know. I don't want to deceive Mama. That's not what I mean to do. I want my own life is all."

"I've known that feeling."

"How can you? You're a *man*."

"True enough, but why do you say it like that? Like being a man is a bad thing."

"Not bad, exactly. I'm just exasperated." She blew the curl out of her face, but it just sprang back. Did she dare take both hands off the reins? No. Sweetie was as gentle as a horse could be, but doom had a tendency to follow her around. She had no intention of letting anything else go wrong.

"Meredith often gets exasperated," Minnie explained with a little girl's seriousness. "Mama says it's because nothing is quite to Meredith's liking."

"That's not true," she hotly denied, as she always did. "Okay, so maybe it's true sometimes. It's just that boys have it easier. They can do what they want."

"That depends." Shane's voice dipped low, butter-smooth and warm with amusement. "My mother thought I should join my father in business and one day follow in his footsteps. Carry on the family legacy."

"Drifting from town to town?" The quip escaped before she could stop it. What was wrong with her?

"I wasn't always a saddle tramp." Those crinkles around his eyes deepened, drew her closer and made her want to know more.

She shouldn't be curious, not one bit, not one iota. The dashing, mysterious, slightly dangerous young man was not her concern. Although it was easy to imagine him lassoing wild horses, fighting to defend the innocent or performing some noble act. Beneath the stubbled jaw and traveling coat, he might be full of honor, a real-life hero with the rain washing away the mud on his boots.

She tried to imagine what her best friends would say. Earlee, the most imaginative of the group, would pen him as an intriguing hero of a fantastic tale. Lila, ever the romantic, would compare him to the most handsome boy in their high-school class, Lorenzo. Kate and Scarlet would heartily agree and start dropping hints about the status of their hope chests, the reason they met every Saturday afternoon to sew for a few hours. A sewing circle of friendship and of hope, they tatted doilies, embroidered pillowslips and pieced patchwork blocks for the marriages they would all have one day.

Yes, this chance meeting was going to be a huge topic of conversation come Saturday.

The rain turned colder, falling like ice, striking the great expanse of prairie with strange musical notes. Beauty surrounded her, but she could not take her eyes from the handsome wanderer.

"What did you do in your former life?" Was that really her voice, all breathless and rushed sounding? Her face felt hot. Was she blushing? Would he notice?

"Back home, my father and grandfather are lawyers, although now they have many partners to manage the firm." He let his horse fall back, to keep pace beside her. "As the oldest son, I am a great disappointment traveling around on the back of a horse."

"I think it takes courage to follow your own path." Courage was what she was trying to find for herself.

"Could be courage. My father called it stupidity.

My mother said it was stubbornness. She was none too happy with me when I left, since she was in the middle of planning my wedding to a young lady of their choosing."

"You ran out on a wedding?"

"I never proposed, so I didn't see as I had an obligation to stay for the ceremony." Dimples belied the layer of sorrow darkening his voice.

"Your parents had your whole life mapped out for you?"

"Mapped out, stamped and all but signed and sealed." Understanding layered the blues in his eyes and softened the rugged, wild look of him. "Something tells me your parents adore you. They want the best for you, and that's not a bad thing, as long as it's what you want, too."

"Tell that to Mama."

"Sounds like our mothers are cut from the same cloth."

The howl of wind silenced and the veil of rain seemed to vanish as he leaned over in his saddle, close and closer still. The sense of peril returned, fluttering in her stomach, galloping in her veins and did she turn away?

Not a chance.

"No one I know has a mother like mine." Strange they would have this similarity between them. "Is yours overbearing, impossible, full of dire warnings and yet she'd throw herself in front of a train to save you?" she asked.

"Yep."

"Does she drive you beyond all patience with her

meddling and fussing and trying to do everything so your life is easier?"

"That would be an affirmative."

"And you love her so much you can't bear to say no and disappoint her?"

"In the end, I did say no and it broke her heart." No way to miss the regret. It moved through him, deep like a river, reflecting on his face, changing the air around them. "It was hard for her to let go, but I wouldn't be the man I wanted to be unless I made my own life. She'll come to see that in the end."

"So she hasn't forgiven you?"

"Nope. Not yet. But I'm confident she will come to see I was right."

"That wasn't the answer I was hoping for." If only following her own path would not potentially cost her her mother. "I'm praying my experience will be different from yours."

"Your mother doesn't want you to be a teacher?"

"She doesn't want her daughters to work." She hadn't corrected his misimpression of her as a simple country girl, so how did she explain her mama's view of society and a woman's role in it? "My only hope is that Papa will understand."

"Then I'll pray for that, too." Serious, his words, and so intimate that it was as if they were the only two people on the entire expanse of the plains. Completely odd, as she'd never felt this way with anyone before. It was as if he'd reached out and taken her hand, although they did not touch. A tug of warmth curled through her, which was sweet like melting taffy and enduring in the way of a good friendship.

"Meredith!" She felt a tug on her sleeve. "Don't forget to turn."

She blinked, the feeling disappeared and the world surrounding her returned. Wet droplets tapped her face, the jingle of the harness and the splash of the horse's hooves reminded her that Minnie was at her side, home was within reach and the time to say goodbye to this man had come.

"Is this your driveway?" Shane broke the silence between them, one brow arched with his question.

Did he feel this way, too? As if he did not want the moment to end?

"Yes." The word rasped past the regret building within her. She drew Sweetie to a stop, knowing he would go his way, she would go hers and she would never see him again. Her spirit ached at the thought. "Where are you headed?"

"To a ranch somewhere in these parts." He knocked off the rainwater gathering on the brim of his hat. "Since we're running late, we might as well see you to your door. Braden, is that okay with you?"

"Goin' this way anyway," came the answer as the older, gruff man pulled his mount to the roadside and consulted the telegram in his pocket.

"Guess that means we don't have far to go." He shivered when the wind lifted, knifing through his wool coat. Nearly wet to the bone, he ought to be eager to get into dry clothes and thaw out in front of a fire. Gazing down at Just Meredith, he wasn't in much of a hurry. "You ladies must be freezing. The temperature is falling. I could dig a blanket out of my saddle roll. Might keep you warmer."

"That's very gentlemanly of you, but we'll be fine."

"Meredith!" Minnie protested. "I'm cold. Look. It's starting to *snow*."

"No wonder I'm half an icicle." Nothing like a joke to warm a fellow. He twisted in his saddle to tug on the ties and pulled a folded length of red wool from beneath the oiled tarp protecting his things. "This ought to keep you two ladies a little more comfortable."

"Thank you, Shane."

He liked the way she said his name with a touch of warmth—unless he was imagining that—and a bit of respect, which he didn't mind at all. He gave the blanket a snap, settled it over the ladies' skirts, nearly falling out of his saddle to hand over the edge to Meredith so she could tuck it around her and Minnie. Leaning close, an odd sense of warm curled around his ribs, something tender and fine like first light on a spring morning.

Once she had the blanket settled, she gathered the reins in her slender, smooth hands. In retrospect, maybe he would have thought about that more and realized it was a sign. That a country girl's hands wouldn't look soft and pampered instead of callused and rough from work. But the bit of warm felt cozy in his chest, a nice and wholesome thing, so he didn't think too much as he followed the buggy off the main road and down a narrower drive curving between a copse and tall fencing.

Braden signaled him. "I don't want you gettin' too friendly with any of the neighbors."

"Are you tellin' me you want me to be rude?" He

angled his brim against the driving snow tapping against his hat and stinging like icy needles on his jaw.

"Not rude, no. But I want your mind on horse business."

"It will be." The chance to keep learning at Braden's heels was all he wanted. So why did his gaze stray to the buggy? Although he couldn't see Meredith from this angle, he wanted to, as surely as he sat in the saddle. That could *not* be a good thing.

"I know how it is. It's only natural to take interest in a pretty gal. But remember, we move on. Our commission here is only two months at the most."

"I know that." He knew what was important and why he was here. He had learned a lot, and on this assignment he would have more responsibility and a real opportunity to use what he had been taught. "I know what you're asking, Braden, and you can count on me. I'm not going to leave you with all the work while I chase after a pretty calico. I'm not that kind of man."

"I'm still waiting to see the brand of man you are." Braden, tough for his years, iron-strong and jaded, had a look that could pare like the sharpest blade. "You have potential, Shane, but you're a blue blood. I'm waiting to see which wins out."

"I'm not playing at this. I'm here to work." He still had a point to prove. Right now his work was the only importance in his life. He squared his shoulders and did not flinch when arctic blew in on the wind. The curtain of snow thickened, obscuring Meredith's driving buggy and the rest of the world from sight.

* * *

Home was nothing more than a hint of a roofline and a glint of windows through the whiteout. The weather could often be a surprise in Montana Territory and she liked that about this part of the country. Here, you could build a fence, but you couldn't fence in the prairie. The adventurous part of her, the one Mama did her best to lecture right out of her, thrilled in the feel of the icy wind and violent snow.

"Uh-oh." Minnie stood up, gripping the dashboard, to squint in the direction of the front porch. "That's Mama. Do you think she will notice the mud?"

"How could she not?" Meredith drew poor snow-covered Sweetie to a stop and set the brake. Beneath the blanket, the mud thick on her coat and skirt had frozen, crackling as she moved. The good news was that snow had iced over it, so it was almost impossible to see the dried brown beneath.

Please, Lord, let Mama be understanding. She laid the reins over the snowy dash and squinted into the white haze. She saw nothing but shadows and no sign of handsome Mr. Connelly.

"Allow me." His voice rolled through the storm. A gloved hand caught hers, and in the thick of the storm she could make out the cut of his wide shoulders and the hint of his square jaw.

When her hand settled against his broad palm and she felt the power there, awe thrilled her. He was a perilous man because he made her feel both safe and in jeopardy in the same breath. Simply allowing him to help her from the buggy was like taking a grand adventure. For a moment she floated, caught in midair as if defying gravity before she flew downward and her shoes touched solid ground. The veil of snow had thickened, obscuring him completely, and when his hand released hers she felt alone.

"Girls!" Mama's shrill voice dwarfed the howling late-spring storm. She barreled into sight, well-wrapped against the cold, marching down the walkway like a general at battle. "I have been worried sick! Where have you been? And who are these *people?*"

Although it was hard to tell in the snowfall, Meredith could well imagine Mama's curled lip. Mama did not approve of strangers, particularly strange men who were not in the same social class. Meredith winced, picking her way through the ice toward the lee of the house, where the snowfall thinned.

"We wanted to make sure your daughters arrived home safely." Shane Connelly appeared, dappled with snow, safely seeing Minnie onto the pathway. He faced Henrietta Worthington as if he were not intimidated by four-star generals. "The storm has turned treacherous."

"Indeed!" Mama disregarded him with a turn of her shoulder and hugged Minnie against her. "I have been half ill with worry. Where have you been?"

And today had started out so well, she thought. "We had a bit of trouble with the mud."

"Did I not warn you? Don't think I didn't notice the mud caked all the way up to the dash, young lady. I knew it was a mistake to let you drive." Mama grabbed Minnie protectively and pointed her toward the steps and the front door with a motherly push. "I suppose I owe these people some sort of thanks for seeing you home."

How embarrassing. Meredith's face burned. It was not respectful to correct her mother, but the argument sat on her tongue. A muscle ticked in Shane's jaw, and she felt his muscles bunch in his arm. Tension. Maybe a sign of hurt.

"I'm sorry," she said quietly but he seemed so far away. Maybe it was the snow's veil putting distance between them, but probably not. Mama's opinion of him had altered everything. The closeness and the taffy-sweetness within her had died. Was there any way to repair it? "I am grateful for your assistance, Mr. Connelly."

"It was nothing."

"It was gallant. And muddy."

"In truth, I did not mind the mud." Any hint of a smile was gone. His striking blue eyes had shielded, his handsome face as set as stone.

Of course he would be unhappy with the way Mama treated him. Who wouldn't be? Anyone would be offended. Meredith ached to set things right, but how could she? She would have to speak to her mother later for all the good it would do, and that wouldn't mend things at this moment. She longed to say something to Shane, but he stepped quickly, deliberately away. His unflinching gaze hardened.

This was why she wanted to be her own woman and not her mother's daughter. She wanted to stand tall for what she believed in without apology. She loved her family, but she was embarrassed by them, too.

"I can have Cook reheat some stew," Mama

announced in her superior way, thinking she had been so kind to the rough-looking men. "You may circle around to the back door. Take off your wraps and boots first. Be mindful of your manners. I'll expect you to keep your hands to yourself, no pilfering the silver, and you must leave as soon as you are finished eating."

Meredith watched another muscle jump along Shane's clenched jaw. If only she could melt into the snow and disappear. She couldn't believe Mama had said such a thing. Whether these men were down on their luck or simply passing through, they did not deserve to be spoken down to. "Mama, you must mean to say how happy you are that these fine men offered to help Minnie and me. It probably inconvenienced them and since it's nearly dark, perhaps they would like to join us for dinner—"

"That is not what I meant!" Mama gripped her shoulder and firmly guided her up the steps. "What has come over you, Meredith? In the house, now, and start your homework. I'll deal with you later."

"But, Mama—"

"And change that dress. I want this understood. You will never ask to drive that buggy again." Her mother drew herself up full height, not in an understanding mood. "Now, inside before you catch your death of cold. I must have a few words with these people."

"I'm sorry." It was all Meredith could offer Shane. She watched a hint of understanding soften his iron gaze before she stumbled over the threshold and into the warmth of the house. The door slammed shut behind her and she felt Minnie's hand curl into hers.

"It's too bad we'll never see them again." She sighed. "But wasn't it something to see his Appaloosa?"

Chapter Three

Shane swiped snow from his face, ignoring the icy pinpricks against his skin and the letdown within. He might have known. Just Meredith, as she'd claimed, was a far sight more. This was the Worthington estate and although he couldn't see more than a hint of a roofline, the long stretch of lamplight windows gleaming through the storm suggested not a simple house but a dignified manor. Meredith was no country miss.

"I'm Mr. Shaw," Braden attempted to explain to the dismissive Mrs. Worthington. "I'm the horse trainer."

"The man my husband hired?" The woman drew her chin up and looked down her nose at the rough and ready pair. "And the one who gave my daughter special attention? Is that your assistant?"

If looks could maim, he would be in need of a pair of crutches. Shane stepped forward. He was no longer Aaron Connelly's grandson, not in these parts. He was a horseman and proud of it. "Yes, ma'am. I'm Shane Connelly."

"You were being awfully forward with my daughter." Mrs. Worthington barreled fearlessly farther into the snowfall to meet him, her apple-cheeks pinched severely and her gaze hard with accusation. "Tell me I am wrong."

"I was helping her out of the buggy and through the storm. That was all."

"And that's the way it will stay if you wish to work here. Do we have an understanding?"

He held his ground, fighting down the urge to argue and correct her misimpression. He may have been enjoying the pretty miss's company, but that was all. If he felt anything more, then he refused to admit it. It stung to be reprimanded when he'd done nothing wrong, and he couldn't explain the tightness within his chest. Nor could he remember being offended by a woman so quickly. He wanted the job here and he did not wish to disrespect a lady. He was not raised that way, so he did not argue with her. "Yes, ma'am."

"Fine. Mr. Shaw? If you two will take the mare and buggy to the stables, you'll find Eli waiting. He'll show you around, get you acquainted with our expectations before he leaves us for good at the end of the day. I'll tell Cook to keep the stew warm for when you're ready. Use the back door only."

"Yes, ma'am."

Although Shane couldn't see Braden's expression, he could sense a wariness. The hardest part of their job wasn't the horses but the people who owned them. He swiped snow from the old mare's forelock, taking care to keep the cold wet from falling into her eyes. She was a sweet thing, watching him patiently with a liquid brown gaze and a quiet plea.

"You did a fine job today," he assured her as he took hold of her bridle. It was the mare that had fooled him into believing Meredith's pretense. This was no fine pedigreed animal, but an elderly mare with a slightly swayed back. Strange that she was the driving horse of choice for the Worthington girls and not some fancy pony.

His nape prickled as if Meredith Worthington was watching him from one of those dozen windows. He studied what he could of each glowing pane but caught no sight of blond curls or her big gray-blue eyes. Probably just his imagination or the wish that people—especially women—could be what they seemed at first sight. That was why he wanted to spend his life training horses. A horse didn't put on airs, put you down or figure they were better than you because of the quality of their possessions.

"I plan to tell Worthington I want a trial period." Braden fell alongside, leading both horses by the reins. "I'm not sure about that woman."

"She was protecting her daughters." Akin to the way a mother bear defended her cubs.

"Sure." Braden nodded, his jaw tense. "But one thing needs to be made clear to Robert Worthington. I came to work with the animals, not to be nitpicked to death by a lady who has nothing better to do with her time."

"You're still ticked from our last job."

"True enough. After those difficult people, we deserve an easier assignment." Braden shook his head and rolled his eyes. "Not sure if we're going to get it this time."

"No, I don't think we are."

Lord, please let this work out.

The first outbuilding they came to was a well-built barn with a wide breezeway marching between big box stalls. Several horses poked their noses out into the aisle to nicker a welcome to an old friend and to greet new ones. Hobo sidestepped, head up, cautious as he looked around.

"Whoa there, buddy." He left the old mare standing to lay a hand of comfort on his boy's neck. Snow tumbled from his black mane.

Best to get these horses rubbed down, dry and stabled and no sense in hurrying. His stomach might be rumbling, but he wasn't looking forward to heading up to the main house to eat. Meredith would be there. That made his gut clench tighter.

Maybe it would be best to avoid her, he decided, if that could be possible as long as he had a job here. That young woman had as good as lied to him. He'd had enough people in his life being less than honest, and he wasn't looking for more of the same.

"Ho there." A man about his same age with a friendly grin and a trustworthy look hiked down the main aisle. "I'm Eli Sims. You must be the new trainers. Good to meet you. Let me lend a hand with your horses."

Braden stepped forward to ask a few details about Mr. Worthington, as Shane knelt to uncinch saddles and unhook harnessing. He kept half an ear to their conversation but couldn't seem to concentrate. At least he hadn't been fooled by her for long. Not that the not-so-country girl was on his mind. He was doing his best to purge every thought and image of her from his brain.

Whether or not he was successful was another question entirely.

Meredith couldn't forget the look on Shane's face when Mama had spoken down to him, which was by her guess the exact moment he realized she was not the country miss he'd assumed her to be.

Did he hate her? Was he the kind of man who would understand? She hadn't meant to mislead him. Was her parentage her fault? Hardly. They lived in the country, so she technically was a country girl. It wasn't a lie she had let him believe, but she hadn't corrected him.

She regretted that now. She stared out her bedroom window instead of at the history book open on the desk. She could not concentrate and let her gaze wander over the roll of high prairie and the rugged Rocky Mountains hugging the horizon. Sunset dusted the snow-capped, craggy peaks with dabs of mauve and streaks of purple.

"Meredith." Matilda, her older sister, poked her head around the door frame. "Mama wanted me to come fetch you. Dinner is about to be served."

"Dinner." She was not in the mood. "I don't suppose I can have a tray sent up here?"

"Mama is mad enough as it is. I wouldn't ask if I were you." Sympathy softened Tilly's features, making her almost pretty in the lamplight.

If only a fine beau could see Matilda as her sisters did, with a beauty of spirit, a sweetness of temperament and a generous soul that made her the finest catch in all of Angel County. Men were notoriously shallow, as Meredith had decided, and so dear Tilly was still unmarried and, worse, unbeaued at the age of twenty. Not a single man had come courting, when marriage and a family were all that her sister desired.

"Then I suppose I'll survive dinner." With a wink, Meredith closed her textbook, pushed back her chair and climbed to her feet. The sun was going down on the day and on her hopes. Her one chance to prove herself as a sensible driver to her parents was over. "Do you think it will be the topic of conversation? My big failure as a driver."

"You may have to endure a few comments from Mama, but Papa believes a woman should know how to drive," Tilly encouraged. "Remember how he bought Sweetie for me, so I could be more independent? And that means—"

"You can drive me," Meredith finished, reaching out to squeeze her sister's hand. "The certification exam is coming up. Will you find a way to help me take it?"

"I'll drive you there and back myself, even if I have to defy both our parents to do it." Voices at a whisper, they meandered down the long stretch of hallway. "There is always the hope that the new horseman will be as helpful as Eli has been."

Eli was a gem and while it was a boon to him that he was joining his brother's teaming business, she seriously doubted that Shane Connelly was going to go out of his way to help her. The disbelief on his face flashed back to her as they'd stood in the falling snow.

Would he understand, especially after the way Mama had treated him?

She hoped so. There had been a spark of something between them on the ride home. She shivered remembering the warm taffy sensation his nearness had brought her. She was still dazzled by his dimpled smile, the snapping connection when their gazes met and the tender touch of the rough and rugged man.

"I hadn't realized Papa hired two horse trainers." Matilda's comment echoed in the stairway as they descended to the main floor. "Minnie says the older one is a little scary."

"Not scary exactly, just distant and in charge." In truth she hardly had an impression of the older horseman. Shane had so dominated her senses at the time that no one else could matter. She could not tear his image from her thoughts, and her gaze shot to the windows hoping to catch a single sighting of him.

"Girls, there you are." Mama bustled toward them, skirts swishing, floorboards shaking, cups rattling in their saucers on the dining-room table. "Hurry. We are waiting the meal on you."

"Sorry. I was lost in my studying." And wondering about the new horse trainer, but she kept that to herself. She felt Tilly's hand on hers give an encouraging squeeze. Glad she wasn't alone, she headed toward her chair. Papa and Minnie were already seated. Meredith cast an apologetic look at her father, who looked stern as she slipped into her chair next to Minnie. Definitely not the best of signs.

"I heard you had some trouble today, young lady." His deep voice seemed to fill the room, although he spoke softly. Papa had a presence, too, a formidable one when he wanted it. "Something about nearly ruining the buggy and being covered with mud."

"We came back in one piece." The last thing she wanted to do was to disappoint her father. She set her chin, determined to accept with grace the loss of her driving privilege, which was sure to be coming. She tried to be upbeat. "All's well that ends well."

"It certainly was not." Mama's chair scraped as she settled up to the table. "Anything could have happened to you. You could have been killed or maimed."

"I was careful. We are fine." Humiliation rolled through her. She was a sensible girl who got good grades. She needed practice driving, that was all. She swallowed hard against the rising sense of failure that seemed to fill her to the chin.

"Not fine enough," her mother argued. "Your dress was near to ruined, Meredith."

"I know." Mortified, she folded her hands, preparing for grace. She felt bad enough, seeing herself from Shane Connelly's point of view. She could have had "loser" painted on her back in scarlet letters. Not merely a loser, but a failure and a disappointment. Papa appeared so grave and Mama furious.

"I'm sorry." The apology wasn't easy. "You are right. A more experienced driver would not have gotten stuck."

"It was all the mud's fault." Minnie spoke up. "Meredith isn't to blame. It could have happened to anybody."

"Not anybody." Was that a hint of amusement in

Papa's voice? "For instance, I drove that stretch of road home and I had no problem avoiding the mud holes."

Doom. Meredith hung her head, knowing the official pronouncement was imminent. She would be banned from the family's horse and buggy forever.

"Dear Father," he began to pray instead using his most serious voice. The room fell silent except for the creak of the back door opening, muffled by the closed kitchen door.

Was it Shane coming in for his dinner? Were those his boots thudding with authority against the floorboards in the other room?

"Please bless this food we are about to partake and know that we are grateful for Thy bounty." Papa's brow furrowed in concentration, his face set with sincerity.

I should be paying attention. She did her best to rope in her thoughts, but her disobedient ears continued to strain for the texture of that low, deep voice talking with Cook. It had to be Shane's because her soul knew it, the rise and fall and rumble.

Please help him to forgive me, Father, she asked silently.

"Although we are far from perfect," Papa continued, "You forgive us and continue to bless us with Your loving kindness."

Was it her imagination or did Papa wink at her? It was hard to tell because he was so very somber as he finished his prayer.

"Guide us to Your will, Lord, and Your eternal light. Amen."

"Amens" rang around the table, but the faint low rumble of Shane's chuckle was the only sound she heard. It rolled through her like a spring breeze, welcome and refreshing. Why did he affect her so?

"Meredith!" Minnie nudged her with an elbow. "Pass the gravy."

"Right." She shook her head, trying to scatter her thoughts, but Shane remained front and center, the tap of his boots against the floor, the deep note of his "thank you," and the final squeak of the closing door more drawing than the delicious scents steaming up from the serving platters and her family's conversation.

"I know how you feel, Henrietta," Papa said to Mama as he plopped a spoonful of mashed potatoes onto his plate. "But this is the best horseman around. Even our dear Thad recommended him. Braden Shaw and his apprentice are genuine wranglers. They've broken and trained horses from Texas all the way to Canada. They've been all over the West. Can you imagine? Just like in my favorite novels."

"Novels are made-up fiction," Mama pointed out as she always did from her end of the long table. "Just you mind that. Real horses kick and bite and run away with their drivers. Remember what happened to you? You were nearly killed handling an unbroken horse. I hardly think we need animals like that in our stables."

"That's why we have a horse trainer, my dear. Besides, I'm fit as a fiddle and fully healed. As Meredith says, all's well that ends well."

"All ends well only with eternal vigilance, heaven's guidance and common sense." If a corner of Mama's mouth upturned as if battling good humor, it had to be Meredith's imagination. "I know where this is going,

Robert, and no, I refuse to reconsider. Meredith will not be driving that buggy again anytime soon."

Meredith was certain Papa winked at her as he handed Minnie the bowl of mashed potatoes.

"I would like to learn to drive." Minnie dug into the potatoes with unladylike zeal. "Do you think Shane could teach me?"

"Wilhelmina!" Mama's fork and knife tapped against the rim of her dinner plate. "Such talk! You are far too young, and no, I know what is coming next. You may not learn to ride horses either. A Worthington lady does not resort to such behavior."

"But, Mama, I don't want to be a lady."

The back of her neck tingled, as if someone were watching her. Shane? His path from the kitchen door to the bunkhouse would take him through the garden and right past the dining-room windows. Sadie, their maid, would have given them their meals in a basket. Hired men were not allowed to eat in the house. Was he standing outside looking in, and what was he thinking of her?

She craved the opportunity to talk with him. She glanced over her shoulder, searching through the glass for the sight of his black Stetson and his striking face. But all she saw was the turn of his back and the impressive line of his shoulder as he strode away.

He had understood about her mother when they had spoken before. Surely he would do so again. And if she ought to be wondering why his opinion of her mattered, she didn't want to analyze it and took the potato bowl from Minnie instead.

"Why don't you tell us all what Lydia's letter said,"

Papa began as he cut into a slice of roast beef. "I brought home the mail today and there was an envelope from our girls."

"And another letter from the school's headmaster." Mama's mouth pursed as she held out her hand, waiting for the potatoes. "Angelina is on warning. She was caught smoking behind the outhouse again. Another stunt and she will be permanently suspended."

"Did you truly think finishing school would change her?" Tilly said in her gentle way. "She doesn't want to be there, Mama."

"I know how that feels." Meredith handed over the bowl and accepted the beef platter from Minnie. She forked a slice of meat onto her plate, remembering how restricted she had felt, how smothered. "Sometimes a girl just has to be who she is, or she feels as if her heart will die."

"Nonsense." Mama dished up with a clink of the spoon against her china plate. "We have a family obligation and standards to uphold. We may have moved out West for practical purposes, we are still considered a part of good society. We must not allow our conduct to slide."

Mama cared far too much what certain people thought about her. Life in St. Louis had been much different, and her mother had been happier with her numerous clubs and charities there. They had moved to take care of cousin Noelle when she had been blinded in a buggy accident, and her parents—Mama's brother— killed. But what the Worthington girls had seen as an adventure, Mama had viewed as a necessary duty, a hardship she struggled to rise above.

"I hope you do not rue the day you dropped out of that fine school." Mama's pronouncement was punctuated by another dollop of mashed potato hitting her plate. "Now, back to Lydia's letter. Your dear sweet sister writes that she loves her teachers and her coursework this year is most enjoyable."

Meredith glanced over her shoulder again. The pathway was empty and all sight of Shane gone. She felt as if something important, something she couldn't describe, had slipped away.

The bunkhouse smelled like fresh lumber, coal smoke and boiling coffee. Shane pushed back his now-empty dinner plate on the plank table and took in his new home. Much better than their last place with separate rooms for sleeping and living, comfortable chairs near the generous windows and a woodstove. Cozy enough to spend a comfortable evening reading and plenty of room for at least a half-dozen hired men. The place echoed around them.

"Looks like Worthington is hoping to be a major operation one day, judging by the size of this place." Braden ambled over with the coffeepot and filled both ironware cups. "Good for him. I had a chance to ride around the spread. He's got some prime land for raising horses."

"And plenty of it." That took money, and judging by the looks of things, the Worthingtons were rolling in it. Memories of the life back home, the one he'd been dying to get away from, hit him like a slap to the face.

"Tomorrow we look over the horses we've come to

train." Braden set the coffeepot on the stove with a *clunk*. "Caught sight of the two-year-olds in the paddock. Fine-looking bunch. Robert Worthington has a good eye. Shouldn't be too hard of a job, if we can answer to Worthington only. That wife of his..." Braden didn't finish the sentence, shaking his head.

Shane didn't need to be a mind reader to know what his boss was thinking. Braden had issues with women, especially the domineering type. Thinking of his own mother, who managed her family and alienated his father with her overbearing determination to have everything her way, Shane couldn't blame him. It was the reason he'd chosen his own path in life. He pushed out of his chair and opened the door a crack. With the fire going full bore, the well-built house was sweltering. "At least we can leave when our work is done, and sooner if you decide to."

"There's nothing better than freedom," Braden agreed, swinging into his chair. He dug into the sugar bowl and stirred a couple teaspoonfuls into his coffee. "It's why I'll always be a bachelor."

"Always? That's a mighty long time."

"And well worth it. I can come and go as I please, do what I want without being henpecked to death by a woman." He slurped the steaming coffee, a man content with his life.

"Or lied to." Hard not to talk about what had been on his mind all afternoon, since they'd come upon the young ladies in the road. Just Meredith, she'd been then, pretty as a picture in her pretty yellow dress and gold locks tumbling down from her hood, flyaway curls that framed her beautiful heart-shaped face like a dream.

She looked sweet with that swipe of mud on her peaches-and-cream cheek and wholesome, so determined she was to help free the buggy.

Captivated, that was a word he might have used to describe her effect on him. That was before she'd gone from Just Meredith to a Worthington daughter, one of the richest families in the county and, according to Braden's research, the territory. The way she'd tricked him taunted him now, reminding him of how easy it was to get the wrong impression about someone. He tugged the sugar bowl closer to his cup and stirred in a heaping spoonful. Coffee steamed and the strong rich brew tickled his nose.

"You aren't thinking about the Worthington girl, are you?" Braden stared at him over the rim. The rising steam gave his piercing look a menacing quality.

"Don't worry about it." He had been, so he couldn't lie. "It's nothing."

"Make sure it is. This is the first time I've seen you show interest in a calico since I've known you." Braden took another slurping sip. "I feel beholden to warn you to stay away from her. She's the boss man's daughter. That's a brand of trouble you don't want to get tangled up in."

"Not intending to." The hot coffee scorched his tongue and seared his throat and shook him out of his reverie. He was here to work and to learn. Braden was one of the best trainers in the country and he wasn't going to mess up this chance to work with him. "I suppose Meredith Worthington is eye-catching enough, but I've seen who she really is. Nothing she can do from this point on can make me see her differently. She's not pretty enough to distract me from my work."

"Good to know." Braden nodded once, turning the conversation to tomorrow's workday, which was scheduled to start well before dawn.

Shane didn't hear the muffled gasp on the front step or the faint rustle of a petticoat. The gentle tap of the falling snow outside and the roar of the fire in the stove drowned out the quiet footsteps hurrying away through the storm.

Chapter Four

Meredith shook the snow from her cloak at the back door in the shelter of the lean-to before turning the handle. Clutching the covered plate, she eased into the busy kitchen, where Cook scrubbed pots at the steaming soapy basin and barked orders to their housemaid, Sadie, who scurried to comply.

Sadie never missed anything and glanced at the full plate Meredith slid onto the edge of the worktable. "They don't like cookies?" she asked.

"Something like that." Still smarting from the conversation she'd overheard, she numbly shrugged out of her wraps and hung them by the stove to dry. Shane's words rang in her head, unstoppable. He wasn't going to understand. He didn't want to be friends. He didn't think she was pretty.

She squeezed her eyes shut, facing the wall, glad that her back was to the other people in the room so no one could see the pain traveling through her. It hurt to know what he thought of her.

"Meredith?" The inner door swung open, shoes beat a cheerful rhythm on the hardwood and Minnie

burst into sight, cheeks pink, fine shocks of dark hair
escaping from her twin braids. "There you are! You
are supposed to help me with my spelling. Mama said
so."

"I'll be right up." Her voice sounded strained as she
arranged the hem of her cloak. She could not fully
face her sister. Pressure built behind her ribs like a
terrible storm brewing. Shane's tone—one of disdain
and dismissal—was something she could not forget.
He'd said terrible things about her. So, why did pieces
of their afternoon together linger? The way he'd swiped
mud from her cheek, leaned close to tuck his blanket
around her and the steadying strength of his hand when
he'd helped her from the buggy hurt doubly now. Why
it tormented her was a mystery. She didn't know why
she cared. She no longer wanted to care. A man who
would say that about her was off her friend list.

"Meredith?" Minnie asked. "Are you all right?"

"Couldn't be better." Fine, so it wasn't the truth, but
it would be. She was an independent type of girl, she
didn't go around moaning the loss of some boy's opinion. She was strong, self-reliant and sure of her plans
in life, and those plans had nothing to do with some
horseman who was too quick to judge. He undoubtedly
had a whole list of flaws and personality defects.

"Good, because you looked really unhappy." Minnie
crept close and took her hand, her fingers small and
timid. "Are you terribly upset at losing your driving
privileges?"

"A little." A lot, but she would deal with that when
the morning came, when she had to be driven to town

like a child. With Eli gone, Shane would be the logical person to take his place.

Oh, no. No, no, no. Her pulse stalled, her knees buckled, and she grabbed the wall with her free hand for support. However could she endure being close to him and, remembering what he'd said about her, pretending not to? Sitting there next to Minnie on the backseat through the silence of the drive to the schoolhouse staring at the back of his head?

"I think Papa understands." Minnie's grip tightened, the melody of her voice ringing with loving sympathy. "Maybe he will let you drive again after the roads firm up. The mud won't last forever."

"Yes, sure." She squeezed her sister's hand, so little and trusting within hers. She loved her sisters; she was so blessed to have each and every one of them. "Now, let's get you upstairs and we will see how well you know your spelling lesson."

"I studied and everything." Minnie wiggled her hand free and skipped ahead, rattling the china in the hutch.

"Minnie!" Mama admonished as the kitchen door swung open. "No running in the house. How many times must I tell you?"

"I forget." Minnie meekly skidded to a stop in the dining room, although her fast walk held quite a bit of a skip as she headed toward the staircase.

"Walk like a lady!" Mama peered around the edge of the sofa in the parlor, her sewing on her lap. "Do not forget you are a Worthington. We glide, we don't gallop like barnyard animals."

"Yes, Mama." Minnie grabbed the banister and

pounded up the steps, perhaps unaware how her footsteps thundered through the house.

"Quietly!" Mama's demand followed them up to the second story, where Minnie popped into the first doorway on the right and jumped onto the foot of her bed. The ropes groaned in protest.

Did Minnie's window have to have a perfect view of the new bunkhouse? Meredith stopped at the small desk, pushed up to the sill and stared beyond the greening leaves of the orchard to the glowing squares of lamplight. Behind those muslin curtains was the man who'd maligned her, who'd judged her and whose words she could not get out of her mind.

I've seen who she really is, he'd said. She wrapped her fingers around the back rung of the chair until her fingers turned white. The pain returned, digging as if with talons around the edges of her heart. How could he judge her like that without giving her the chance to explain?

"Meredith? The list." Minnie bounced impatiently on the feather mattress.

The list? She shook her head, an attempt to scatter her thoughts, but they remained like hot, red, angry coals glowing in her skull. She glanced at the book lying open on the desk before her and concentrated on the words printed there, forcing all thoughts of Shane Connelly from her mind.

She chose a word randomly from Minnie's spelling assignment. "Insularity."

"Insularity," Minnie repeated, taking a deep breath, pausing as she wrestled with the word. *"I—n—s—"*

It wasn't fair. He wasn't fair. Her gaze strayed to the

windows of the bunkhouse, where the bracing scent of fresh coffee had filled the rooms and carried out the cracked open door.

"—*i*—*t*—*y*," Minnie finished. "Insularity. It means to be narrow- or small-minded."

Not that a certain horseman came to mind. She cleared her throat, grateful when no emotion sounded in her voice. She chose another word from the list. "Supposition."

"*S*—*u*—*p*—" Minnie's dear button face furrowed in concentration.

Meredith did her best to stare at the word on the page, checking carefully to make sure her baby sister got the spelling right. Was it her fault her eyes kept drifting upward? It was as if there was something wrong with them, as if Shane Connelly held some sort of power over her ocular muscles tugging them in his direction.

"—*n*." Minnie sounded proud of herself. "It means to draw a conclusion or an assumption."

That was exactly what had happened today. Shane had met her mother, seen the family's rather extravagant house and assumed she was the same, a pampered young lady of privilege who was not good enough for an honest man like him. The talons of pain clutched tighter, as if wringing blood. She didn't want to think why this mattered so much.

"Prejudice," she squeaked out of a too-tight throat. She felt as if she did not have enough air to speak with. As if all the surprise and shock of what she'd overheard had drained away, leaving no buffer. She had not leaped to conclusions about him, although she was happy to do so now.

"*P—r—*" Minnie paused, scrunching up her face as she tried to visualize the spelling. "*—e—j—*"

What was she doing, fretting about a saddle tramp? She didn't care what he thought of her. He was clearly not the type of person she wanted to befriend, and if a tiny voice deep within argued, then she chose to ignore it. He'd insulted her, hurt her feelings and now her dignity. Well, she was hurting, and she had better things to dwell on than a man like that.

"*—i—c—e.*" Minnie finished with a rush. "Whew. I almost always get that one wrong."

"It's tricky," Meredith agreed, gathering the book with both hands and turning her back to the window. Forget Shane Connelly. That was certainly what she intended to do from this moment on.

A knock rapped against the open door. Her oldest sister hesitated in the threshold. "Hey, are you busy?"

"I've spelled three words in a row correctly!" Minnie gave a hop, beaming with pride.

"That's what happens when you study first," Tilly teased in her gentle way, love obvious on her oval face. Her brown curls bounced as she bounded forward with a sweep of her skirts and plopped on the free corner of Minnie's bed. "I overheard Papa and Mama talking. I have a suspicion Papa will be able to make things right."

"In time for school in the morning?" Meredith asked.

"Probably not that soon."

Of course not. However soon her father talked her

mother into changing her mind, it could not come fast enough. First thing tomorrow she would have to face Shane. Dread filled her. The thought of him waiting for her alongside the buggy, reaching out his hand to help her up, being able to listen in on her conversations with Minnie from the front seat, filled her with a burning mix of confusion, hurt and rage.

Well, she didn't care about his hurtful words. Her pride was wounded, that was all. So what if he didn't like her? Why would she want him to? She simply didn't have to like him. She pulled out the chair and sat down, her spine straight, her back to the window. What she needed to do was to banish all thoughts of the man from her head.

Pleased with her plan, she could focus on her sisters' conversation.

"No, Minnie, I can't drive you tomorrow." Tilly smoothed a wrinkle in her skirt. "I wish I could, but I promised Mama I would help her finish your new dress. You are growing like a weed, little sister."

"I am." Pleased, Minnie grinned, showing off her adorable dimples. "Pretty soon I ought to be tall enough to ride a wild mustang. Then I could help break next year's new horses and Papa wouldn't have to hire anyone to do it."

"I don't think that's likely to happen, not if Mama has anything to say about it." Worrying the discussion would turn to the hired men, Meredith changed the subject. "What about the day after tomorrow? Can you drive me then, Tilly?"

"I have a meeting at the church that afternoon, but I think we can work it out. Unless Mama has objections about the road conditions. After all, you can't miss going to your weekly sewing circle." Her older sister stared at her intently, as if trying to see at something beneath the surface, something Meredith did not want anyone to know. Tilly shook her head, as if she could not figure it out. "I understand not wanting one of the new hired men to drive you. I'm shy around strangers, too."

Shy? That was hardly the problem. She thought of how she'd bantered with Shane, how he'd made her blush and laugh and quip. She feared her face was heating and her emotions would show and her sisters would guess at the truth.

You don't like him, Meredith, she reminded herself. *It's impossible.* He's *impossible.*

"Oh, Meredith wasn't one bit shy when they met up with us on the road," Minnie burst out. "She and Shane talked practically the whole way home."

"Is this true?" Tilly studied her again, her curiosity greater and her scrutiny more intent.

Heat burned her cheeks. She could feel her skin across her face tighten. Surely she was blushing. A dead giveaway. "I was polite to him, nothing more. I assure you of that."

"But you're blushing."

"Because I feel uncomfortable." That was true. Uncomfortable with the way Shane made her feel, with her hurt dignity and with this discussion. "You know I have plans that have nothing to do with finding a man to marry me right out of school. What would I want with an iterant horseman who is here for two months at the most and then he'll leave, never to be seen again?"

"I wasn't thinking of that." Tilly shrugged, her slender shoulders sagging a notch. The hint of sadness that overcame her was heart-wrenching. "I was wistful, that is all, hoping that true love would come your way, since it is sure not to be coming to mine."

"Don't say that." Meredith slipped onto her knees before her sister, gathering her slim hands in hers. "There is always hope for true love. Emmett is simply busy with his business."

"Oh, he was never truly interested in me. I was the one. It was all me. I mistook his politeness for more, that's all." Although her chin came up and she pasted on a smile, there was no disguising the hint of heartbreak on Matilda's dear face, a sorrow she kept hidden. "A girl has to have wishes, or what else does she have?"

"God. Family. Principles." Mama thundered into the room. They had all been so engrossed they hadn't heard her until she towered over them, glowering. "Some men are more appropriate to love than others, my girls. Now, why aren't you studying? And, Matilda, shouldn't you be downstairs sewing?"

"Yes, Mama," they muttered in unison, Meredith leaping to her feet, Tilly pushing off the bed and Minnie bouncing once before hopping two-footed to the floor.

Meredith glanced over her shoulder, drawn by the lit windows gleaming in the dark evening, unable to stop a deep pinch of regret and, to be honest, a wish that Shane had not been Papa's hired man. That they had parted ways at the driveway and he had kept riding so she would have been left with the romantic tale of their brief meeting, a moment in time when she could have

forever believed in the man and his dimples, his good
humor and character. She could have lived the rest of
her days with the legend of their meeting and what she
had believed him to be.

Now that she knew the truth, there was no legend, no
sweetness, no tale of romance. Just the broken pieces
of what had never been.

In the long gray shadows of dawn, Shane dragged
on his boots by the back door, head pounding and eyes
scratchy from what fell far short of a restful night's
sleep. He'd been fitful, unable to drift off on the top
bunk of what was a comfortable feather tick, in clean
muslin sheets and plenty of blankets. After a hard day's
ride he should have slept hard enough that only Braden's
rough shaking by the arm could have woken him.

"Quit dragging your feet and let's get the morning
started." Braden growled as he jammed one arm and
then the other into his riding jacket. "We've got work
to do."

Not that he minded work. No, he thrived on it. He
loved every aspect of horse care from the shoveling to
the riding. But this morning a dull ache stabbed his
temples as he finished tying his boots, winced when
the wind caught the door and smacked it against the
wall. He grabbed his coat.

Dawn hadn't yet softened the night's shadows, but
already the horses were stirring, some more enthusiastic
than others, nickering for attention and feed. Braden
led the first animal out of her stall—a demure white
mare—and cross-tied her in the breezeway.

"Get to work." Braden handed him a pitchfork and left him to take care of business.

A lot must have been on his mind last night because it tried to surface as he worked. He dug the tines into the soiled straw and hiked it into a pile. He worked with quick, even strokes, lifting and turning the fork, making fast work of the roomy stall before moving onto the next. Was Meredith far from him mind?

Not a chance.

Worse than that, he couldn't stop thinking of home. As merry golden light fell through the cracks in the walls and the double doors open on either end of the barn, he lost his battle to keep sad things buried. Maybe it was this place, he conceded, with its impressive stone-and-wood manor house. The no-expenses-spared stables and fine pedigreed horses reminded him of his family's stable back home. Not that Father was a horseman by any means, but he took pride in owning the best driving horses in White Water County. Appearances were everything in his family.

His guts still twisted up remembering the pressure he'd felt as the firstborn. The love he'd tried so hard to earn most of his childhood until he finally figured out that if you had to earn it, then it wasn't love. Not the real thing, anyway.

Although he'd been gone a while, he missed his family. Just because he couldn't get along with them didn't mean a lack of love. He thought of Grandmama and her kitchen full of delicious smells and her plain house full of blooming flowers. Mother with her narrow view of the world and her belief that she ought to control what she could of it. His younger brother who was always in and out of one scrape or another. Hard to imagine him buckling down to work in Father's and Grandfather's firm and being groomed for politics. He missed the boy's constant ribbing and antics.

Homesickness tugged at him. There were good things he missed—wrestling with his brother, riding with his dad, his mother's cookies and his grandmother's understanding. Sure, he missed home, although he did not want to be there.

"Time to harness up the gray mare for the school-girls." Braden's announcement rang through the barn like a death knell.

Shane grimaced. In truth, he'd been hoping to put that task off as long as possible. Nothing to be done about it but put aside his pitchfork, leave the rest to Braden and go in search of the old, placid mare.

Sweetie greeted him with hopefulness. Recognizing the gleam in those big brown eyes, he searched his pockets for a sugar cube. She took it daintily from his palm, a polite girl. Hard not to like her. Her beauty wasn't in long, perfect lines or the quality of her breeding, but in something far more important. He led her gently through the barn to the buggy he'd washed while his hands froze in yesterday's last bit of daylight and slipped a collar over her neck.

"Whatever happens—" a voice broke the silence behind him "—don't let Meredith talk you into driving."

"Yes, Mr. Worthington." He'd met the patriarch of the family late last night after all the barn work was done. He didn't have an opinion of the man one way or the other. Worthington hadn't been as off-putting as his wife and was far friendlier. Shane gave the mare a pat. "I expect the roads to be tough going, so I'd like to get an early start."

"Wise. I'll inform the girls." Robert hesitated like a man with something on his mind.

Here it comes, Shane predicted. He buckled the gray mare into the traces, bracing himself for whatever warning or judgment the wealthy man was about to make. Most likely a threatening warning to stay away from the Worthington daughters.

"It was hard to let Eli go. He had been a fine employee. Always took care of my horses and my girls. I never gave either of them a moment's worry when they were in his care." Robert cracked a smile, a masculine hint of Meredith's, and he had the same stormy blue eyes.

This job meant a lot to him so he would take the warning on the chin. Not let insult to injury show.

"I can read between the lines," Worthington went on. "The mud on the girls. Mud on the buggy. And poor Sweetie was barrel high. I noticed you cleaned the buggy, boots and tack without saying a word. You helped the girls when they needed it, and I'm much obliged. I can rest easier knowing they are in safe hands with you at the reins."

Sometimes folks surprised you, Shane thought as he gave the last buckle a tug. Maybe this would be a better assignment than he'd figured, not that he was looking forward to driving Miss Meredith Worthington around town. But this was what Worthington wanted, so he would do it to the best of his ability. "I won't disappoint you, sir."

"You say that like a man who has no clue what he's in for." Worthington shook his head, retracing his steps. "Meredith is not happy about this. Consider it a word of warning."

Meredith. As if his thoughts had summoned her, she bustled into the barn, dusted with snowfall and clutching a big stack of schoolbooks in the crook of her arm. If the scowl on her beautiful face was any indication, she was about as thrilled with the situation as he was.

Chapter Five

Her plan to banish Shane Connelly from her thoughts backfired like a Winchester with a jammed cartridge. Meredith swiped snow from her face as she took smaller and smaller steps toward the waiting buggy. He was there, as remote as stone, as unmoving as marble. He did not even seem to be breathing.

Perhaps it was especially difficult for him to be anywhere in proximity to her. She pushed Minnie ahead of her, gently nudging her along so she would reach the buggy first. She'd worried over this moment all night long, whenever dreams would pull her from her sleep, taunting dreams of Shane's smile, his dimples, the snap of aliveness she'd felt in his presence. Regret had chased her all night long, keeping her sleep fitful and dawn a welcome release. She'd risen out of bed, dreading each step she took, each word to her sisters, every bite at the breakfast table because it led her all inexorably here to this unstoppable moment as he helped Minnie into the buggy's backseat and then held out his gloved hand.

Memories of that hand in hers mocked her. Worse, he gazed past her, as if she didn't exist to him. Much worse than she'd anticipated. She didn't have to worry about meeting his gaze and being reminded of his words last night. She ignored his hand and clamored into the buggy of her own accord, settling her skirts and reaching for the lap robe before he could help.

You can be tougher than this, Meredith. She set her chin, focused her gaze forward, aware of his hesitation, so near to her she could hear him breathe. His gaze scorched her, raking the side of her face like a touch. If she turned and dared to face him, would she see regret softening the rugged angles of his handsome face? Or would she see his disdain?

His opinion of you doesn't matter, she told herself, curling her fingers tightly around the hem of the robe. She was independent. She should not need any man's regard, and it irked her beyond all reason that his opinion did matter. Somehow the air turned colder, the morning less bright as he took a silent step away and settled with a creak of leather onto the front.

"What about the roads?" Minnie scooted forward and laid her arms against the back of his seat. "Are we going to get stuck again?"

"We'll have to wait and see," came Shane's reply, warm and friendly as he gathered Sweetie's reins. "The snow is too wet for the sleigh and the road is too soft for the wheels. It ought to be interesting."

"I trust you." Minnie grinned at him, flashing her adorable dimples. "I know you're a really good driver. I can tell because Papa hired you."

"Then I'll try not to let you or your papa down." Shane released the brake and gave the thick leather straps a careful slap. The old gray mare stepped out into the yard, eager to lift her nose to the flyaway snow-flakes tumbling from the sky. An arctic wind fluttered her mane and ruffled the edges of the lap robe, letting in a cold blast of air.

"That's good, because I don't want to be late. I have a spelling test this morning and I can't miss it," Minnie chattered on. "I really worked hard and I know every word perfectly."

"You do?" Shane seemed interested in a kindly, brotherly way.

If Meredith didn't have her heart set against him, then she would have liked how he treated her little sister.

"It's the very first time I have studied so hard." Minnie swiped snow from her eyes. "I always pretend to study, but Mama keeps getting really mad at my grades. I have to go to finishing school in two years, and my marks are abysmal. That's what Mama says. I don't think they are all that bad. I would rather be riding horses than sitting in school."

"That's the way I felt, too, shortcakes. I finished school first, and *then* I started working with horses." He turned his attention to the road ahead of them, the half-frozen mud clutching the buggy wheels like glue. The old mare struggled, lowering her head to dig in with all her might.

"You called me shortcakes." Minnie's grin stretched from ear to ear. She knocked the snow accumulating on her pink cap. "How come?"

"'Cuz you're cute and you're sweet."

"I am?" Pleased, her grin went dazzling. No doubt

about it, in a few years she would be breaking more than a few young men's hearts.

"I would appreciate it if you were not so familiar with my sister." That cool voice could only belong to Meredith. How he could ever have mistaken her for a sweet country miss was beyond him. He didn't have to look over his shoulder to know she had her chin up and a regal look on her beautiful face.

"The apple didn't fall too far from the tree?" he asked.

With a gasp, she fell silent. He gave thanks for the whipping wind and thick snow sailing into the buggy. He had his opinion on many things, such as a fancy summer buggy being used for winter driving, but he kept his tongue. He tried to convince himself it didn't hurt that she obviously didn't like him. As he guided the mare down the snowy landscape, doing his best to guess where the higher ground beneath the snow might be, he felt her disregard like the beat of the wind.

Admit it. You don't like disliking her. He'd been captivated by the country beauty in the road yesterday, but what he'd told Braden was also true. These days he was a working man, not his father's son, and pretty debutantes like Miss Meredith Worthington had to stay out of his reach. He'd learned his lesson about debutantes the hard way. His brief fiancée, Patricia, had only cared about having material things and more of them than her friends, and he did not want to go down that path again. Regardless of how beautiful Meredith was or how fascinating, she was not the kind of woman who could capture his heart.

Not that he was looking for one.

The mare heaved, struggling with the weight she pulled. The ground was not fully frozen, and mud sucked at the wheels, making the going rough. Without a word of reassurance for the fine Worthington girls in the backseat, he hopped out of the buggy to lighten the load and gripped the icy trace. He walked beside Sweetie the rest of the way to town, glad to be battling snow and the road instead of thoughts of Miss Meredith and her cool disdain.

The school's bell tower could be seen from the town of Angel Falls's main street, rising like a ghost above the two-story buildings and playing peekaboo through the veils of snowfall. Meredith thought of her friends and wondered if they would already be gathered in the schoolhouse, or would Providence be with her and she would arrive first so that no one would be able to notice the new driver. Watching the stiff line of his back and the way he purposefully ignored her had not put her in a pleasant mood. She wondered if she should ask him if she could help, too, but could not summon up the will to speak to him. If only she was as tough as she wished to be.

They turned the corner and the schoolyard came into view. Well-bundled students marched along the streets. Horses and vehicles clogged the roadway as parents dropped off their children for the day. Screams and shouts rose like shrill music as snowball fights domi-nated the well-covered lawn, gangs of girls clustered together to laugh and share news, and the first series of bells tolled from the tower.

"Shane is a really good driver." Minnie clutched

the lap robe and shivered in the cold. "We didn't get stuck once and we got here really fast. Ooh, look, there's Maisie." She leaned over the side to wave at her friend.

Not only was he a good driver, but he was kind to their dear mare. His soothing tone, his care when she struggled, the way he laid a hand on her neck when a snowball from the schoolyard flew into her path all spoke well of him. She'd paid attention to the way he'd handled the horse all the way to town, realizing that as a driver he had done so much more than hold the reins and tug on them now and then. It bothered her greatly that she could learn much from him, the one man she did not ever want to talk to.

Sweetie stopped in front of the school. Finally. Meredith hopped down, not bothering to wait for the new driver's assistance, and slung her book bag over her shoulder. She did not require his assistance. Her dignity may still be smarting, but he did not seem the least bit affected. He stepped away from her and gave Minnie his attention.

"Meredith!" Fiona waved, trudging through the snow, her lunch pail swinging from one red-mittened hand, her book bag from the other. "I just finished blanketing Flannigan. Could you believe all the vehicles stuck on the road? I didn't think you would make it."

"We have a new driver who is surprisingly competent." Surely Shane could hear her. He was merely feet behind her, helping Minnie from the buggy, so close the hair on the back of her neck tingled.

"So I see." Fiona, happily engaged, glanced curiously

at the hooded figure who was mantled with snow. "Oh, he's good-looking."

"Is he? I thought so when I first met him, but then I changed my mind." He was beyond what a sane woman would call handsome; he was magnificent. The steady strength, the quick world-changing grin added to his gentle manner would make the toughest female look twice. But she could not bear to let him think she thought him so fine.

"Isn't he your type?" Fiona asked. "Handsome, rugged, very manly?"

"My type?" *Please, don't let him have heard that, Lord.* She glanced over her shoulder to see Shane handing Minnie her lunch pail with a big brother's kindness. A smirk tugged at the corner of his mouth.

He *had* heard her.

"Oh, he's all right," she said, letting her voice lift on the wind, knowing full well Shane could hear her. "But he's not fine enough to interest me."

"Meredith! What a thing to say, and I think he heard you." Dear gentle Fiona was shocked. She skidded to a halt, jaw dropped, eyes wide with a sad censure. "I've never known you to be mean before."

"I—" The excuses died on her lips. Cold quivered through her, burrowing deep into her bone marrow and further, as if into her soul. She'd only meant him to know that she hadn't been thinking about romance, that she hadn't been hoping he was interested in her. She wanted him to know that he'd hurt her, but the words had come out wrong, and now she'd made matters worse.

The man drove her crazy.

Shane's gaze fastened on hers, holding her prisoner as time stilled. Snowflakes tangled in her lashes, but she could not break away from the compelling mix of hurt and sadness darkening the wondrous blue of his eyes. She could feel his emotions as clearly as her own. It was the oddest sensation. The connection they'd forged upon first sight remained, but it was wounded, no longer light and full of laughter but of something grave.

I'm sorry, she wanted to say, but before she could, he broke away. The wind gusted and the snow fell harder as if even God were ashamed and trying to steal him from her sight.

"Fiona! Meredith!" Scarlet Fisher emerged from the storm, her bag swinging from her shoulder, her beautiful red hair dusted with snow from her walk through town. "Who was that?"

"Nobody." The word was out before she could stop it. Meredith drew her scarf over her face. She could hide her humiliation from her friends, but not from herself. How could she have done such a thing?

"He's almost as handsome as Lorenzo." Scarlet shook the snow from her knit cap and fell into stride alongside them. Snowballs flew over their heads and little kids darted into their path as they waded through the yard toward the schoolhouse's front steps. "Is he Eli's replacement?"

"He must be," Fiona replied, "although Meredith doesn't seem to like him."

"What's not to like?" Scarlet asked. "Did you see his shoulders? He looks like a hero out of a novel."

"You always say that." Fiona rolled her eyes, although

she was smiling. Ever since she had become engaged at Christmastime, she had been a lot happier. It was good to see. "Sometimes men like that are even real."

What they needed was to change the subject, Meredith decided and took charge of the situation. "Did either of you figure out the last math problem in our homework assignment?"

"Who cares about our homework?" Scarlet grabbed Meredith's hand, staring in the direction of the school steps. "Lorenzo."

Sure enough, Lorenzo Davis stood off to the side, chatting with a few of his close friends. Their nemesis, Narcissa Bell, was easy to spot as she laid a possessive hand on Lorenzo's arm, as if staking claim.

Fiona said something, words lost in the wind and snow and the fuzz in Meredith's brain. Of all the sounds in the school yard, it was a single note of baritone, low and gentle, that rumbled to her ears. It was Shane speaking to the old mare, encouraging her through the combination of deep mud and spots of ice the busy road had turned to.

The snowfall hid him, but she could picture him perfectly, his straight impressive posture, powerful and so caring as he walked alongside the mare. Other horses neighed in frustration, other drivers shouted in exasperation, and even a whip crack or two snapped out. But Shane's comforting voice did not show impatience or frustration or cruelty.

You do not like him, Meredith. She stared at the ground where the snow grabbed at her shoes and her ruffled hem, sick with regret. She'd never been so disappointed in herself. Had he taken her words to heart, the way she had his? Or was he tougher, able to disregard the hurtful comments from a girl he'd found less than worthy?

From a girl who had just sounded extraordinarily like her mother. The realization punched through her like a physical blow. Her knees weakened, shock rolled through her and she'd never felt so bad. One thing was for certain: Shane Connelly brought out the worst in her.

Perhaps it was her duty to bring out the best.

"Meredith." A sneering voice broke into her thoughts, a familiar and unfriendly voice. Narcissa Bell gave her perfect blond ringlets a toss. "I heard your father hired a new horse trainer. When my father was looking for a new trainer, he had considered the same man but found someone much better. Too bad your papa couldn't afford to do the same."

"Leave her alone." Scarlet, fearless as always, shouldered up to Narcissa hard enough to knock her back a step. "You ought to be more careful. Your jealousy is showing."

"As if I could be jealous of her." Narcissa dropped her tone, so it wouldn't carry to the crowd she had been with. "Lorenzo is as good as my beau. I don't see him hanging around with your circle. Meredith isn't so much."

"If you can't say anything nice, then maybe you shouldn't say anything at all." Fiona led the way up the stairs. "C'mon, Meredith."

"Poor Lorenzo." Meredith followed her friends, her shoes slipping on the icy step. She was aware of Narcissa's glare, the quick glance up and then down at her new hat, her elegant traveling coat and the new dress Mama had finished the other day with the ruffled and embellished hem finer than even Narcissa's.

She had learned a lot of lessons living in this small town, ones she had never learned at finishing school where Mama had wanted her to turn out so fine. Clothes did not make the person, material possessions did not matter, certainly not in the way that God cared about. As she shrugged out of her wraps in the crowded vestibule, she was aware of each rustle of the green velveteen gown, every ivory button, every inch of imported French lace.

"This time she's probably telling the truth," Scarlet said as she hung up her practical brown coat. "You know, one of these days, she's going to snare him."

"Poor Lorenzo," Fiona agreed, hanging up her old dove-gray coat with care. She smoothed the wrinkles from her plain gingham dress. "It's important to be with someone kind you can trust to be good to you."

"You would know all about that," Scarlet answered, gathering up her book bag, adorable in her blue flannel plaid dress, trimmed with wooden buttons and matching ribbon. "Your wedding is three weeks away. Are you getting excited?"

"Nervous. Marriage is a big change. But I'm excited, too." Fiona reached out, taking Meredith's hand. "You are off in a daze again. Are you still worried about your homework?"

"I'm always worried about my schoolwork." At least that was true, and a good way to avoid admitting her most cherished goal had not been on the forefront of her mind. Shane had.

Right now he was battling the road and weather conditions right along with Sweetie, his shoulders as unbowed as his spirit as he guided her on the long trip home. His work was harder because Papa would not let his girls be seen in the serviceable but plain sled with the right runners for this weather, a vehicle made for hauling hay to the animals.

I wish I were a simple country girl, she thought, because then Shane would still like her and she would not feel as if she stuck out here, among her friends and the place she loved.

"Meredith." Lila, keeping her voice low, opened her bag and pulled out a comb. She began to fluff at her sleek cinnamon-brown hair. "Love your dress. Is that the one your mother just finished?"

"No one can embroider like Mama." She felt self-conscious of the fluffs and the flourishes and the rose embroidery in matching silk thread that adorned the bottom tier of the skirt. It was lovely, but it didn't fit the image of the one-room schoolteacher she wished to be—the woman she wanted to be. She set her book bag on the desk, which she shared with Scarlet, and gestured toward the empty seat where the rest of their friends should be. "I guess both Kate and Earlee are having trouble making it."

"Kate has a long way to travel on worse roads," Scarlet agreed. "I notice none of Earlee's sisters and brothers are here. They have to walk all the way in."

"I wonder how Earlee is?" Lila asked, leaving unsaid what they were all thinking. Her lot in life was the hardest among them. If she was on the road right now attempting to reach town, then perhaps she would be meeting Shane on the way.

Shane. Even the thought of him weighed on her. *It doesn't matter what he thinks of you,* she told herself, but she knew that it was a lie.

It mattered, and much more than she could explain.

Meredith Worthington was a piece of work. Shane blinked hard against the snowflakes diving at his face and eyes, swiped them away with the cuff of his coat sleeve and tightened his trip on the trace. Not even the weather of the morning's hardship could drive her from his mind.

The morning's traffic to town had broken the crusted ice and churned up doughy mud that grabbed hold of his boots with every step. A mean wind sliced through his layered garments, cutting clean through to his bone marrow. A sky cold as steel and as light as snow made the world one ball of white, except for the mud tracking ahead of them.

Sweetie nickered and stopped in her traces, her harness jingling. The mare shook her head, snow flying off her mane, as she surveyed the road ahead. She remembered the exact spot and direction she had become stuck the day before. Nervous, she didn't want to take another step forward. He patted her neck, hoping to give her comfort.

"You're scared of that happening again, but I'm with you this time." He kept confidence in his voice so the mare would hear it. "Trust me, girl."

The mare nickered, leaning into his touch. Her

brown eyes and curled lashes searched his, tentative and worried. She must have been frightened, held captive by the buggy she could not budge. She was trying to let him know it.

"We'll keep to high ground as best we can," he promised, putting all his understanding in his voice and gentle pressure on the bridle, waiting until she was ready before he whistled and led her through the muck. Snow crunched beneath one boot as he took to the shoulder, eyed a deep ditch, and felt thick mud ooze beneath his tread. Sweetie quivered with nerves as she picked up her pace, half in a panic as she clamored and slipped in the icy and slick mixture.

"That's a good girl," he praised, stepping fast to keep up with her. Something grabbed hold of his toe and with a sucking sound, his boot slipped right off. His stockinged foot squished in the freezing muck.

"Whoa," he called out, holding on, ignoring the stunning cold of his exposed toes as each step he took made his sock wetter and icier.

Great. Just what he needed. Once he had the mare safe on firmer ground, he set the buggy's brake and splashed back to tug his boot free. Bending over, vulnerable in the road, awareness snaked down the back of his neck. Unarmed and defenseless, he whirled in the road, sensing he was no longer alone.

Chapter Six

"That almost happened to me!" A little boy who couldn't be more than six or seven broke through the veil of white. A knit blue cap crowned his head and matching mittens covered his hands, where he held on to a small bundle wrapped against the weather—schoolbooks, Shane guessed. The family was on their way to school. The boy skidded to a stop in the mud. "What are you gonna do about your sock, mister?"

"Probably take it off before I put my foot in my boot." He liked kids, and this one with a single tooth missing and a dimple in his chin looked as likable as can be. "You're mighty late for school."

"We all are."

We? Shane glanced as far as the snowfall would allow. Sweetie nickered, sensing what he could not see. A few seconds later shadows began to appear in the whiteness. A row of children stair-stepped year by year, a family of nine brothers and sisters, mostly sisters.

"Well, gotta go." The boy grinned up at him, wiggled a tooth with his tongue that was getting loose and plunged ahead into the mud, choosing the deepest puddle to wade through with more splashes than a rampaging buffalo could make.

"Edward! How many times do I have to tell you?" A slightly amused voice rose above the whispering wind and tapping snowflakes. "Stay out of the mud."

"But I couldn't help it, Earlee!" The little guy called over his shoulder as he splashed along, not repentant in the least. The storm closed around him until he was a shadow and then nothing at all.

"Pardon us, please," a young lady, tall and willowy, halted next to him. Other children said a simple country howdy as they passed. The oldest one of the bunch squinted at him carefully. Blond curls peeked out from beneath her knit cap. "That's Meredith's family's horse and buggy. You must be Eli's replacement."

"Lucky me." He didn't believe in luck, he believed in the Lord, but it was the only comeback he could think of. Eli was the fortunate one, blessed enough to be well away from Meredith Worthington.

"I'm Earlee Mills, one of Meredith's friends. You aren't from around here, are you?" She knocked a thick pile of snow off her hat and curly bangs, studying him with clear gray eyes.

"Nope." He took a step back, boot in hand, sizing up this friend of Meredith.

She was obviously no debutante, he decided, noticing the old wool coat fraying at the hem and the simple calico dress, unadorned by any lace or ribbon beneath the coat's snowy hem. Although mud obscured most of her shoes, what he could see of them looked worn and aged, as if those shoes had been handed down more than once, as did the cap and mittens she wore, the red yarn fading in places.

"I don't suppose it's a good sign that you have Sweetie. Meredith's first day of driving must not have turned out too well." The other children had disappeared, but this young lady lingered, concern wreathing her oval face. "Oh, dear. Poor Meredith. Driving meant so much to her."

"So I've heard." This was Meredith's friend? Something didn't add up. Wouldn't Miss Hoity-Toity want a more socially prominent friend? "You must live just up the road?"

"Quite a ways. Our farm is almost a mile beyond Meredith's."

"That's quite a way." A farm? No doubt about it, this was a country girl, unlike Meredith of the sad eyes and sharp retorts. "But you are friends?"

"Of course." She took a step away from him. "Why wouldn't we be?"

"No reason. Just fact-gathering." He looked down at the muddy boot he held. "Meredith is an interesting character, isn't she?"

"Interesting? She's fantastic." She glanced over her shoulder. Her brothers and sisters were out of sight, but she felt the pull of responsibility. She didn't have time to figure out this stranger. "I didn't catch your name."

"Connelly. But I doubt Miss Meredith will use my Christian name if she talks about me."

"Why not?"

"She's a tad angry with me, although I don't know why," he confessed.

Was that a twinkle in those dazzling blue eyes?

Something glinted deep in the iris, beyond flesh and all the way to the spirit. He was a charmer, and if she wasn't mistaken, he held a spark for Meredith.

There I go, weaving stories again. She took a step backward, slogging through the sludge. She was given to tales of romance and fancy. Her mind had always been prone to it. But she had not imagined the hint of warmth when this Connelly character had spoken her friend's name. A warmth and a reserve, a strange combination. She would have to get the full tale from Meredith at a later time.

"I'm late, so I had better go. It was nice meeting you, Mr. Connelly." She lifted a hand in farewell, the snow already closing around her. Aside from the echoing pattering footsteps of her siblings on the road ahead, she could have been alone as she walked on, cocooned by the storm. Perhaps that was why her thoughts turned to the letter in her pocket, the one she hoped to post after school. Although it was only two pages of parchment, it weighed down her pocket and the corners of her heart as if it were two hundred.

This was the consequence of harboring a secret crush. No one, not even her circle of best friends, knew she had started corresponding with a man. Last February a letter had come to her family addressed to her cousin, who was no longer living with them. Since she did not know where Euen had moved on to, she returned the letter with a note of her own to the sender, Finn McKaslin.

Even thinking his name sent little tingles of life through her soul. He was twenty-one to her eighteen, and she well remembered him from the days when he'd attended Angel Falls's public school and all the times she spotted him around town. Folks called him trouble and he was surely that, but she could see the pain in him, the heart and the tenderness. He was capable of so much, and she believed a great goodness lived inside the man. In spite of his mistakes, she cared.

While Finn had met a sad end, he had once been funny and full of life. Handsome didn't begin to describe him. With his midnight-blue eyes, thick dark brown hair and his strong frame, *magnificent* would be a more fitting word to describe him. *Superb* would do nicely, too. Even *extraordinary*.

The letter in her pocket felt heavier, and Earlee supposed she could not hide the truth from herself. *And certainly not from You, Lord.* She was ignoring one teeny-eensy fact. Finn was currently incarcerated in the territorial jail over in Deer Lodge. He had responded to her letter, he'd written her in return, asking for news of the town. She had written to him with friendliness only, but she couldn't deny that in her soul, in places she did not dare look, were buried tiny seeds of hope for more.

"Earlee!" Her sister Beatrice called, her annoyance echoing through the storm. "Hurry up! We're late enough. Don't make it worse."

"Coming." She strode out, walking faster, forcing her thoughts to the school day ahead and the arithmetic lesson she was likely missing. Her friends would already be warm and tucked into their seats at school. Her steps lightened simply thinking of them.

If only she could get him out of her mind, then she could do a better job at her schoolwork. Frustrated,

Meredith blew a curl out of her eyes and stared at her slate, wishing she could make sense of the scribbles of the vocabulary words she was supposed to be learning. Too bad the letters were incomprehensible squiggles and lines her brain did not want to decipher. And why?

Because Shane Connelly would not vacate her brain.

I could never like a man like him, she told herself. Why couldn't she feel this way toward Lorenzo Davis? It would give Mama fits of bliss. She peered through her lashes across the desk, past Scarlet bent over her vocabulary list to the handsome young man who her mother had deemed the most acceptable boy in town. The Davis family had come from Connecticut and a respectable banking fortune, and since Papa owned the bank in Angel Falls, Mama had blessed the match.

The only problem was, Lorenzo, as cute as he was, had never turned her head, not seriously, and she had never done the same for him. No, if he had eyes for anyone, it was Fiona, but as she was marrying someone else, he was likely to be single for a long while.

Someone bumped her elbow, startling her out of her reverie. Had she been staring at Lorenzo? She hadn't meant to. She noticed Scarlet inching her slate closer on their shared desk. A note was written there.

Lorenzo? Scarlet winked, and the sparkle in her eyes put a nuance to the word.

No, Meredith wrote on her slate. She was not sweet on the poor guy.

The horse driver guy? Scarlet scribbled.

"Class, your attention please." Miss Lambert stood to

ring her handbell. "It is three-thirty. You are dismissed for the day."

Shoes thundered against the floorboards as several dozen students flew out of their desks, talking all at once. Meredith grabbed her book bag and shoved her slate into it. She moved fast, but she already knew it would be nearly impossible to evade Scarlet's curiosity. Or Earlee, who had mentioned meeting Shane on the road this morning when they had been eating lunch.

Just because she had managed to change the subject at the time did not mean she was free from questions about the man. As much as she loved her dear friends, they had one-track minds when it came to boys. How long she could delay having to mention anything more about the horse driver guy was anyone's guess. She grabbed her last book and launched out of the desk.

"Minnie!" She spotted her sister in the crowded vestibule where the girl was chattering away with her friend Maisie. "I've got to run up to Lawson's. Tell Connelly to come fetch me there."

"Why don't you do it yourself?" Minnie tugged on her mittens. She beamed adoration for the horseman. "He's so nice. I'm sure he will. He's right outside waiting for us."

"You have him take Maisie home first." That ought to keep him busy for a while and delay having to face him. "Then you can swing by the mercantile."

"I'm surprised you aren't rushing out to meet the guy. Talk about handsome. Wow." Earlee sidled up to her, coats in hand. "Here, I fetched yours, too."

"Thanks, Earlee." Resigned, she accepted the garment and slipped into it, making her way toward the door. A glance over her shoulder told her that the rest of the gang wasn't far behind. "I'm going to pick out more material for my quilt. I've changed my mind about the border fabric."

"Hey, I can come with you. I've got an errand at the post office." When Earlee smiled, the whole world shone. "Besides, I have to come lend a hand. You know how I love looking at all the fabric."

"You and me both." Snow pelted her face as she tugged up her hood. The steps were slick beneath her shoes as she trudged down to the yard along with a long line of students. Kids ran off screaming and laughing, snowballs filled the air and a long parade of horses, vehicles and waiting parents lined the road. Judging by the tap-tapping of her pulse, Shane Connelly had to be close.

Best just to keep walking and not look to the left or right. Straight ahead, that way she could ignore him. She didn't have to remember how she'd acted this morning as long as she didn't have to see his face.

"The horse driver guy is amazingly gorgeous," Scarlet said. "He's waving at you, Meredith."

"So? It's my plan to ignore him." Forever, if she could get away with it.

"Why?" Lila fell in stride beside her. "He looks nice. Not as handsome as Lorenzo, but who is?"

"I suppose that's in the eye of the beholder." Fiona joined the group, pulling on her mittens as she waded through the snow. "I happen to think my Ian is the most handsome of all."

"True love will do that to a girl," Earlee commented with a dramatic sigh.

"Do what? Make her blind?" The words were out before Meredith could stop them, sarcastic and cynical even for her. What was the matter with her today?

There was only one answer. Shane Connelly. He was what had happened to her, stirring her up, twisting her inside out, making her sound like her mother. She could feel his pull like gravity tugging against her, and she set her chin, refusing to look at him. Did it stop her from wondering about him?

No. What was he thinking as she marched past? Was he glad she kept going?

"Meredith." Lila laughed. "What has happened to you? You've gotten cynical."

"Unrequited love can do that to a girl," Scarlet answered before Meredith could.

"It's not unrequited love." Honestly. Where had Scarlet gotten such an idea? "For your information, Shane Connelly isn't the slightest bit interested in me."

"He sure has eyes for no one else," Earlee commented with a sigh. "Look at the way he watches you. I could pen a story about this, with love triumphant and a happy ending."

"Love triumphant?" Her shoe slipped in the snow, sending her off balance. She caught herself and remained upright, although she felt as if she were falling as she turned to catch a glimpse of the man.

Across the expanse of snow and distance, she spotted him standing tall and regal, the wind tousling his dark locks and whipping the hem of his coat. His gaze hooked hers, shrinking the distance, silencing the noise, arrowing straight to her soul. She felt touched, impossible from such a great distance, but she could not halt the sensation. She felt exposed in places she never knew existed within her, the corners of her heart, the rooms of her soul.

"I think we have another romance on our hands," Lila announced, hands clasped with glee.

"And another wedding to sew for," Fiona added with a happy lilt, as if she were smiling all the way to her soul. "Who would have thought Meredith would be the next of us to marry?"

"I'm not marrying anyone." Really. She was a practical woman these days and she would prove it, if only she could pull away from Shane's gaze, from the sight of him offering his hand to her little sister and helping her onto the backseat. Minnie chatted with him a moment, and try as she might she could not rip her attention away. Through the tumbling flakes and the span of the road, she felt close to him and the sight of his smile traveled through her like music and hope.

But hope for what? She believed in true love, but knew how rare it was. A chance for such a blessing came perhaps once into a person's lifetime. She did not begin to think for one minute that Shane was that chance.

"But you want to marry someday, right?" Lila asked.

"Sure, when the time is right. In the meanwhile, I have plans. You all know that. I've been studying for the teachers' exam for months."

"Which you will pass easily." Earlee, ever sweet and supportive, took her arm and gave her a squeeze. "You will make a great teacher, Meredith."

"That's the plan." She focused her attention on the

intersection ahead, but her senses were still off-kilter and she could feel Shane's presence like a physical tie stretching between them. Was he watching her? The back of her neck prickled and would not stop.

"Just because you have planned one future, it doesn't mean something better can't happen." Fiona's tone held a smiling quality, and it reminded Meredith that once she'd said the same thing to Fiona. "God might have other plans for you. Better ones. That is exactly what happened to me."

"Shane Connelly is not my future. You all know we have something better to talk about. Fiona's impending wedding." Meredith rolled her eyes, hoping that would effectively divert her friends' attention and her own thoughts from the handsome horseman.

The conversation changed tracks as they walked together, laughing and chatting down the town streets, but her thoughts and her sense of Shane did not.

He could see her through the mercantile's front window at the fabric counter, chatting with one of her friends from school, the one with brown hair. The others must have gone on their separate ways while he'd been delivering Minnie's best friend home. Because the girl lived a few blocks behind the town's dress shop, he figured the purpose of such an errand was so the little girls could chat and giggle together a bit longer before being parted for the day. Even now, Minnie was in the backseat scribbling a note to the friend they'd just dropped off.

Females. He shook his head, deciding they were an enigmatic bunch. He pulled his watch from his shirt pocket and frowned. Braden had expected him back by now. They had been evaluating the yearlings, two-year-olds and the new horses Worthington had purchased earlier in the year. Work was waiting and Miss Meredith did not seem to care, concerned as she was with fabric. She did look a fine sight at the counter in her beautiful dress and soft bouncing curls trailing down her back.

You are not going to let her distract you from your work, Shane. He'd made that promise to Braden and to himself. But she could tempt the sun from the sky with her loveliness. Her words this morning had hurt him, but they had shown him something, too.

"Does she always take this long?" he asked, glancing at his watch again.

"Yes." Minnie rolled her eyes. "Sometimes she takes longer. She's taking her time on purpose, you know. She's mad at you because you're driving instead of her."

"I don't think that's why she's mad at me." He shivered as the wind gusted, and he felt the cold driving through his layers of wool and flannel, more than he usually did. He'd spent the morning feeling her contempt with every step, every block and, finally, every mile between them.

"Trust me," Minnie confided. "She's real upset about the driving thing."

"Yep, I noticed that."

"Except she's not very good at it." Minnie put down her pencil, glad to have someone to share her secrets with. "Yesterday after school, she had to have one of the boys at school help her rehitch Sweetie to the buggy and then she backed into the hitching post in town. That was before she got stuck in the mud."

"That's one tough day." Why couldn't he look away? It was as if every molecule he owned longed for the sight of Meredith. She was pure as spun sugar with her pretty face bright in laughter. Unaware he was watching her, she accepted a wrapped bundle from her friend behind the counter and lifted a long slender hand in goodbye.

She has captured me, he thought, as surely as if she'd hobbled him like a horse at the ankles. He watched, enchanted as she whirled toward the front of the store, giving him a perfect view of her flawless face, the breadth of her smile, the shimmering brightness of her merriment. Her long skirts swirled and swished as she paced closer to the door. She shined as if she brought the lamplight with her.

This was a Meredith he'd never seen before, another side of the puzzle that was the woman. A bell jangled as she opened the store's glass door, waltzing toward him like sunshine on the darkest of days. As her shoes tapped on the damp boardwalk, he launched off the seat and, with a bow, held out his hand.

She lifted a slender eyebrow, perhaps sensing his sarcasm. He could not stop the rolling crest of emotion threatening to take him over. The snow did not touch him, the wind did not chill him as she laid the palm of her hand softly against his. Time stopped, his soul stilled and her gaze found his.

Wide-eyed and startled, she did not move. Nor did he. A second stretched into a moment without heartbeat or breath, and he felt as if eternity touched him. It was only her stepping up into the buggy. She looked away, her hand slipped from his and it was as if the contact had never been. They were once again separate. She, with her chin in the air and he, standing below her on the boardwalk with weak knees.

"Shane?" Minnie gripped the back of the front seat bouncing in place as he took his place at the reins. "Can we swing by Maisie's house again? Please, please, please? I've got to give her this."

"A note? But you just saw her." He released the brake, trying to pretend he was not shaken, but his voice came out thick and raw.

"But it's important," Minnie pleaded. "Please?"

"You were in school all day with her." He gave the reins a snap, checking over his shoulder for traffic as the mare moved out, pulling them along behind her. "Can't it wait until tomorrow?"

"No, or I wouldn't have asked you."

What he would give to be as thick-skinned as Braden. Then it would be easy to disappoint the pixie with the fairy-tale freckles and eyes just like Meredith's.

If he turned his head, he could barely see Meredith out of the corner of his eye sitting as regal as a princess clutching the wrapped bundle on her lap.

"Fine," he said to the little girl. "But I'm going to need something in return."

"Whatever can I do for you, Mr. Connelly?" Minnie asked primly, bouncing on the seat.

"I'm partial to molasses cookies. Put in a good word with Cook for me, would you?" While Minnie laughed in agreement, he noticed the hook in the corners of Meredith's rosebud mouth. She fought a smile she could not fully suppress, and to him it was as if spring had returned.

Chapter Seven

The shady outline of the house appeared in the twilit snowfall, telling her they were home. She gathered her things the moment the buggy stopped rolling and hopped down before Shane could reach her. He looked busy enough tending to Sweetie; perhaps she had a rock in her shoe with the way he knelt, the mare's hoof resting on his knee.

Ignoring the temptation to gaze upon him a few moments more, she offered Minnie a hand. She had to make sure the girl did not slip as she landed with a two-footed thud. The flakes were larger and wetter, hitting like little slaps against her hood and her face, smacking in imprecise rhythms against her coat and the ground. Warming, the snow had grown slick and dangerous.

"Sorry I couldn't help you," Shane shot over his shoulder, apologetic and sincere. A furrow dug into his forehead. Worry for the horse?

"Is Sweetie all right?" she asked, concerned. She adored their little mare.

"Just a little heat is all, I think." The concern returned

to narrow the hard ridges of his face and made more prominent the high cheekbones and the straight blade of his nose. "Tomorrow you fine ladies will not be riding in that buggy."

"You mean we have to use the barn sled?" Minnie skipped over to the kneeling man and rubbed her hand across Sweetie's flank. "The one used for hauling hay?"

"Depends on what the weather brings." Shane gently returned the mare's hoof to the ground, rubbing her comfortingly. "If there's more snow, then yes. If the weather warms, it will be on horseback."

"That would be great. Wouldn't it, Meredith?" Minnie's dimples flashed.

"Either choice would give Mama the vapors." She should be turning on her heels and putting as much distance possible between her and Shane. So why were her feet carrying her toward him?

Dumb decision, she told herself. The man was nothing but trouble. The kind of trouble she knew best to avoid. "Papa won't allow it."

"The mare is fine today, but drive her tomorrow in worse conditions and she could founder." The disdain evaporated, replaced by a grim set of his expressive mouth, and she realized his feelings were over the horse's welfare and not because she was anywhere near him.

A tiny fission of relief rippled through her, like the wind through the snow. Odd, the effect this man had on her.

"What's founder?" Minnie asked. "It sounds bad."

"It means to go lame." He rose to his full six feet.

"Don't worry, I'll take good care of her. She needs a bit of rest and some pampering. She's an old mare and we don't want to ask too much of her. Unless you don't care what happens to her."

"Of course we do." She stroked her fingertips along Sweetie's neck, smiling when the animal leaned into her touch with a nicker. Such a sweet girl, really. "We want the best for our Sweetie."

"Don't let anything happen to her, Mr. Connelly." Minnie wrapped her arms around the mare's front leg, holding on tight. The horse lipped the brim of her cap with affection.

"I won't, shortcakes. And you might as well call me by my given name." He gave her braid a tug. "Don't forget your promise to me, now."

"Not on my life." Minnie flushed, gazing up at him between her long curling lashes. She released the horse and took off, book bag bouncing on her shoulder. "I'll go talk to Cook right now!"

Fine, so he was kind to Minnie. He was probably the kind of man who was great with children. She could admit that he wasn't *all* bad. The deep fading notes of Shane's chuckle rumbled through her, scattering her senses, drawing her to him like the snow to the earth. Vaguely, she heard Minnie shut the front door with a thud and she realized they were alone. With the curtains of white cocooning them from sight of the house, they could very well be the only two people on the high Montana prairie.

"Thank you for being so nice to my sister."

"No need for thanks. She's a good kid, and I'm not as bad as you think." Dimples hinted, bracketing his mouth with the promise of more. "I don't know how, but you heard what I said about you last night. Isn't that right?"

It was hard to read the tone of his voice, for it was dangerously light and bordering on amusement, but the set of his features and the lines of his face remained like stone.

"The bunkhouse door was open," she confessed. "The cookies were still in the oven when Sadie bundled up your meals. She wanted you to have dessert, but she was busy helping Cook with the dishes, so—"

"You volunteered." He finished her sentence, nodding slightly. He laid a hand on Sweetie's withers, a touch to let the mare know he hadn't forgotten she was standing hot and lathered in the icy winds. His attention did not flicker, his gaze latched on to Meredith's in understanding. "You came to serve us dessert? You? Did your mother know?"

"Don't act so surprised. I wanted to ease Sadie's workload a bit, that was all." Snow flocked her curls, enveloping her with purity and drawing the feelings he had refused to acknowledge a little closer to the surface. She flushed, as if embarrassed. "I wanted to apologize for how Mama treated you. That's why I volunteered. I felt so bad about what she said to you, and the way she said it. But things didn't work out according to plan."

"That's fairly obvious since I never did get any of the cookies."

"I'll make sure you get double dessert with your supper tonight." She cast her gaze downward at her shoes, where she toed the snow. Her hair fell around her, soft bouncy curls around the most beautiful face he had ever seen. She appeared troubled, and vulnerable.

"Braden was concerned you would distract me from my work. That's what you overheard. Do you want to apologize for what you said about me in the school yard?" He had to ask. He had to know if she forgave him.

Her toe stilled. She pulled herself up like a ballerina, elegance and grace, and her blue eyes began to sparkle like an ocean storm. The corners of her mouth tipped into a full-fledged grin, dazzling in its honesty. Trouble glittered there along with a measure of amusement.

"*That* I am not sorry for," she trilled, spinning in the snow to waltz away from him. "Now we're even."

"Even?" The way a woman's mind worked puzzled him greatly.

"We've both agreed we are not interested in the other whatsoever, so now we may as well call a truce."

"A truce?" He knew from the sound of her gait that she was on the steps.

"As long as it's not terribly disagreeable to you." She disappeared into the storm, lost to his sight, her voice as buoyant and as warm as a May breeze.

"Not too terribly disagreeable," he admitted. "Marginally bearable."

"Good. Then we're in perfect agreement."

He searched for the hint of her shadow, the movement of her skirts. The lamplight at the window glinted off a golden curl, the only sign of her in the storm. He did not know why she drew him. But if the grin on his face and in his soul were any indication, he was in trouble. Big trouble.

"Have a good afternoon, Just Meredith."

The door swung open and heavy footsteps tapped onto the porch. "What is going on out here?" Mrs. Worthington demanded. "Meredith, why are you speaking with this person? You could catch your death standing in the cold. Get inside before you freeze clean through."

"Yes, Mama." There wasn't a contrite note to her words as they died on the wind. The door creaked shut, and she was gone. The brightness within him, the one she had put there, remained.

"C'mon, Sweetie." He knelt to unbuckle the traces. "Let's get you washed, rubbed dry and tucked in your warm stall. What do you say?"

The mare nickered in agreement, and they headed off together, side by side as the snow warmed, and crystal drops of ice rained down on them.

"It's lovely fabric, Meredith." Tilly's gentle alto chased away the icy remains of Mama's mood. Their mother had long since retreated from the parlor although her reprimand had not.

"Meredith, it would please me if you did not talk with the hired men." She could still hear the authority and ring of Mama's footsteps as she'd crossed the wooden floor of the parlor. "I'm in the middle of tea. Now I do not wish to be disturbed again."

She had disappeared down the hall to the solarium in the north wing. Now and then women's voices merry with conversation drifted down the long hall that separated the wings of the house. Mama was hosting another gathering of her friends, all the finest wives of

the wealthiest families in Angel County. She knew her
mother meant well, but how on earth was she going to
avoid speaking with Shane? Especially now that her
pride was no longer hurting?

"I liked it better than the silk Mama insisted on."
Meredith turned her thoughts back to the fabric she
was showing her sister. She thumbed the purple cotton
fabric with the tiny sprigged rosebuds. "Lila pieced a
patchwork quilt years ago done in calico fabrics and
I've always admired it."

"Calico quilts can make a room feel cozy and snug."
Tilly's understanding was worth more than all the
money in the world. "It will make a nice addition to
your hope chest."

"My far-in-the-distant-future-perhaps chest," she
corrected, lifting the folded fabric and giving it a shake.
The plentiful yards tumbled over the sofa in a cascade
of ivory cotton and miniature green leaves. "Maybe
it will be for my first place when I'm on my own as a
teacher."

"Your plans may change." Tilly took an end, holding
it out. "The right man may come along and save you
from my fate."

"You are not a spinster yet, Matilda." She ached for
her poor sister, whose beauty ran deep, but it was a
sad state of the world that many men did not measure
a woman for her internal beauty. The one slight interest Matilda had from Emmett Sims, a local teamster,
had faded away. While she had never expressed her
disappointment, Meredith knew it was there, a secret
sadness her older sister did her best to hide. She did
not know how to comfort her and sighed. "And even

if we both grow old without husbands, there are much worse fates."

"True. There is pestilence and plagues." Tilly gathered up the material in her arms, drawing yard after yard into a messy bundle. "Or we could take up smoking."

Thinking of their rebellious younger sister, they burst into laughter. Their peals echoed against the coved ceiling.

"Can you imagine?" She helped Tilly with the last bit of fabric. "Mama would burst."

"If we did that, we would have to take up horseback riding, too."

"Maybe chewing tobacco."

"We could learn to spit."

"So much for the family's reputation."

"From couth to uncouth in sixty seconds." Tilly gasped, sputtering. "It would be a total waste of our finishing school."

"True." She led the way through the dining room, the last vestiges of laughter fading. "Have you ever thought how different our lives would be if we weren't Worthingtons?"

"Now and then." Tilly's smile remained, but it had turned sad. "Emmett and I—"

She didn't finish. She didn't have to. Events might have turned out differently for Tilly. He was a teamster, a common occupation about which Mama had made her opinion very clear. Meredith couldn't help her suspicions. "Do you think our mother said something to discourage him? The way she's treated Shane makes me wonder. Do you think she did the same with the Sims brothers?"

"Who knows?" Tilly shouldered open the kitchen door. "If Emmett didn't care enough about me to stand up to Mama, then…" She said no more, turning away, disappearing into the kitchen.

Meredith caught the door. She didn't know what to say to ease her sister's devastation. She wished there was a way to piece those broken dreams back together for her.

"I'll be happy to get this washed up for you, Meredith." Sadie's voice rose above the clatter Cook was making at the stove. The scent of baking pork roast filled the air. "This is lovely fabric. It will be a perfect match with those blocks you are piecing."

"Thanks. I think so, too. Would you like the scraps when I'm done?"

"Oh, I would love them. Thank you." Sadie curtseyed, her accent sweet as the delight on her face. Soft auburn curls tumbled down beneath her ruffled cap. "It will go well with the scrap quilt I'm making."

"You've started a quilt?" Sadie was another sad story. The girl was the same age as Meredith and her friends, but she was an indentured servant, working off the cost of her steamer and train fare from Ireland. She was poor without family to help her and without the chance for an education. The difference in their lives, although they were a month apart in age, reminded Meredith how fortunate she was. Why the Lord had blessed her well and not Sadie, she did not understand. "I would love to see it."

"Truly? I can show you on Sunday." Her only day off. "I've just started piecing my first blocks."

"The beginning is always so exciting."

"Yes, and—"

"Sadie!" Cook bellowed. "I'll not have you wasting time like a lazy lout. Get over here and scrub these pots."

"Yes." Sadie bobbed her head in acquiescence, shot Meredith an apologetic shrug and gathered the big ball of fabric into her arms. She disappeared into the lean-to where the washtubs were kept.

"Out!" Cook commanded with a straight-armed point. "I have work to do."

"Sorry." Tilly and Meredith together backed out of the kitchen. Pots clanged and banged, the sound chasing them through the dining room.

Against her will, her shoes skidded to a stop at the wide windows. She could not say why as she looked over the garden and glimpsed at the barns. Ice clung to everything, sheeting the glass panes, dripping from exposed tree branches and varnishing the great expanse of snowy ground. Shane was out there, lost to her sight. She didn't know why her thoughts returned to him now, but thinking of him made quiet joy whisper through her. She was Just Meredith to him again.

He caught glimpses of her through the rest of the afternoon. When he hauled buckets of water from the pump behind the main barn, the windows of the house glowed golden through the gray, catching his attention, a haven of light and shelter in the freezing storm. Ice beat against his face as he caught sight of her sewing industriously while Minnie paraded around the parlor with her slate in hand, perhaps practicing her spelling homework.

Later, after nightfall and several trips with the wheelbarrow to clean the stalls, he saw Meredith at the dining-room table, bent over her schoolbooks. The ice-glazed glass made the scene ethereal, as if out of a dream. The way she sat, spine straight, arms folded primly on the table before her, made her endearing, an image he carried with him back into the horse stables when he took up his pitchfork.

"Tomorrow we start working with the yearlings in the morning. The two-year-olds in the afternoon." Braden sauntered up to fling forkfuls of clean straw into the newly mucked-out stall. "We'll be up and at work by five to get a full twelve-hour day in. I want to get our work done as fast as we can. The missus paid a visit to me today, and I'm already eager to be outta here."

"Can't blame you there." He could well imagine what the woman had told a rough-and-ready like Braden. All he had to do was to imagine what his own mother would have said. She looked down on anyone who performed manual labor. According to her last letter twelve months ago, she looked down on him, too. "Some folks put a lot of importance on the wrong things."

"That's why I work with horses." Braden shook the last of the straw free from the tines and backed down the breezeway. "Horses make sense to me. People don't."

"Some people," he agreed. He forked soiled bedding from the adjacent stall into the wheelbarrow, and the yearling filly he'd tied in the aisle watched him curiously as he worked.

"I'll have this done in a jiffy, girl." He kept his voice low and friendly. Tonight she was interested in him, someone fairly new. The sweet little thing had been well-treated. She didn't shy when he'd approached and she showed no fear now of the pitchfork or his swift movements as he tossed the last of the bedding into the barrow. "Are you going to let me teach you all about a bridle tomorrow, pretty filly?"

Her brown eyes sparkled, liking the sound of his voice. He leaned the pitchfork safely against the wall out of her reach and curled his hands around the worn wooden handle of the wheelbarrow.

"At least you've been well-treated here," he told her as he puffed on by. A full load of dirty straw was a heavy one. "I have a feeling that's the only reason Braden and I are staying."

The filly nickered once as she reached out with her nose to try to grab the hat off his head. Her whiskery lips clamped on his brim, but he was quicker, dodging her just enough that his Stetson escaped any teeth prints.

"That's the truth," Braden called out, his boots pounding closer, and fresh straw landed with a rustling whoosh in the filly's stall. "Any serious trouble from that woman and we're gone. So don't get too attached to this place. Or, more importantly, to anyone here."

"What makes you say that?" Shane set down his load to heave the end door open.

"I got eyes." The force of Braden's frown could be felt all the way down the aisle.

"I'm not attached. I'm not going to get attached."

"See that you don't. Final warning."

"Don't need for a warning." Shane gripped the handles and put his back into setting the wheelbarrow in motion. The front wheel squeaked across the threshold. Stinging pellets of ice slapped across his nose and cheeks and bulleted against his coat.

The instant he was free of the door, where did his gaze inexorably go? To the big window where Meredith now stood beside the dining-room table, gathering up her books and slate, chatting away with her older sister, laughing and full of life.

His chest hitched. Surprised, he shook his head, forced his attention away from her and swiped ice off his brim. Braden didn't know what he was talking about. He and Meredith were worlds apart. More than social status divided them.

He manhandled the wheelbarrow across the crackling ice, his boots sliding out beneath him as he went. Perilous going. Keeping himself upright and in control of the wheelbarrow ought to be enough to keep his mind off the girl but it wasn't. Ice skidded down the back of his neck, needled through the layers of his clothes and numbed the tips of his fingers while he worked, emptying the contents of the wheelbarrow into the manure pile, one forkful at a time.

His teeth were chattering when he finished. Only a single lantern burned in the end aisle of the stable. Braden had gone through and carefully put out all the others, making the horses safe for the night. Shane stowed the fork and the wheelbarrow in the stable, and after waiting for Braden to lock up, led the way back to their quarters. The ice was softening, the downfall changing to freezing rain rather than ice, making the going so treacherous they skated the last ten yards to their front door.

"I'd best go fetch our meal." He didn't want Sadie coming out from the main house and risking a fall on his account.

"I was young once, too." Braden almost cracked a smile before he turned stoically into the bunkhouse and kicked his boots against the door frame to beat off chunks of ice.

It was worth the inclement weather and the near fall into a berry bush for the chance to see Meredith's smile one more time. He didn't figure she would be in the kitchen—she wasn't. But she was nearby. He could hear the low alto of her voice through the kitchen door. That was enough.

He took time checking through the heavy basket to make sure nothing was missing. He made sure there were two servings of pork roast, mashed potatoes and dinner rolls and went in search of the dessert. Molasses cookies, just as he'd asked for. Two dozen of them, just as Meredith had promised.

Happiness he didn't understand accompanied him through the storm. Rain tapped off his hat as he reached the bunkhouse door. He spotted her in the dining-room window, ready to draw the curtains. He couldn't be sure but he thought he saw her smile. A truce, she'd said.

That sounded mighty fine to him. He was looking forward to it. He stomped the ice off his boots, stumbled through the front door and into the bunkhouse.

Chapter Eight

"I'm sorry," was all that Tilly had said the moment they'd spotted Shane seated on the high front seat of the buggy, driving two of the draft horses kept for farm work up to the house. "I know I promised to drive, but with the roads in a worse condition than ever, I just don't feel up to it."

"It's all right. I have set my mind to endure the man." Meredith had closed the front door behind them, seized her sewing basket and clomped down the steps into the cold rain. Framed by a silent, steel-gray sky, he'd tipped his hat at her as solemn as a judge except for the mischief sparkling in his eyes of midnight blue.

Mama had waved them off with dire warnings about the road conditions. The moment Shane extended his hand to her to help her onto the seat beside him, summer washed over her. She settled her skirts, taking care to smooth the blue flannel fabric so it wouldn't wrinkle. When Shane leaned close to tuck a warm blanket over her, she took the length of wool from him and tucked it in herself. Just because she'd declared a truce did not mean she wanted him any closer than he had to be.

The ride had been a bumpy and a muddy one, and with Shane sharing the seat with them, she and Tilly didn't take time to chat. Fiona's little rental house came into sight and the usual excitement trilled through her. She couldn't wait for the wagon wheels to stop turning and had the blanket off her before Shane could lend her his hand. As his strong fingers wrapped around hers, the sense of summer returned.

Surely, a flitting sense of whimsy, that was all. Nothing to worry about.

"Have a good time, Miss Meredith." His dimples ought to be against territorial law for the effect they had on a girl.

"I intend to, Mr. Connelly." She shivered in the wind, waiting for him to hand down the food hamper and her sewing basket. She hardly had time to think of him again because the front door flew open and Fiona rushed out to meet her.

"Meredith! We were beginning to worry." She wrapped a shawl around her shoulders, hurrying through the mash of melting snow, ice and thawing ground. "But you're here safe and sound after all. Thanks to your very capable driver."

"He's just doing his job." Honestly, she had to set her friends straight about the man before they started planning her and Shane's life together. She waved to her sister, let Fiona wrestle the food hamper away from her and they tripped up the steps together. "Don't get any ideas. Shane is here only for a few months. Maybe less if their work is done sooner."

"He's gallant." Fiona tumbled through the doorway into the cozy front room. "Did you all notice Meredith's new driver? He's escorting her around again today. On a Saturday."

Before she could get a word of explanation in, Scarlet called out from one of the chairs set in a circle around the tiny sitting area. "Fortunate for you, Meredith. I wouldn't mind a handsome driver of my own."

"Wouldn't we all?" Kate glanced up from her embroidery work. "I love my dad, he's such a dear to drive me all the way to town and back, but I wouldn't mind my own driver. Let's say he could be a tall handsome stranger with dark eyes and a mysterious past."

"Oh, I could write a story about that." Earlee squinted as she threaded a needle.

"That's the only way I'm going to have a happy ending considering the boys at school. We don't have much to pick from," Kate quipped. "Aside from Lorenzo, who else would you marry?"

"Luken Pawel," Lila answered immediately, setting down the calico dress she was basting. "What? You all don't need to look so shocked."

"You're always going on about how Lorenzo is utterly too-too." Meredith shrugged out of her coat and sat in the chair by the door to unbutton her muddy shoes. "I thought you only had eyes for him."

"*Aside* from Lorenzo, she said," Lila clarified, eyes twinkling. "If he and his family moved back east, I would have to set my sights lower, to be sure. It would take me a while to get over the heartbreak, but I would eventually move on. There are other handsome men in town."

"Not *that* handsome." Kate giggled as she pulled a long strand of green embroidery thread through her hoop, fussing with it so it would lie just right. "Face it, the pickings are slim."

"That's because we've known everyone forever," Earlee added. She tied a slipknot at the end of her needle and thread. "This is a small town, and we've grown up with the same guys. It's hard to foster any romantic feelings over the boy who spilled ink on your favorite dress, or put a salamander in your lunch pail."

"James Biddle did that." Scarlet set down her crochet hook. "I was seven and I may have forgiven him a long time ago, but forgetting is another thing. If Lorenzo moved away, then I would simply pine for him and grow old as a spinster. We may as well face it, girls. There is a shortage of decent, solid bachelors in this town. If you're picky about looks, then it's even slimmer pickings."

Meredith took a moment to gaze at the circle of best friends. Five of them had been together since their first day of Sunday school when they were just little girls. When her family moved to town over five years ago, she had been welcomed into their midst with loving arms. She felt as if she had always been a part of their friendship, the kind of bond that would always endure. As she slipped into the last available place beside Earlee on the horsehair sofa, overwhelming gratitude breezed through her.

God had been looking out for her the day He led her to their circle, and she felt His presence greatest when they were assembled together.

"We all can't have handsome strangers ride into our lives the way Fiona and Meredith have." Kate debated the placement of her needle before pulling it through her hoop.

"Whoa there." Meredith pulled out her latest patchwork square and her threaded needle. "Don't put me in the same category as Fiona. There's a big difference. She's about to be married. I am trying to make peace with a man my father hired. There's a big difference between the two."

"Make peace?" Fiona returned from the kitchen with two cups of steaming honeyed tea. "Are you two getting along now?"

"I'm trying, but he's an impossible man," she quipped. She smoothed her sewing on her knee and studied it as if it held all the importance and Shane Connelly none. *Here it comes,* she thought, *the place where her friends begin imagining what isn't there.*

"That's what I thought, too, when I was getting to know Ian." Fiona set one of the cups on a nearby footstool that served as their coffee table. "He was impossible and maddening and wonderful. And that part of things hasn't changed."

"But your feelings toward him did," Lila pointed out, returning to one of the long skirt seams of her new dress. "The same thing could happen with Meredith."

"I wouldn't hold my breath if I were you." Meredith pawed through her basket for a stack of small fabric squares she had cut out over several sewing circles past. She considered the different colors of calico and chose a blue piece to add to her square. "He isn't at all interested, just like I'm not interested in him. He's said so."

"Not interested in you?" Fiona straightened, taking

care not to spill the cup she held. "I don't believe that for a second."

"Believe it. He said he can't be distracted from his work."

"Oh, Meredith. I'm sorry." Fiona's dear face wreathed with concern. Her sympathy was mirrored on the rest of her friends' faces. Needles stilled. Sewing projects were set aside.

"So that explains what you said about him." Fiona nodded, as if it were all making sense to her. "Well, he doesn't sound like the nicest man."

"Yes, that's what I thought, too. But I think he really is all right. We've called a ceasefire of sorts." Meredith blushed, feeling too many curious and caring gazes on her. She carefully pinned her piece into the block, eyeing the quarter-inch seam allowance. "Like I said, he'll be gone soon, and that's enough about me. Fiona's wedding is coming up. Are you starting to get nervous?"

"Not one bit. I've never been more sure of anything in my life." Her beloved friend wasn't fooled, judging by the way the sympathy on her face changed to understanding. "A few more weeks, we'll all be graduated, I'll be married and then Ian will be able to move in here as my husband. Let me take this tea in to Nana and I'll be right back."

Fiona swept from the room to open one of the doors that opened from the sitting area. Meredith caught a glimpse of a well-appointed bedroom. Ian had moved his grandmother out to live with them, and Fiona cared for the elderly woman who was in fragile health. Never had her friend looked so happy. Becoming engaged was a definite improvement to Fiona's life and Meredith knew the marriage would be a great blessing for her.

"The right man will come along one day for each of us. I have to believe that." Earlee's head was bowed over her work as she stitched a simple princess collar to the child's dress—she worked on her family's sewing as often as she worked on projects for her hope chest.

"Amen." Scarlet double crocheted, the lacy doily taking shape as she turned it, double crocheting again. "Isn't that why we're all sewing? We have hope."

"Hope." Meredith repeated the word as she took up her needle. Words from Scripture came to mind. *Now faith is the substance of things hoped for, the evidence of things not seen.* She had wishes for a happy future. Maybe one day a handsome, good man who would ride into her life at just the right moment with midnight-blue eyes and a dashing grin, the man who would capture all of her heart.

Why was she picturing Shane? She should not be remembering the scent of hay on his coat and sweet mystery she felt whenever their hands touched. He was still a stranger, a saddle tramp—he'd admitted that himself—someone simply passing through.

She wanted so much more in a man, in a husband, than that. Fiona took her place at the circle and the conversation turned to the wedding plans. While they sewed and talked, rain drummed on the roof and tapped at the windows, making their ring of friendship cozier.

He could see her through the small front window of the shanty, golden hair burnished by the lamplight, transformed by happiness. She might look like a country miss with her simple braid trailing down her back sitting in a typical country home with her sewing on her lap, but when Meredith relaxed and in laughter let her true beauty show, she was extraordinary. She shone like a single star in a sky without light, her luminous goodness a guide for a man alone in the dark.

He waited in the rain until the gathering was over. As the front door opened and the young ladies tumbled out into the cold, gray world, they brought their laughter and life with them. Bonnets and skirts swirling beneath their coats brought color to the dismal afternoon, and their merry farewells and promises to keep for Sunday school tomorrow rang like music. A pair of oxen and a wagon pulled up, loaded with fence posts from the lumber yard. A fatherly man tipped his hat in greeting before extending a hand to one of the girls and driving off with her. She kneeled on the wagon seat, facing backward, waving goodbye to her friends.

A pair of Meredith's friends disappeared around the corner to the stable. A buggy waited in the shelter, perhaps the vehicle they had driven from town. Meredith waved gaily to them before grasping the last girl by the arm and pulling her to the wagon.

"We're giving Earlee a ride," she explained as she handed up the hamper and basket.

"Fine by me." He nodded at the familiar blonde. "We met in the road the other day."

"We did. Thank you for letting me come along this afternoon. It will save me a good mile of walking." She climbed onto the seat beside Meredith, casting her a secret glance. Females were such a mystery to him, he didn't even try to guess what either of them were thinking. Braden was right. Horses were better. You knew where you stood with horses.

He gathered the reins, directing the matched bay Clydesdales around in a circle and back toward home. As he listened to the girls talk about someone named Fiona and a sweet grandmother, he kept his eyes on the road. He ought to be wondering about how Braden was fairing. They were not making the desired progress without the two of them working side by side. Worthington had him driving his daughters all over the county, or at least it seemed that way. When Meredith's laugh trilled, warming the air, a piece of loveliness he enjoyed listening to, he had to admit he didn't mind. But it was a distraction from his work.

She was a distraction, her voice stealing his focus and forcing him to listen to her. Maybe it wasn't the girl that lassoed his attention, but what was missing in his life. He had been lonely this past few year, leaving all his family behind and some friends who hadn't understood his decision. Moving place to place every few months didn't make it easy to establish new friendships.

Maybe loneliness was the reason he felt drawn to her. Maybe it was as simple as that.

"This is where Earlee gets off." Meredith turned to him, her shoulder brushing his arm, the brief contact sweet and comfortable as homecoming.

"Whoa." He drew back, slowing the big animals, who pranced in place and huffed great clouds of breath in the cold. The girls exchanged goodbyes while he gave Earlee his hand. Shyly she avoided his gaze, thanked him and splashed to the ground. She waved, hurrying down an intersecting road, a small figure on the roll and dip of the vast high plains, leaving him and Meredith alone. As he picked up the reins and guided the horses on, he was acutely aware of the rustle of her skirts as she resettled them, the small sigh as she swiped rain off her nose, the faint scent of rosewater.

He should not be noticing such things.

"Do you want to take the reins?" He handed them out to her, when he should have stayed silent. But the hope splashing across her dear face told him he'd done the right thing.

"Do you mean it? You would let me drive?" Her gloved hands were already reaching out, eager for the lines. "I might have to alter my opinion of you."

"No need to go to such extremes."

"I wasn't intending a radical change. Just a tiny step up in my tolerance of Shane Connelly." She bit her bottom lip, as if doing her level best not to break into laughter.

"Tolerance?" He could joke, too. He laid the thick leather straps across her palm. "I thought we agreed to be friends."

"I don't remembering using that word, and I certainly didn't mean we should become kindred souls." Mischief teased the corners of her mouth as she leaned forward to take the reins. Her slender fingers took hold just behind his, and for a moment—one brief span of time—it was as if they were connected by more than the leather straps. "I knew a man like you has his uses."

She was baiting him on purpose. She could not disguise the merriment dancing in her gorgeous blue eyes or the curve of her mouth that she could not hold straight.

"Is that a hint of regard I hear in your voice?" He shook his head, scattering rain off his hat brim.

"No, perhaps the wind is distorting my words."

"It is not distorting my eyesight." He released the lines, leaving them in her dainty hands, hands that he suddenly wanted to cradle within his own. A crazy wish. "You have to know the impact you have on a man."

"Me? What impact could I have?"

"The sight of you can distract a blind man from a mile away." He moved his hands over hers, to adjust the tension of her grip, ignoring the wish taking form and life. "Women with your beauty put us men at a disadvantage. You have been so angry with me, and it wasn't fair. You were the one who caused it. You're pretty enough to befuddle the most stoic of men."

"You think I'm pretty?" Astonishment rounded the soft contours of her mouth. Didn't she know what she was? As beautiful as a princess in a storybook.

"No." He said the word with much emphasis, doing his best to hide the feelings he could not possibly have. "*Pretty* isn't a word I would use to describe you. *Stunning* and *amazing,* maybe. But no, not *pretty.* Remember that the next time you come upon a poor man trying to hold on to his senses."

"Is that what you're doing now? Holding on to your senses?"

"No, because we have a truce."

"Can I ask you something, Shane?"

"Sure." He'd bared enough of his soul. A little more wouldn't hurt.

"Are you in need of glasses?"

"Not to my knowledge."

"A doctor's examination?"

"Nope, I'm fit as a fiddle and my mind is, too." He reached over to draw on the left rein. "Perhaps it's my good taste that is questionable."

"There's no accounting for taste?"

"Yes." The smile blooming through him was like nothing he'd known before. Being with her was like Sunday morning and Christmas Eve all rolled up into one. He leaned to tug on the right rein, guiding the horses. "Best to keep the wagon out of the mud this time."

"It's worse today with the thaw." Up ahead was the mud hole that had claimed her buggy. The entire way was soupy and sloppy from the fence pole marching down the field on one side all the way to the section posts on the other. "There is no way to see the worst of it. It's danger lurking in the depths. That's what I discovered the last time I drove."

"You want to keep to higher ground." He leaned closer yet and the brush of his arm to hers became a steely pressure that scattered her wits. His breath fanned the loose tendrils from her braid. He tugged on both reins, taking charge of the horses. "You see the wagon tracks on the other side of the bog? Keep your eye on them."

"I'd rather keep my attention on the mud." It felt as if no space separated them, as if he were pressed up against her from the powerful length of his thigh to the forceful curve of his shoulder. Her wits were definitely gone right along with every lick of sense.

"Look beyond the problem, Meredith." He guided the horses to the left, toward what she was sure was danger. "Try to get the wheels out of the ruts. Line them up and give the horses more speed."

"Speed? I would rather go slower when the wagon mires down and tips and we go flying out of the seat and onto the ground." Had she really said that? She heard shades of Mama. "It's true. When a girl grows up she turns into her mother. It's happening already."

"Then you had better start listening to me."

"I don't think that's a good idea either." The quip died on her tongue as his hands closed over hers, bands of warm strength that felt intimate in spite of his gloves and her mittens. It was as if they touched skin to skin.

When he gave the reins a smart snap, the movement traveled up the lines through the bones of her fingers, along her arms and inexplicably working its way into her heart.

"We're going to turn over." She felt dizzy and off balance. Was it the wagon? Or her senses?

"We're going to be fine. Trust me."

Trust him? The notion sent her into a panic. The wagon bounced, the wheels splashed and mud flecked up from the horses' hooves. The horses charged forth, trudging through the mud hole with grim determination. One wheel rose up on the high side of the shoulder, tilting the vehicle to the side. She definitely felt as if she were falling, but then the wagon settled with a thud, level and safe. They were on the other side of the mud hole. The horses plodded forward, and Shane released her hands.

"You did it, Meredith. Good job." He didn't move away.

This close, she could make out the gold and green flecks in his stunning blue irises and see the faint hints of a day's growth beginning along his rock-solid jaw. If she looked hard enough, she could see deeper into him. There was a sadness like shadows in his eyes and a hint of lonesomeness she did not understand. Why could she sense these things about him, things she did not want to know?

"Would you come with me to Sunday school tomorrow?" She blurted out the question, surprised by her boldness. Heat stained her face, so she turned her attention to the road ahead and the horses ambling along, the reins heavy in her hands. She felt the tactile brush of his gaze on her face, his curiosity and something deeper she didn't understand.

"Why are you asking me?" He sounded as surprised as she was.

"I know what it's like to move to a new place and to feel as if you are on the outside looking in." She liked to think that was really the reason why she had asked him. "Everyone knows one another and have friends, but not you. So I thought you might like to come along. As a friend and not as my family's hired man."

"I would like that very much." Buttery warm, that baritone, ringing so low she could hardly hear it.

"I only ask because you've been so nice to me," she told him, hearing the defensiveness in her words, feeling it creep through her. It had to be the truth. It wasn't as if she was sweet on the man. He had been kind to let her drive. She needed the practice and she appreciated his help.

"Sure, I understand that." He didn't sound troubled by it. "I have need of a friend, Meredith. I'm starting to like you."

"You're not too bad, yourself." They shared a smile as the house came into sight, their ride together at an end.

Chapter Nine

There was something sacred about the light on a Sunday morning, something special that no other day in the week had. Glad to soak in the peace, Shane guided the Worthington family surrey down the muddy town street. The shops were dark and the boardwalks empty. Only those headed to church followed the road through town to the white steepled church on Third Street where families flocked toward the front steps and children raced around in their Sunday finest on the sodden lawn. He drew the vehicle to a stop near the front stone walkway and hopped into the road with a splash.

"Hurry, young man." Henrietta Worthington held out her gloved hand. "I will not be late for my ladies gathering."

"Sorry, ma'am." He ignored the censure in her voice. She had been the one running late, forcing the horses to wait and criticizing his driving all the way to town. On top of that, the roads had slowed them. The church bells pealed, tolling the hour, as he aided the woman over to the grass, leaving her to help down the oldest daughter, Tilly, who thanked him primly, and Meredith, who did not thank him at all. Her gaze met his like a punch, and he did his best not to reel from it as he released her elbow.

"I'll be waiting for you at the bottom of the basement stairs," she whispered to him, leaning close enough so that only he could hear. Her breath fanned his cheek pleasantly, and the wind lifted that faint scent of rosewater. The fragrance teased his nose, reminding him of sharing the wagon seat with her, closer than he'd ever been to anyone.

Henrietta cleared her throat, and he broke away. Tiny tremors of nerves skidded through him. He wasn't sure if he could hide them completely as he swept the littlest Worthington girl out of the surrey and swung her over the mud.

"Oh, thank you ever so much, Shane!" Once safely on the grass, Minnie clung to his hand. She was adorable with freckles scattered across her nose and her cherub's dimples. "You are the best driver we've ever had."

"Thank you kindly, shortcakes." He tipped his hat to the girl and bowed, as gentlemanly as he knew how to be. He liked the sound of the child's giggle, and he liked much more Meredith's reaction. For one moment her guard slid away, and she smiled at him without reservation. Her happiness in how he'd treated her baby sister was the best reward he could have.

"Young man!" Henrietta marched toward him, chin up, mouth pursed, her plentiful skirts swirling around her like a whirlpool. "Don't forget to blanket the horses. When Reverend Hadly begins the final prayer, you are to leave the sanctuary quietly and bring the horses around. I'll not have my daughters standing overly long in these unacceptably cool temperatures. It is unhealthy."

"Yes, ma'am." Hard not to recognize the disapproval in the woman's manner. She wasn't going to intimidate him. He met her glare and straightened his shoulders. He had done nothing wrong. He guessed that his friendliness and the familiar look he'd shared with Meredith had not gone unnoticed.

"That will be all." With an air of authority, Henrietta dismissed him like a servant, spun on her heels and marched down the walkway, sending any churchgoers in her path scurrying. The woman was formidable, he had to grant her that. Everyone had faults, but there was no mistaking the look of maternal love on her face as she held out her hand to Minnie and an arm to draw Meredith to her side. Matilda followed, their conversation a part of the general din of the growing crowd, the family's closeness a precious blessing.

Love was something his family had lacked. He'd grown up understanding duty, hard work and loyalty, but he had not known love. His maternal grandmother had been his only example of that emotion in his childhood and she had taken it with her when she'd passed away. He didn't know a whole lot about love except to recognize it in others. Maybe that was why he had chosen a nomad's life. It was easier to move on and never put down roots than to stay and try to be something he was not.

As he watched Meredith, something strange happened. He started wondering about roots.

"You! Hurry up there. We're waiting." An impatient

driver pulled up behind the Worthingtons' vehicle and although there was plenty of space, he seemed annoyed not to be closer to the walkway.

"Hold your horses." Shane barely glanced at the fine surrey behind him, the man scowling at him as if he owned all rights to the road.

"Hi there!" A child's voice called above the noises in the churchyard. Edward, the little boy from the muddy hole the other day.

"Howdy," he called out and tipped his hat. The horses jerked the surrey forward, and in the crowd of so many people it was Meredith his gaze arrowed to. Meredith his pulse slowed for. She was with her friends now, chatting excitedly with them. The swish of her bright pink skirt, the lark song of her laughter, her wholesome joy stood out to him like color in a world of gray. He eased the horses to a stop alongside the road in full view of the woman.

Even when he turned his back to her to climb down and tie the team, his ears searched the winds for the melody of her voice and the music of her laughter. He glanced over the backs of the horses as he blanketed them, captivated by her straight, willowy posture, the tumble of her gold hair and the graceful way she moved with her friends toward a door at the side of the church. He stopped breathing when she disappeared from his sight. He stood aching for her like nightfall missing the sun.

It's not as if I'm sweet on the girl, he told himself as he crossed the road. He could always hope the tangle of emotions locked away in his chest had more to do with his lonesomeness than true interest. And if a tiny voice at the back of his mind wanted to argue, then he simply did not have to listen.

"I saw you at the school yard the other day." A female voice cut through his thoughts.

He blinked, turned on his heel, not knowing exactly where he was. He'd been so wrapped up in his thoughts that he hadn't realized he was standing on the church lawn. The grass squished and squeaked beneath his boots. Someone—one of Meredith's friends?—was hurrying toward him. She had dark hair and finely tailored clothing. Pearls gleamed at her throat. Gold glowed from the rings on her hands and from the expensive brooch pinned to her cloak. With her carefully coiffed appearance and a *Godey's Lady's Book* look, she was the kind of girl his mother would rave over.

Not one of Meredith's friends, if he remembered right.

"Aren't you the Worthingtons' new driver?" She flashed him a coquettish smile and tilted her head to one side, as if doing her very best to appear charming. "I'm Narcissa Bell. I know your name is Shane Connelly because I overheard Meredith say so."

Narcissa Bell. That name sounded familiar. It could have been mentioned in one of the conversations he'd tried not to listen to while conveying the girls around. He scanned the churchyard, looking for help. Of the people streaming past either toward the church's front steps or the basement, not one of them looked his way. Looked as if he was on his own with this problem.

"I couldn't help noticing how you handle horses." Her compliment was a purr.

Great. He knew exactly what she was up to. Not that

a girl of society would be interested in a working man, so there had to be some other motive.

"You have a strong way with them and a gentle touch. I admire that so much." She batted her long dark lashes, gazing up at him sweetly.

"Gotta go." Escape was his only response. He hoofed it away as fast as he could. He didn't want to look back, but he was fairly sure the girl followed him.

"Shane! There you are." Meredith marched through a small crowd of schoolboys, scattering them as she advanced like Sherman on Atlanta. Fire blazed in her eyes and her dresses snapped with the fury of her pace. "What are you doing? I have been waiting to introduce you and here you are making cozy with Narcissa."

"Shane and I were having the most wonderful conversation." Narcissa caught up to him and grasped his arm, holding on with a surprising amount of strength for such a fragile thing. "I'm so sorry he forgot all about you, Meredith, but as you can see—"

"Excuse me, miss." Heat burned across his face as he twisted away from the girl's iron clutches. Never had he been more uncomfortable in his life. One girl using her wiles on him, the other enraged and passersby were starting to notice.

"I'll be happy to walk in with you." Narcissa tripped after him and he moved his arm before she could latch on to it again.

"Go ahead. I don't care." Meredith turned on her heel, her face red, her lovely hands fisted. She stormed away, back stiff, shoulders bunched, her skirts rustling furiously.

"Excuse me." With a curt nod, he broke away from

the manipulative debutante. He had to run. Meredith might be willowy and petite, but she was a powerful force. He caught up to her at the open door.

"It wasn't my fault," he quickly explained.

"When it comes to *boys,* it never is." She emphasized the word with a hint of distaste, as if to make clear he'd gone down a step in her estimation.

"I'm no boy." He settled his hand on her shoulder, knowing she would turn toward him, knowing there were more emotions buried beneath her anger. He wanted her to understand. "I see what that girl is trying to do to you. I'm not interested in her."

"This is not about interest." Pride. Meredith's chin went up and she spun way in a swirl of golden curls and pink satin. "I only wanted to warn you, but I can see you've made up your own mind about Narcissa Bell."

"She approached me. I'm perfectly innocent."

"If you want to resume your acquaintance with her, you might want to sit well away from me," Meredith tossed airily over her shoulder as she led the way down the narrow stairs. "Narcissa and I have never gotten along since she insulted my sisters and spread horrible rumors about me when I was new to school, but if you want to befriend her, be my guest. That's your choice. Maybe you were made for each other."

"I didn't mean to betray our friendship." He gentled his voice. He'd forgotten how childhood rivalries could be, how cruelties could build upon cruelties. He'd felt the sting of those once as a boy. He hadn't forgotten. He hated that Meredith was so upset. Surely she wasn't jealous. He puzzled on that as he held up his hands. "We're in a church. Surely you can forgive me?"

"Only because it is my faith."

Was that a hint of humor warming the chill from her voice? She'd relaxed a little, he realized, as she trailed a hand down the banister and hopped off the last stair. They had entered a great room divided by several different sets of clustered chairs. In the far corner young children gathered around a kindly but harried-looking woman who must have been in charge of the little ones. In the center of the room milled the middle-grade children. The final group in their teens looked up to study the stranger in their midst. He recognized many faces from the school yard and noted a few men who looked to be close to his age, about twenty.

"This is Fiona's fiancé, Ian McPherson." Meredith gestured toward a tall, quiet-looking man with a friendly manner. "He's fairly new to our group."

"Good to meet you, Ian." He held out his hand.

"Good to meet you. We're a small group here, but a friendly one." Ian's grip was firm and there was something about him Shane immediately liked. The two of them might have been friends, if time in this town wasn't so limited. "I hear you have taken over Eli's old job."

"What do you do?"

"I work north of town at the lumber mill." Ian drew a dark-haired young woman dressed in gingham to his side. The couple radiated happiness. An engagement ring glittered on her left hand.

A middle-aged woman clapped her hands. "School is about to start. Come and take your places."

Where had Meredith gone?

"Hi, Shane." Narcissa Bell again sauntered by and batted her lashes.

He could feel Meredith's glare of daggers from six chairs away. Poor Meredith was not having a good day. He stepped around Narcissa, hoping to sit with his chosen girl, but her friends surrounded her, taking all the nearby chairs. He noticed the class was segregated by gender—girls on one side, boys on the other, so he joined Ian and Eli Sims. He settled in, greeting Eli, but his attention remained on Meredith.

She didn't look happy with him. Was she truly worried about that Narcissa girl? Didn't she know that her honest, wholesome beauty was far superior? A strange ache settled deep in his chest, one of admiration and respect, he insisted stubbornly, because it could not be anything else. He could not allow it to be.

As the Sunday-school teacher opened her Bible, all he could focus on was the way Meredith sat straight and proper, her attention devout on the open volume she held on her lap. Was it his fault he noticed the vulnerable curve of her nape, the lovely line of her slender shoulder and the soft angle her arm made as she bent over her Bible?

Lord, what are You trying to tell me? He pondered that question, fighting gentler emotion he did not dare acknowledge.

"'*Strength and honor are her clothing,*'" the teacher read from Proverbs, "'*and she shall rejoice in time to come. She openeth her mouth with wisdom; and in her tongue is the law of kindness. Favor is deceitful and beauty is vain, but a woman that feareth the Lord, she shall be praised.*'"

Meredith remained in his sight and in his thoughts all morning long, as did his gentle feelings for her.

The image of seeing Narcissa hanging from Shane's arm burned like a coal-hot brand. It stung all the way to her soul. The scorching did not abate through the lesson or Sunday service. Meredith fidgeted on the hard pew, frustrated. She didn't know what strange emotion was troubling her, but it burrowed into her and would not let go. It was an unwelcome agony and she did not like it.

This *is what came from dealing with men*, she decided. It was a good thing she had set her sights on teaching instead of settling for the first guy who would propose to her. If she got this agitated over a man she hardly liked, think of what it would be like when she did like one?

She was starting to rethink her views on romance. Maybe being a spinster wasn't such a bad idea.

"Meredith! What's wrong with you?" Mama hissed. "Stand up."

Right. The final prayer. She bobbed out of the pew, the last to stand. But were her thoughts contemplative on this morning of worship?

Not a chance. She wished her gaze would not slip from the reverend at the pulpit, across the rows to where Shane sat. He certainly looked fine in a black muslin shirt and matching trousers. She rarely saw him without his hat, and the thick tumble of his dark hair became fascinating and so did the cowlick at the back of his head.

Stop looking at him, she told herself. If she kept

gaping at him, then people would mistakenly start to think that she liked him. She clasped her hands and bowed her head, determined to let only holy thoughts into her brain.

"Let us pray," Reverend Hadly began. "Heavenly Father, we ask for Your loving guidance. As we go through our busy and demanding week, please help us to remember to put on a mantle of kindness."

Only holy thoughts, she reminded herself. But one broke through, and it wasn't faith-centered. Shane drew nearer. She sensed him like the ripple of a breeze from the windows. Her eyes opened; she could not stop them. He padded soundlessly down the aisle, his wool coat clutched in hand and his Bible tucked into one of the pockets. He honestly was the most dashing man in the church, perhaps in the entire town. Maybe it was his classic good looks and his high cheekbones that made him irresistible. She rather thought it was his square jaw hinting at his good character that made it impossible to look away.

This was not fair. Caring about him was not her fault. She was helpless to stop it. A girl did not have a chance around him. She had tried her best to dislike him and if she could not do it, then no one could.

"Meredith!" Mama hissed again, nudging her arm.

She snapped her eyes shut, but did the awareness of him end?

Not a chance. She felt the touch of his gaze against her cheek as he came closer. His shoes whispered on the floorboards and the air around her shivered from his movements.

Just ignore him, she told herself. Could she help it if the hair on her arms prickled as he passed? Perhaps it was a gust of wind blowing through the church and no possible reaction to him.

Mama's elbow bumped her sternly, more serious this time. Clearly her mother did not understand the consequences of being around a man like Shane. She sighed, forced her attention to the front and gave thanks that Shane was safely out of the church. She knew because her mind could focus on the last of the prayer.

"As You have drawn us with loving kindness, help us to remember to see You in all we meet," Reverend Hadly implored. "Amen."

A chorus of "Amens" rang out. The service was almost at an end.

This was like torture. Meredith opened her eyes, feeling a little light-headed from her ordeal. Rustles echoed through the sanctuary as heads were raised, hands reached for hymnals and Mrs. Tilney at the organ began the first strains of "Amazing Grace." Voices lifted with the melody, but all Meredith could think about was Shane out in the rain.

"Meredith, I've decided to get a new beau." Narcissa leaned across the aisle, not even bothering to sing. "Shane is so handsome. You can have Lorenzo if you want."

"I don't want either of them." It felt as if she were telling a lie, and she wasn't. She didn't want a beau. She certainly did not want Shane. She wanted to be an independent woman in complete control of her heart and her life. "Go ahead and set your cap for him. I don't care."

"I'll have him wrapped around my little finger in no time. Just you wait and see." Narcissa's nose went up in the air. Her face crinkled unpleasantly as she gave a disparaging grimace. "There's a reason some girls can't catch themselves a beau."

What she needed at this exact moment was the perfect comeback. Just this one time to really put Narcissa in her place. But could she think of a single word?

No. Meredith bit her bottom lip. Her feelings simmered and yet her mind was as blank as a clean slate. Completely frustrating. Especially because she'd had no trouble doing the same to Shane the other day.

"Meredith!" Mama nudged her with her elbow, leveled her with a warning look and returned to singing the final chorus with great zest.

"…was blind," Meredith joined in, but she couldn't properly concentrate on the song. Narcissa's smugness kept floating across the aisle to her like a foul odor. Finally, the hymn was done and the service ended.

"I don't know what's come over you, young lady," Mama huffed, shaking her head severely. "You are in church."

"Yes, I realize that." She doubted her mother would ever understand. She felt miserable, and not because Narcissa had declared her intentions for Shane—surely that could *not* be it.

A hand settled on her shoulder, and there was no need for words. Meredith turned around and smiled at Lila, who was with her family.

"Are you all right?" Lila whispered.

A single nod was all she dared, with Mama listening in. Lila's face wreathed with empathy. No doubt she had overheard Narcissa's whispers across the aisle and was offering unspoken comfort. There was nothing like best friends. Lila's kindness and solidarity was the perfect antidote to Narcissa's declaration.

Rustles and voices filled the sanctuary. Worshippers began filing into the aisle, ready to head home. Meredith gathered her Bible and her wraps. She waited until Mama was occupied with Minnie and slipped into the aisle.

"Some people have all the nerve." Fiona fell in beside her. "I heard what she said. Do you really think she's going after Shane?"

"It doesn't matter to me." There was that feeling again, that she was telling a fib. It was the truth—Shane's love life was none of her business. She didn't want him. Correction. She didn't *want* to want him.

"You would think Narcissa would be happy trying to torture us all with how close she is to Lorenzo." Lila slipped into stride with them. "Lorenzo has never beaued her anywhere. Not even to church."

"*You* would notice," Kate added, peeling away from her family to join them. "How long have you had a crush on Lorenzo?"

"Since I was seven. It's a romance that is never meant to be." Lila shrugged.

"Meredith," Scarlet stepped in to say, "you know Narcissa's interested in your driver guy only because she thinks you are."

"Then maybe I should pretend to like Luken so she would throw herself at him and leave poor Shane alone." An extreme plan at the very least, but it sounded very tempting.

"If I were writing the story," Earlee began as she squeezed into line with them, "Narcissa would be the villain who would try to steal the hero away from the heroine, but she would get her just reward in the end."

"What reward?" Scarlet wanted to know.

"Well, that's the fun about being a writer." When Earlee smiled, the whole world brightened. "She could trip, roll down a muddy hillside and land in very thorny brambles. But I would hate to do physical harm."

"It's not terribly Christian," Kate admitted, gesturing around at the stained-glass windows and the crucifix on the wall.

"No physical pain, then." Lila paused, considering. "Maybe the hero could see her for what she truly was, turn his back to her and marry the heroine."

"You aren't saying I'm the heroine, right?" Meredith interjected.

"It's a story," Earlee assured her.

"Based on actual events," Lila went on to say. "I think you should have the mean things she does come back around to her."

"Great idea." Earlee nodded. "And the hero and heroine live happily ever after."

"I don't believe in fairy tales." Meredith broke through the doorway and lifted her face to the sky. A fine gray mist drizzled from leaden clouds, but May's touch was in the greening trees, the spears of daffodils poking up in the border beds and the robins taking flight from the lawn.

The promise of summer was everywhere. And Shane

was waiting for her, watching for her, and lifted his hand. Too bad he looked exactly like her idea of a perfect hero. They were a fairy tale that could never be.

———

Chapter Ten

Shane closed the gelding's stall gate, taking time to double-check the latch. The big Arabian nickered, poking his nose over the half door to make sure there was no grain to be found in Shane's hand.

"Sorry, buddy. You already had your share." He rubbed the animal's nose, laughing as the velvet lips nibbled at his gloves, which very well might have smelled of grain. "I'll be back with your supper later, big guy."

The gelding shook his head, as if he understood perfectly, and nickered to his next-door neighbor, as if to start a horsey discussion. Shane grabbed the empty bucket and damp towels, the curry comb and the hoof pick and headed down the aisle.

"Shane?" Her voice welcomed him, as refreshing as first dawn's touch on a waiting world. She'd changed out of her Sunday best into a simple cotton dress, adorned with dainty touches of lace and silk. She carried a small basket in hand. "I know you are supposed to fend for yourself on Sundays, but since you drove us to church because Papa was busy, we ought to at least provide you with lunch."

"I can't argue with that." His stomach rumbled in agreement as he shouldered open the tack-room door to lay down his load. "That fried chicken smells mighty tasty."

"I made it myself, because Cook has the day off."

"You cook?" He poked his head around the door.

"Don't look so surprised." Her laughter rang like the sweetest music. "Cook taught Tilly and me. Things are different in Montana Territory than St. Louis."

"That's where you're from?"

"Yes. Both Matilda and I are not looking for the socially advantageous marriage our parents think we should have." She untied her hood and shoved it out of the way, revealing her rosy cheeks and sparkling spirit. "Mama is stubbornly holding on to hope, but society seems less important here. Maybe because there are so few families who are rich."

"Is that why you have the friends you do?" He thought he already knew the answer, but he wanted to hear it from her lips, to *see* the measure of her not just to know it.

"You mean because I had no other choice, so I settled for whoever I could find in this small town?" She looked at him as if he were an idiot. "Really. That's what you think of me?"

"I've sat in the front seat of the buggy driving you around. I think I have a notion of who you are." He was close enough to brush one of the many stray curls out of her eyes, of her endless blue eyes a man could fall right into and become lost forever.

"Then you know I love my friends as if they were my own family." She held out the basket to him, blindly, as her gaze was held by his and she was helpless to look away. Maybe she did not want to. "When I moved to this town, my circle of friends welcomed me without question. I remember standing in the basement of the church, feeling unsure and surrounded by strangers. Mrs. Hadly had split up my sisters by age group, and this girl with red hair patted the empty seat beside her and smiled at me. After class Scarlet introduced me to the rest of the gang and when I started school the next day, they greeted me like old friends."

"They welcomed you without question." He tucked the basket in one arm, riveted by her, unblinking. The way his gaze remained locked on hers felt as if a deeper bond, a greater connection was forged. "I've known that feeling before."

"Then you understand."

"Unconditional acceptance and love. The best kind of friendship there is." His stomach rumbled again, breaking the moment. He looked away, as if a hint embarrassed. "I'm obviously starving. Would you want to stay with me while I eat? I'd offer to share, but I'm sure you already ate your dinner. We could keep talking."

"I would like that." She glanced around and spied the ladder ascending to the loft. "How about the haymow?"

"My favorite place."

"Mine, too." Rain tapped lightly on the roof, serenading her as she seized both sides of the ladder and hiked her foot onto the bottom rung. "That's another blessing living in Montana. There are so many opportunities to do different things. Back in the city, we had a small stable for our carriage horses, but that was all. Here we have barns and horses and land to roam."

"And your mother allows this?"

"There are so many of us, Mama can't keep us all in check at the same time." She hoisted herself up to the next rung, carefully moving her hands one at a time. "You'll see when my other sisters come home from boarding school. It's a madhouse when we're all together."

"If I'm still here, that is." He waited patiently on the ground below, with his back turned to her. He seemed smaller from so high up, but not diminished. "Braden says we're making fast progress with the horses' training."

"Yes, I suppose you always have to keep on eye on your next job." Sadness hitched in her throat. Odd, because of course she knew he wouldn't be staying in Angel Falls. She raised her foot onto the next narrow rung and pulled her weight over the lip of the loft and onto the hay-strewn boards. "I'm up. You can look now. Next time I'll borrow a pair of trousers."

"I can't imagine what your mother would think of that."

"She would have an apoplexy for sure. Although Kate wears her brother's trousers when she rides her horse, and Earlee does the same when she helps with the barn work." My, but he could climb quickly. She backed up as he hopped onto the mow, basket and all. She wandered around, looking for the best place to sit. "Now it's your turn."

"Mine?" His forehead furrowed as he carried the basket, hay crackling beneath his boots.

"Your turn to talk." There was already a horse blanket spread on the hay. She watched as he set the basket down on a corner of it.

Light spilled through the cracks in the wall boards and the spaces between the walls and the eaves. This close to the roof, the rain whispered and sluiced with the cadence of a sonnet, rising and falling in the most pleasant way. She spied a small writing desk on the corner of the blanket. *This must be Shane's own hideaway place, where he spends his spare time. Curious.*

"I'm not sure I have anything interesting to say." He unlatched the wide door and drew it open. He didn't seem to realize how fascinating he was. "I'm not a terribly interesting man."

"Interesting is in the eye of the beholder." She knelt and settled her skirts, aware of how impressive Shane looked staring out at the gray-and-green world. His hands were planted on his hips, which showed off his amazing shoulders and the strength in his arms. His feet were braced apart, emphasizing his height and power.

Meredith, you are staring at him again. She blushed, thankful he had his back to her and didn't know. She cleared her throat, hoping she sounded perfectly normal because she certainly didn't feel that way. "What about your friends?"

"Right." He pushed away from the open door, outlined by the falling rain as he paced toward her. "It's a long story. Are you sure you want to hear it?"

"Positive."

"I might bore you." He folded his long legs, swept off his hat and reached for the basket.

"If you do, I'll stop you." As if this man could possibly bore her. He had set her world upside down the moment he'd ridden into it.

"Don't say I didn't warn you." He winked, his manner light, but there was something deeper, something private that remained just out of sight. He lifted the basket's lid. "Just before my twelfth birthday, many of my father's investments went bad and we fell on hard times."

"I'm sorry. That happens to a lot of people."

"And we were no exception." His voice stayed steady, betraying no emotion. "We had to rent out our house in order to keep it, so we moved in with my grandmother."

"And you left your friends behind?" she guessed.

"Worse. I had no friends to leave behind." He kept his face down as he pushed aside the cloth keeping the food warm, speaking casually, perhaps thinking she could not hear the shades of strain hidden behind his words of the lingering hurt he must be trying to hide. He pulled a plate from the basket. "When our financial situation changed, the friends I had grown up with turned their backs on me."

"How awful. You had to be crushed."

"Something like that." He unwrapped the plate of fried chicken. "I can still remember standing in the front yard waiting for Ted and Zachary to come home from school, the school I'd been forced to quit because we could not pay the tuition. It was raining just like it is today, a fine drizzle that wet your face and misted the world. It was cold and turning colder, but I refused to go inside because my mother was upset packing up our house and because I was lonely staying home from school. I wouldn't wait to see my two best friends."

"But your family losing money changed things with them?"

"Yes. When they came down the road driven in their family carriage that day, their driver didn't stop. They didn't lean out the window and wave, shout some remark or even throw a spit wad. You know how little boys are. Ted saw me and turned away, as if he were ashamed of me. Zachary sneered as he rolled past, and called out something unkind. He made it clear I was no longer their friend."

"That had to devastate you."

"I never forgot it." He withdrew a second plate from the basket, hardly paying attention as he set it on the blanket. The memories had changed him, drawing layers of emotion and sadness she'd never seen before. "Two weeks later we moved into my grandmother's house. I was feeling as lonely as a boy could be. Two kids from across the street came over to see what was going on. When they saw I was their age, they invited me to come play tag with them. Neither of them cared about my family's name or what my grandfather did for a living. We're friends to this day."

"Is that what the writing desk is for? So you can keep in touch?"

"Yes. Eventually my family's finances improved, and we moved back into our house a few years later. Warren, William and I have been corresponding ever since. Some friendships are able to survive time, life's events and even great distances."

"Yes, and whenever you're together again it is as if no time has passed and nothing has changed." She leaned forward to help him by lifting the cloth from the plate. "Such is the nature of real friendship."

"I can't argue that."

"You know what this tells me about you?"

"I'm afraid to guess." His dimples returned, edging out the sadness of his story and leaving the hope.

"That you have more character than I gave you credit for."

"Did you just pay me a compliment? Or did my ears deceive me?"

"I'm as astonished as you are."

They laughed together. She couldn't hold back her admiration or the strange power he seemed to have over her affections. Like a rope binding her heart to his, when he felt, so did she. His gladness rolled through her and they smiled together as if in synchrony, as if friends for real.

"And I have even more news," she confessed. "I officially have no reasons left not to like you."

The sunlight broke through the doors, spilling across them like a sign from above. They laughed together, their chuckles echoing in the peaked roof of the loft and drowning out the rise of birdsong from the green fields.

Hitching up Sweetie had not been nearly as difficult as she feared, not with Shane teaching her. She pulled the last strap through the buckle, securing the buggy's traces to the mare's thick leather collar.

"Did I do it right?" she asked.

"Perfect," Shane praised from the other side of the horse. "How does it feel to have hitched up your first buggy?"

"Liberating." The floor bit into her knee, so she stood and dusted off her skirt. Bits of dirt and scraps of hay tumbled off the cotton, swirling like dust motes in the sunshine. "Thanks to you, all the lines and buckles and pieces are no longer completely mystifying. Now I can hitch up any horse, no problem."

"You're one step closer to your plans." Over the top of Sweetie's broad back, he tipped his hat to her. "Well done. Soon you will be driving your own buggy across the plains."

"I wish. I still have examinations to pass, and they are usually very hard." The mare nickered as if wondering why she was standing still if she was hitched to go somewhere, and Meredith rubbed her shoulder comfortingly. "It's getting closer, and I'm getting more nervous. What if I don't pass? I'm starting to see doom. All the ways things can go wrong."

"Don't worry. You will do fine, the same way you do everything."

"You're just saying that. You don't know me that well."

"I know you're smart and hardworking." He laid his arms across the horse's back and leaned close, resting his chin on his hands. "I know you enough to guess you are at the top of your class."

"Earlee always gets the top grades, but I come

close." Just thinking about it made nerves settle into her stomach, hopping around like trapped grasshoppers. "I've been wanting this for so long and suddenly it's almost here. If I pass the exam, I can have my own little schoolroom this summer."

"Summer? Doesn't school usually start in the fall?"

"Yes, but some areas can't afford to pay a teacher or there are too few students for a district. Summer school helps to bring education to the rural areas. It's a great place for a beginning teacher."

"You light up when you talk about it. Why do you want to be a teacher?"

"Because education can better a child's life. I believe everyone should have the chance to learn." A curl tumbled into her eyes, as one always did, and she brushed it away, totally unconscious of the adorable gesture. She tucked the lock behind her ear. "I took my schooling for granted until I moved here and saw life from a different perspective."

"My move to Charleston to live with Grandmother did the same thing for me." His throat closed, full of so many things he couldn't admit or felt too bashful to say. It was fine to have material things, but a man could not build his character accepting inherited money that he had not earned. That was another reason he had walked away from his family. He supposed Meredith felt the same, and he admired her for seeing the work she could do in the world instead of closing her eyes to the need.

The door at the other end of the barn opened with a wrench of wood and a drum of boots. Didn't sound like

Braden back early from town. That meant the intruder could only be Robert Worthington.

"Meredith!" Harsh tones reverberated the length of the structure. "Are you out here?"

"Uh-oh." Across Sweetie's withers, Meredith stepped back, panic pinching her lovely features, animating her in the most darling of ways. "I'm not supposed to be here, but mostly I'm not supposed to touch the horse or buggy."

"I'll take care of her," he whispered back. "Go on. Talk to your father."

"Thank you." Her sincerity washed over him as surely as the spring breeze at his back, and he felt her gratitude in his inner-most heart. She seemed to take the light with her as she scurried away on pretty kid slippers, leaving him as if in winter's gloom.

The mare curved her neck to toss him a questioning look, as if to say, "What's going on? Aren't we going somewhere?" He reached to unfasten the buckles holding the collar to the buggy traces, working fast. Those striking boot steps had stopped midway through the barn, dangerously close. Not that he intended to deceive Worthington if he should question him, but if the horse was unhitched in time and back in her stall, the man might not think to ask a question he would not have to answer.

"But, Papa!" Meredith's protest rang in the breeze-way.

She was probably being sent back to the house. Shane lifted the collar from Sweetie's neck and hung it on the nearby hook. Lighter steps tapped away, her gait diminishing with distance. She must be gone. The barn door squeaked closed and he led Sweetie back to her stall.

"Connelly." Robert Worthington's voice boomed in the stillness, chasing a sparrow from a perch on the grain barrel. Horses stirred in their stalls and many poked their noses over the bars of their gates, nickering and whinnying at the disturbance. A sign of anger in the man's voice.

Even Sweetie skidded sideways, suddenly nervous. Shane laid a hand on her neck, murmuring low to her.

"I'm in here, sir." He opened the gate and Sweetie hurried into her stall.

"I need a word with you." Worthington pounded closer, his boot steps preceding him. He came into sight still in his Sunday's finest—a waist coat, pleated trousers and shining boots. He was no longer the doting, easygoing patriarch, not with anger tight on his face.

"What do you need, sir?" Shane checked Sweetie's latch and pushed away from the stall.

"A moment of your time." Robert glowered. "I don't know how to say this."

"Clearly something is wrong. Let me guess. You were concerned about your daughter being alone in the barn with me without a chaperone. Is that right?"

"That's it." Robert pounded closer, closing the gap between them. With every step he took, the disapproval lining the man's face became deeper and more apparent. "Meredith is a good girl, but she is headstrong and naive."

"I would never do anything to insult or harm her or any of your daughters." He had done nothing wrong, so it was easy to meet the man eye to eye and ignore the tension thick in the air.

"I believe that." Robert came to a stop outside the stall, his tone dark. "Which is why you will understand. I have to insist that you limit your interaction with my daughter to strictly the business I've hired you for."

"You hired me to train your horses."

"No, I hired Braden for that. You, as his assistant, will do the various menial tasks around this place. If you cannot, I will hire someone who can." Shoulders back, chin up, unflinching, Robert looked like a man who meant what he said. "Is that clear?"

"Of course. I don't want to lose this job for Braden." He thought of Meredith in the house. He didn't want her punished for spending time with him. They had been talking, nothing more. Surely no one could believe differently. "I meant no disrespect to you or to Meredith."

"See that it stays that way." Worthington jammed his fists into his pocket, his gaze narrowing as he looked Shane up and down. "Don't take this the wrong way, son, but you're young and you have little to show for yourself. You're learning a trade. For that I commend you, but do not misunderstand my daughter's propensity for befriending those less fortunate than herself."

"Less fortunate?" He blinked, a little puzzled because he had thought the father was concerned they had been alone together and for his daughter's reputation. Apparently the greater issue was their budding friendship. "I don't understand, sir."

"The man who wins my Meredith's hand will not be an itinerant saddle tramp working a few months out of the year, living hand to mouth, with nothing to offer. Now do you understand?"

Now it made sense.

"You are as clear as a bell, sir." Anger built like a fire behind his sternum, but he tamped it down. He should have been prepared for this. He should have seen it coming. He couldn't say it didn't hurt.

"It's nothing personal, son." Robert wasn't a cruel man, and his tone softened a notch. "Things might be different if you had the right family connections and a fine spread of land to call your own."

"I can't say that I do, sir." Not anymore. He had given up that life. He was no longer that man. He was twenty years old. Worthington wasn't exactly wrong. He'd built up a savings, but he had no plans to settle down. He *was* sweet on Meredith. He felt closer to her than he should.

"Otherwise, you have done a fine job for us. I hope there are no hard feelings." Robert dipped his chin in a formal nod before pivoting on his heel.

Hard feelings? Shane blew out a breath, determined to hold on to his dignity. Best to let the man's words roll off him instead of take them to heart. He couldn't say that if he was in Robert's shoes he would have done anything different. Meredith was amazing, worth protecting, worth the sting he felt on his pride.

He was a wanderer, that was part of his job. He was itinerant, he had no home and every material possession he owned could be tied to the back of his saddle. It shouldn't matter that he'd been told not to be friends with Meredith. The weeks would soon be ticking by until it was time to leave. There was no future for them anyway, and he didn't want one. He wasn't looking for anything serious. Not now. Not at this place in his life.

The sting remained like a welt, tender and inflamed, as he headed out into the yard. Leaves rustled overhead and the breeze sang through the blades of grass at his feet as he made his way to the bunkhouse. The sunshine winked on the windows of the house, drawing his attention, forcing him to glance at the big window where Meredith could be seen sitting at the dining-room table, laying out a piece of material. Her oldest sister stood nearby. The two young women commented, studied, furrowed their brows and Meredith moved around a few pieces of fabric. The sisters smiled, as if pleased.

Shane twisted away, realizing he was staring. The woman had more power over him than he'd realized. He forced his feet forward where the bunkhouse and a good book awaited him.

Chapter Eleven

"Girls!" Mama's call rang through the morning stillness. China cups rattled in their saucers as she barreled
into the dining room. "Hurry and get ready or you'll
be late for school."

"I wouldn't mind being late." Minnie dropped her
fork on her plate with a *clink*. "I have a quiz today."

"And let me guess. You didn't study?" Meredith took
one last sip of apple cider before pushing away from
the table. "I would have helped you."

"But I didn't want to do it." Minnie flashed her
dimples and bobbed out of her chair. "What I want is
for summer weather to come, so I can play in my tree
house."

"That is hardly ladylike." Mama drew herself up,
shook her head with disapproval and gave Minnie a
loving nudge. "Off with you, now. Gather your books
and put on your wraps. Sadie! Where are the girls'
lunches?"

The kitchen door swished open and the maid, hair
curling from the kitchen's heat and looking frazzled,

scurried into sight, carrying two small pails. "Here you are, ma'am. Is there anything else you'll be needin'?"

"No, go back to your work, Sadie." Mama took possession of the tins. "Meredith, why are you daydreaming again? Stop staring at the window and get ready to go."

Had she been staring? She hadn't noticed. Meredith blinked, realizing she was indeed facing the window, and launched out of her chair. A strange flickering feeling traveled through her as she followed her mother through the parlor. It wasn't a bad feeling, just a novel one that was as pure as the morning's gentleness and as uplifting as the budding lilacs waving their tiny perfect flowers in the breeze.

Shane. She could see him through the parlor window driving the buggy to the front door. He perched on the edge of the seat and the wind tousled the ends of his dark hair. The new day's light bronzed him as if he'd come straight out of a painting.

"Did you not hear me, child? Goodness, you are preoccupied today."

"Sorry, Mama." She took the coat her mother thrust at her and jabbed her arms into it. Something was definitely wrong because it was the strangest phenomenon that the closer Shane came to her, the more she was aware of him. The tug he held on her heart increased. Her thoughts centered on him. Her senses filled until he was all she could see—not the door opening, not Minnie jumping down the steps and skipping along the walk, not Mama kissing her cheek and wishing her a good day—just him.

Only him.

It was as if something had gone wrong with her entire brain and she was helpless to stop it. She hardly felt the bricks at her feet or the change in the wind that May day brought. The air evaporated from her lungs, leaving her breathless as her hand settled into his. His fingers closed around hers, and the connection between them became more powerful, as it did every time they touched. She did not recall climbing into the buggy or settling on the cushioned seat, only that his hand released hers, he moved away and she felt the purest of lights the heavens had to offer.

It wasn't until she was halfway to town that she realized Shane hadn't bid her good morning or greeted her with a smile. He hadn't turned around once in the seat in front of her. His attention remained focused on the roads. Mud still splashed beneath the wheels, but the sun was out and drying the land. Everywhere mist rose in great cloudy ribbons from earth to sky, and beside her, Minnie scribbled a note to her best friend, preoccupied with the secrets little girls shared.

Town came into sight with children straggling toward the school. The bell was ringing by the time Shane pulled to a stop behind a long line of buggies. Horses stomped impatiently, parents called out goodbye and students scurried toward the front steps as the last toll of the bell clanged.

"We're gonna be tardy, Shane!" Minnie folded her note into her pocket and held out her arms.

"Sorry about that." In his big-brother way, the man swooped Minnie safely from the seat to the soggy grass and gave the ribboned end of one braid a tug. "Do good today, shortcakes."

"I will!" Minnie beamed up at him as if he'd been personally responsible for hanging the sun. She spun away and sprinted across the lawn. "Maisie! Wait for me!"

Chuckling, Shane turned back to the buggy, back to her, the essence of him so attractive and powerful it was nearly too much to bear. She felt ensnared by invisible bonds she could not describe or understand, and she wanted nothing more than to capture the closeness they had shared yesterday in the barn. To reestablish their fun banter and trade a laugh or two.

The trouble was, he did not seem to feel the same. He did not meet her gaze. His smile faded as he held out his hand dutifully, as silent as stone.

"I hope you have an enjoyable day with the horses." She floated instead of stepped from the buggy. When her shoes touched the ground, it came as a surprise. Being near him scrambled her senses, there was no denying it, even if he did not feel the same. She could no longer deny she liked him very much.

"I hope your day is enjoyable as well." Oddly formal, he didn't look at her as he spoke. He turned away and climbed into the front seat, intent on straightening the reins, which were straight and orderly to begin with. What was going on?

The male brain made no sense at all to her. He was simply going to drive off as if they were complete strangers, and after the time together they had shared? Fine, let him. A smart girl wouldn't give the guy another thought. A sensible girl would march to the schoolhouse, where class was about to start any minute.

Because her shoes were not taking her in the direction of the front steps, she was obviously neither smart nor sensible. Her feet took her right back to the buggy and Shane. He looked up from releasing the brake, startled to see her standing there when he'd thought she had gone. His arresting blue eyes could stop the sun from rising, which was probably why she was standing in front of him and not acting like herself at all.

"Is this because I said I liked you?" she blurted out, wishing for the first time she had paid attention to her roommate Elizabeth Barker back at finishing school who had much experience and endless advice on dealing with the male gender. Shane paled, so perhaps she had been a bit overly bold. Did that make her fall silent?

Not a chance.

"You hardly so much as glanced at me this morning." She gripped the side of the buggy and met his startled gaze. "You were talkative with Minnie and friendly with her. Then in nearly the same breath you became with me as formal as a judge."

"I'm doing a job, Meredith. That's all." Strain bracketed his mouth, a poor imitation of the dimples that she liked so well. Apology shone in the depths of his irises and in his heart, which she could feel.

"I don't understand. Of course you're doing a job. Why else would you be driving us around?" If hurt lodged like a stone behind her rib cage, she did her best to ignore it. "You're one of those fly-by-night men, aren't you?"

"Fly-by-night?" A corner of his mouth quirked upward.

GET 2 BOOKS

IF YOU ENJOY A HISTORICAL ROMANCE STORY that reflects solid, traditional values, then you'll like *Love Inspired® Historical* novels. These are engaging tales filled with romance, adventure and faith set in various historical periods from biblical times to World War II.

We'd like to send you two *Love Inspired Historical* novels absolutely free. Accepting them puts you under no obligation to purchase any more books.

HOW TO GET YOUR 2 FREE BOOKS AND TWO FREE GIFTS

1. Return the reply card today, and we'll send you two *Love Inspired Historical* novels, absolutely free! We'll even pay the postage!

2. Accepting free books places you under no obligation to buy anything, ever. The two books have combined cover prices of at least $11.00 in the U.S. and at least $13.00 in Canada, but they're yours to keep, free!

3. We hope that after receiving your free books you'll want to remain a subscriber, but the choice is yours—to continue or cancel, any time at all!

EXTRA BONUS

You'll also get two free mystery gifts! (worth about $10)

FREE!

If offer card is missing, write to The Reader Service, P.O. Box 1867, Buffalo, NY 14240-1867 or visit: www.ReaderService.com

BUSINESS REPLY MAIL
FIRST-CLASS MAIL   PERMIT NO. 717   BUFFALO, NY

POSTAGE WILL BE PAID BY ADDRESSEE

THE READER SERVICE
PO BOX 1867
BUFFALO NY 14240-9952

NO POSTAGE
NECESSARY
IF MAILED
IN THE
UNITED STATES

"You think a female is getting too close and you race off like a mustang being chased by a mountain lion."

"And why would I do this?" The other corner of his mouth twitched, as if he were fighting amusement and, judging by the set of his eyes, sorrow.

"Because I said I liked you yesterday. Remember?" She couldn't believe it. She smacked the flat of her hand against the side of the buggy, mad at herself. "I was talking about friendship. That was all. Surely you know that."

"I do." He swallowed hard, a man wrestling with something important. "I'm not sure friendship between us is a good idea."

"Why not? You don't like me?"

"Not like you?" He took in the endearing look of her, the vulnerability revealed in her question and in the wobble of her lush bottom lip. "Impossible. Life is better around you, Meredith. But as your father reminded me, I am here to do a job, not to make friends."

"My father? Papa talked to you?" She looked angry. "I made him promise not to."

"He was only looking out for his daughter." The wind tousled a row of bouncy corkscrew curls into her eyes and before she could brush them away, he reached to do it. His fingertips grazed the petal-soft curve of her cheek, the shell of her ear and felt the impact of her sweetness. Tenderness, unbidden and new, rose up in him like a hymn too beautiful to quiet, too reverent to stop.

"What did Papa say?" Worry crinkled her forehead in the most darling way. "He insulted you, didn't he?"

"He said nothing that wasn't true. You have plenty

of friends." The words tore at him, but he managed to say them with a shrug. He was a man unaffected. "You don't need me."

"I do."

"No, you don't." He hated doing it because he didn't want to hurt her, but he raised the reins and shielded his heart. "In a couple weeks, you will be teaching school somewhere far out on that prairie, and Braden and I will be working in Butte. There's no sense in getting attached."

"But, Shane, I don't see why—"

"Have a good day, Miss Meredith." He slapped the reins. Sweetie stepped forward with a slow plod. The buggy rolled a few yards away from her, shielding him from her sight.

All she could see was the black back of the vehicle slowly maneuvering away from the crush on the road— and away from her. Just like that, he'd driven away. Cast aside their friendship because her father had spoken to him.

Not exactly a man capable of great friendship.

"Hey, handsome!" A superior-sounding, very familiar voice lifted above the noise of the street and the shouts of kids scrambling toward the schoolhouse. Narcissa Bell stepped onto the side of the road and waved boldly. "What's your hurry? I'll see you later!"

Had Shane waved back? Had he acknowledged her in some way? Meredith worried, seeing red as Narcissa smiled. A satisfied look passed across her smug face.

"Shane is utterly the cutest." Narcissa's chin went up in the air, her narrow smile triumphant as if she knew exactly how deep the barb went.

Anger roared through her, but she held it in and kept the lash of the anger inside her, silent and hidden. The last thing she wanted was for her archenemy to know how much it hurt. How could Shane end their friendship, and go looking for another? And with Narcissa of all people.

No, he wouldn't, she decided, remembering the strength of character she'd witnessed in him. Narcissa was simply going after what she wanted. No need to be upset over her. It was enough to watch the buggy rolling farther away down the street, hesitate at the corner and then turn out of sight. Why did it feel as if her very essence longed after him? As if her spirit wished for the company of his?

They weren't even friends anymore. She brushed at the curls that had fallen in her face again, remembering the blissful kindness of his touch.

"Meredith? Are you all right?"

She felt a tug on her sleeve. Kate stood beside her with concern on her face and a question in her eyes. Was she really standing here pining after a man for all to see? The sun was in her eyes, causing them to tear a little, and she blinked hard, turning on her heels, lifting her chin, shoring up her dignity. "I'm all right. Just lost in thought."

"You're going to be late. We'd better go in."

"What? Oh, right."

The school bell had long silenced. Narcissa was the only other student in sight scurrying up the front steps. Miss Lambert held the door open, gesturing impatiently. "Hurry, girls! You don't want to be marked tardy."

Meredith felt Kate pulling her along. She was aware her feet were moving. The schoolhouse loomed up ahead and so did the disapproving countenance of their teacher.

"Guess what?" Kate whispered as they rushed up the stairs. "There's a new girl in school today. She's got the desk behind Earlee and me. She looks nice."

"Great." It was as if Kate's words had no meaning, for nothing seemed to be able to penetrate her Shane-centered thoughts. She darted past the teacher, shucked off her coat and hurried to her seat.

He couldn't get Meredith out of his mind. Hours had passed since he'd driven away from her, and still her image of vulnerability and hurt stuck with him. He tipped his hat lower to shade his face against the cresting sun and checked the tension of the longe line. The black filly walked in a large circle, ears up, head up and her gait as smooth as silk.

If only he could enjoy the moment with the horse, the sense of accomplishment he got from seeing an animal progress and the shared camaraderie. He ought to be at peace, happily at his work. But he felt twisted up inside. Losing Meredith's friendship tore him apart. He'd only been doing them both a favor. Mr. Worthington was right. It wasn't practical to form attachments when both he and Meredith had plans to move on.

This wasn't about friendship, he admitted to himself, but something more. That was why he'd agreed with Robert Worthington. The father had recognized what the daughter had not. Shane had never been in love, but he suspected he had taken the first stumbling steps on that path.

"Pretty day, isn't it?" Braden sauntered over from the barn and leaned on the corral rails, eyes on the horse. "I didn't think warm weather would ever come."

"I was beginning to think the same." Shane glanced around. It was hard to believe that snow had blanketed the ground days before. The grass sprang beneath his boots as he turned in place, handling the longe line, keeping the filly at a disciplined walk.

Around him the landscape was stunning, some of the most beautiful he'd seen of all his travels. The roll and draw of the prairie and hills were pleasing, the depth of green in the fields unparalleled, the perfect blue of the cloudless Montana sky breath-stealing.

He could get used to it here. Birds chorused as they perched on the branches of the trees in the orchard. In the next paddock over, the spring's crop of foals stretched their long legs in bright green grass and budding buttercups. Even the wind felt warm as he shucked off his coat and kept the line he held taut. The filly had come a long way, stepping up to a trot when he commanded it.

"Good girl," he praised. "That's it, nice and easy."

"You've done a good job with her, Shane." Braden ducked between the fence boards and into the corral, a coiled lasso in hand. "She's come along very well, but you would do better if you kept your mind on your work."

Guilty. Shane winced, because he couldn't deny it. "I know. If I'm distracted, the horse will be, too."

"Right. When you're done here, come help me saddle

up the white gelding. You're doing good work, Shane. I'm handing over half the two-year-olds to you. We'll see what you can do on your own." With a wink, Braden strode away, his compliment a strange contrast to the frustration and sense of loss Shane had been wrestling with.

Keep your mind on your work and not on the woman, Connelly. He whistled to the filly, watching her gait change as she slipped into a graceful canter. As much as he loved his work, he could not get lost in it. Meredith remained as if she were a part of him.

Concentrating on her schoolwork proved haphazard at best. Meredith rubbed at the dull ache in her forehead, turned the page of her spelling book and stared at the word on the top of the page.

"Time for lunch." The teacher's handbell jingled merrily, and all around her students burst out of their desks, conversation erupted and footsteps pounded down the aisle to the front door, where warm sunshine beckoned.

Finally. She closed her book, blinked to refocus her eyes and gave thanks that she had an hour to rest her weary brain. It took an astonishing amount of energy to keep her mind on the day's tasks.

"At least we don't have school tomorrow." Scarlet stacked her books on her side of the desk. "A day off."

"For you, not for me." She hopped to her feet, glad to leave her work behind, and grabbed her book bag from beneath her seat. "This time tomorrow, I'll be halfway through my teachers' examinations."

"Me, too." Earlee hooked her bag over her shoulder. "While you all are playing, Meredith and I will be finding out if we have what it takes to be teachers."

"As if the answer isn't already perfectly clear." Fiona smiled sweetly.

"Yeah, you two are the smartest in our class. You will do fine." Lila rolled her eyes. "The rest of us will be the losers because you both will leave us behind to get your own little schools. You will have your own careers."

"You make it sound so romantic." Kate sighed as she fished her book bag out from under her desk. "I have no idea what I'm going to do after we graduate."

They hadn't taken a step down the aisle before they heard a familiar, sharp-toned voice.

"Don't even look at me." Narcissa's words were pitched to rise above all the other sounds in the emptying schoolhouse. "Does it look as if I want to be friends with you? What is your name?"

"R-Ruby." It was the new girl, seated in the last desk of the row, looking miserable with her head bowed. Meredith had been so involved with her worries and her work that she had forgotten about the morning's addition to their school.

"I'm going to call you Rags. Look at that dress." Narcissa sneered, pleased with herself as she turned up her nose. "C'mon, girls. Let's go."

A few giggles and twitters filled the air as Narcissa and her group of friends clomped down the other aisle, leaving behind the lone girl with her head still down. A blush stained her fair face as she closed her tattered spelling book, clearly a volume handed down many times. She wore a faded red calico dress, which did not look as if it had been made for her because the fabric was bright red where the seams had been let out. The cuffs of her sleeves did not reach her wrists. The several patches on her skirt were made from a different fabric and were impossible not to notice.

Meredith stopped in mid-aisle. Kate lifted one eyebrow in silent question. Lila gave a little nod. Earlee and Fiona smiled. Scarlet, ever bold, turned on her heels and marched back to the new girl's desk, shoes striking like a hammer in the otherwise empty classroom. "Ruby?"

"Y-yes?" The girl didn't look up at them. Her face was still red as she kept her hands busy with a battered bag she had in her lap.

"Would you like to sit with us at lunch?"

Meredith saw the surprise and then gladness on the new girl's face. Ruby was really very lovely with porcelain features and wide, unguarded eyes.

"Oh, yes. I would like that very much." She swept into the aisle with her bag in hand. She had the friendliest smile. The dress she wore didn't fit much better when standing. The tops of her patched shoes were visible, as were her white stockings. "I'm afraid I've never been to a place like this before, so I don't know what to do with myself."

"You've never been to school?" Meredith had to ask, curious.

"No, I learned at home. My family used to live up near the Canadian border. There was no school nearby." Ruby blushed again. "I resolved not to make a fool of myself, but I think I just did it again, didn't I?"

"Not at all," Meredith assured her.

"Not a bit," Earlee seconded.

"Not even a little," Lila chimed in.

"Come on. We always eat lunch in the shade of the maple trees," Kate explained.

"And when we're done eating, we work on our sewing projects," Fiona continued.

"And talk," Scarlet finished, leading the way down the aisle.

"You all sew?" Ruby's face lit up as she followed them. "I'm not very good. What are you all making?"

"A quilt." Meredith plucked her lunch pail from the shelf above the hanging coats. "What's your current project?"

"Me? I'm afraid I don't have one right now." Ruby blushed again, perhaps embarrassed, hiding her face as she chose a battered tin pail from the shelf. "I did it again. I can't believe I said that. I'm just really nervous."

"It's okay." Earlee gestured at her own dress as they all trooped down the front steps and into the sunshine. "I get nervous like that, too. I'm letting out a dress for one of my younger sisters."

"Do you live in town?" Scarlet wanted to know.

"No. My pa took up a claim on a farm." Ruby shrugged shyly. "This is such a big town. I've never been around so many people."

A big town? Meredith bit her bottom lip to keep from pointing out that Angel Falls, while a nice place to live, was a small settlement and their school humble enough to house all classes in one room.

"You must have lived in a very small town," Meredith said as they settled on one of the benches beneath the circle of maples. The younger children were cross-legged on the grass, pails scattered about, nearly done with their lunches. Some of the boys were already playing kickball.

"There was only a mail stop and a general store," Ruby explained as she took a spot on the bench next to Earlee. "It was a day's drive from the ranch Pa worked on, so we didn't go there very often."

"This must be a big change for you here." Lila empathized.

Meredith took the last space on the edge of the bench and tugged the lid off her tin while Ruby answered.

"Have you told your mother about the test tomorrow?" Scarlet leaned close to whisper.

"No. I've been dreading it, so I put it off." As if she didn't have enough eating her up inside with Shane on her mind. "It appears as if I'm out of time. I have to tell her before I leave to take the test in the morning."

"What if she forbids you to go?"

"I don't know." Meredith looked unhappily down at the meal Cook had prepared and Sadie had packed. Delicious aromas lifted from the cloth-wrapped food, but she wasn't hungry. Her stomach was tied up in far too many knots.

"You will think of something," Scarlet encouraged.

"I had better." Her plans for her entire future were at stake. Good thing Shane had taught her how to hitch up the buggy. If worse came to worst, she could drive Sweetie to town on her own.

Bless him for that. She plucked a leg of fried chicken out of the pail and did her best to join in with her friends' conversation.

Chapter Twelve

Not being pals with Meredith was like slow agonizing
torture. The instant he'd spotted her tripping down the
steps, her school day done, he read her unhappiness.
Her head was down, her walk sedate. He hated seeing
her like that. When she waved goodbye to her friends
as they all parted ways, they promised to send prayers
her way. Battered with regret, he hopped from the seat,
boots striking the sun-kissed grass, seeing the crinkle
of tension at the bridge of her nose and bracketing her
rosebud mouth.

"Hi! Can we take Maisie home today, too?" Minnie
reached him first, hand-in-hand with her best friend.
The little girls giggled, twin braids bobbing,

"Sure thing, shortcakes." With an eye on Meredith,
he helped the little girls into the backseat.

"Thanks ever so much." Minnie beamed at him, as
cute as a button.

"You are ever so welcome." He winked to make her
beam brighter. Hard not to grow fond of the kid. He
would miss Minnie when he had to move on. He never

had a young sister, but he reckoned it would have felt something like this.

He felt Meredith's approach. Every step she took closer seemed to move through him like meter through a poem, the rise and fall of the cadence like that of his heart.

Don't let her know you are broken up, too. He tucked his feelings down deep and drew himself up to his full height. He was a disciplined man, but his resolve wavered as she glided to a stop before him. She did not hold out her hand, and he did not reach for her.

She pushed past him, gripped the side of the buggy and handily hoisted herself up, skirts swinging, lunch tin clanging, school bag dangling. Her silence said everything. She didn't need him, didn't want him. He couldn't say it didn't hurt. She smiled warmly at the little girls on the seat next to her, laughing at something Maisie had drawn on her slate.

Hardening his heart, he took his seat and the reins and sent Sweetie into the street. He was the driver, nothing more. That was what he had told her he wanted. If he felt the sting of her gaze on his back, he did his best to ignore it. If she was unusually quiet, he told himself it was not the sound of her voice he missed.

The streets were busy now that the warm weather had decided to stay. He had to wait at the intersection, enduring Meredith's glares and her silence. It felt as if ten years had gone by before the long queue of horses, wagons and buggies ahead of him dwindled, and he could finally turn onto the main street.

In front of Maisie's house, the little girls said goodbye. Meredith didn't so much as glance at him. He knew because he kept her in the corner of his eye.

There was no doubt she was mad at him. But that was not the reason she worried her bottom lip. Maybe she was anxious about her examination tomorrow. She had so much on her shoulders. A friend could help her by listening, maybe getting her to grin. He was not a friend, so he could not. He hated that no smile touched her rosebud-shaped mouth.

That he should even notice her mouth. It gave the sweetest smiles on earth and, he reckoned, perhaps the sweetest kisses.

Definitely don't think about kissing her, Connelly. If being friends was banned, then kissing would be absolutely prohibited. But as Minnie waved, hanging out the window, and he nosed the mare down the street, he could think of nothing else. Meredith's kiss would be soft as sun-warmed silk, as sacred as the most cherished of hymns. If he were allotted only one kiss in his entire lifetime, then hers would be the one he would choose.

He took the back roads to the church, where the oldest Worthington daughter was waiting on the top step. Tilly gathered her things and offered him a cordial smile that did not touch her eyes. She hopped in beside Minnie, hardly taking his hand. She didn't look any happier than Meredith did. But he was the driver and nothing more, so he gathered the reins and guided Sweetie toward home.

"How did the Ladies Aid meeting go?" Meredith's words penetrated his senses. Of all the noises in town and on the street, he could not shut out the sound of her voice.

"It was okay," Tilly said in the way women did when things weren't all right.

"What happened?" Meredith's question held tender sympathy, and that was what he liked about her the most. That she held a beautiful capacity to care.

He halted Sweetie at the end of the street, checked to see the way was clear and chirruped to her. The wind gusted through full leaves of the trees lining the road, and the music of children's laughter blotted out the older Worthington sister's answer. His every sense strained to hear Meredith's response, but the outside world seemed to work against him. A shout rang out from the main street, and several horses began to bay angrily. A woman came out her front door three houses up and began shouting for her children, her angry calls completely drowning Meredith's side of the conversation. Disappointment twisted through him, leaving him more frustrated than he'd started out.

Maybe he shouldn't be listening in. He knuckled back his hat brim, let the breeze fan his face and gazed up at what he could see of the blue sky beyond the buggy's fringed top.

Father, I'm feeling a tad lost. Please guide me. Even the smallest sign will do. No answer came on the summer-like air scented with green growing grass. They'd left the town behind them, where fields grew green and lush and the river roared on one side. Meredith was talking about an unnamed teamster Tilly was sweet on. The rushing roar of the upcoming falls drowned out the girls' conversation again.

Maybe that was sign enough. He didn't want to admit it, but perhaps he ought to work harder to close off his feelings and keep his desire to right what was wrong for her under control.

"What are you going to tell Mama?" Minnie asked, her words audible as soon as they'd left the falls behind them.

"I don't know," Meredith said, her lovely alto made him come to attention, spine straight, shoulders set. Maybe this was none of his business and he oughtn't be eavesdropping, but did that stop him?

Not a chance.

"I'm going to take the exam, whatever she says."

Yep, he wanted to help her. He wanted to be more than a friend to her. He wanted to be the man she turned to. But it wasn't meant to be. Just the driver, he gripped the reins more tightly and kept his attention on the road. Only on the road. Now and then an occasional note of her voice rose up to him like a little piece of music.

He'd never been so glad to see any building as he was the sight of the Worthington estate. Relief rolled through him. He pulled the mare to a stop. Tilly was out of the buggy before the wheels stopped turning. Minnie leaped out on her own, hollering a thanks to him. Only Meredith moved slowly, reluctant to face her mother, he reckoned, and not to prolong the presence of his company.

He could have wished her good luck, assured her he would say a prayer for her. He could simply reach out to squeeze her hand.

He did not. He sat straight as a fence post on the seat listening to her go. It was the little things that got to him now—the rustle of her skirts, the tiny intake of her breath that was nearly a sigh and the tempo of her gait on the walkway as she left him behind.

"Get a move on," Braden drawled, peeking around the garden gate. "We get the two-year-olds saddle broke, and I'm thinking it's time to reevaluate. Maybe make the decision to move on."

"Because of Mrs. Worthington?" He kept his voice quiet so it wouldn't carry to the house as he drove Sweetie toward the barn.

"That woman sat down with me today and gave me a lecture." He shook his head, looking as if he'd had enough. "I won't be impolite to a woman, but I was sorely tempted. She decided to have a say in how the horses are being trained."

"Does Mr. Worthington know about his wife's involvement?"

"He's about to." Braden, voice pitched low, pushed away from the gate. "I'll be waiting in the small corral."

"I'll be there."

He drove Sweetie into the shade of the barn. Looked as if he didn't need to worry about being here for much longer. He swung down and freed the reins through the loops on the dash. The wind gusted, carrying the faint murmur of women's voices from the house. Meredith's.

"Mama, no. Please. I have to do this." The gentlest plea he'd ever heard sailed over, wrapping its way around him. Heaven knew how anyone could say no to her.

"A Worthington daughter does not work." The

mother's pronouncement rang with unyielding certainty and loud enough to clearly carry all the way from the parlor, across the flower garden and to the barn. "I expect you to deport yourself in a way that's appropriate to this family. A common schoolteacher, Meredith. Really. Where do you get your ideas, my precious girl?"

Whatever the woman's flaws, there was love there, too. He could not fault the mother for that.

Work was waiting, so he led the horse into the barn by the bridle bits. His sympathy for Meredith remained throughout the afternoon and long into the night, keeping him from a sound sleep.

The last thing she wanted to do was to disappoint her parents. Meredith set her morning cup of tea onto its saucer with a clink and tried to will the fog from her brain. After an upsetting evening with her parents, she'd tossed and turned most of the night and had awakened tired and groggy. Not the way she wanted to start this day, of all days. She listened to the mantel clock ticking off the minutes, knowing every moment that passed brought her closer to acting on her decision. Mama was so not going to like it.

"Meredith, why aren't you eating?" Her mother's tone jarred her out of her thoughts. "You haven't touched your breakfast."

"Sorry." She gathered knife and fork and stared at her plate. The food was delicious. Her stomach growled. She couldn't very well take her test without breakfast, so she cut into the stack of pancakes and took a bite.

"That's better." Mama approved with a nod. "A good girl doesn't mope if she doesn't get her own way."

"Although you've been known to, my dear," Papa quipped lovingly from the head of the table.

"I certainly have never moped, Robert." A tiny hint of amusement snapped between them. "I've been disappointed, perhaps, but a Worthington does not sulk."

Papa's chuckle was his answer as he turned back to his morning paper.

If it was only her mother who was against her becoming a teacher, then she knew she could have taken her pleas to her father. Papa had a hard time denying his daughters anything. But he'd sided with Mama on the subject, saying no girl of his would work. If she defied them, what would happen? She loved her parents. She didn't want to risk losing their regard. But neither could she let this opportunity pass her by.

I really hate being eighteen, she thought. Too young to be on her own, too old to let her parents decide the course of her life. She forked another bite of pancake into her mouth. The good food turned to sand on her tongue, nearly impossible to swallow. The clock had progressed another five minutes. If she wanted to get to the schoolhouse in plenty of time, she had to leave soon. Her palms went damp at the thought.

"You keep looking at the clock, Meredith." Mama and her eagle eye. She didn't miss much. "Do you have someplace to be? You know there isn't school this morning."

"I want to take the exam. You know this, Mama."

"And you know I forbid it. Don't think your father will take you to town with him on his way to work.

He and I have already discussed that. Matilda will be staying home with me this morning to finish reading for our book club. And since you are not allowed to drive, I'm sorry to say you have no choice but to spend your morning helping Sadie in the vegetable garden."

Was there any way to make her mother actually listen? Why was Mama's way always the right one, regardless of the consequences? "Times are changing. A lot of women are working. Earlee wants to be a teacher, too. Lila works in her parents' store."

"If your friends jumped off a cliff, would you jump, too?" Mama demanded. "I think not. Don't compare yourself to those girls, Meredith."

"Why not? They are my friends."

"They are not like our family. They don't have our responsibilities—"

"That is *such* an old-fashioned way to think." She pushed away from the table, torn apart by her wish to do as her parents wanted and by her own conscience. China rattled with the force of her feet hitting the floor. She drew herself up tall, hands clenched, pulse pounding. She felt as if she were tearing apart from the inside out. Why couldn't they understand? She wished more than anything that they would take a moment to see her—just Meredith—and not the daughter they intended to mold her into.

"Where are you going, young lady?" Mama's chair scraped. She was on her feet, her face blushing with anger. "You come right back here and finish your meal."

Her feet seemed to be moving of their own accord, taking her to the front door where she'd left her book bag packed last night. Ready to go, she unhooked her coat from the tree. She glanced over her shoulder across the long stretch of the parlor, and into the dining room where her family watched her, shock frozen on their faces.

She had never denied them before. Papa's newspaper had sagged to the table. The disapproval in harsh lines on his face hurt more than any punishment could. Tilly's fork had stopped midair and her sympathetic look was what gave Meredith the courage to slip one arm into her coat. Tilly understood. Minnie was the first to move, bowing her head to drag a strip of bacon through the syrup puddle on her plate, her shoulders slumped, upset by the discord in their home.

I'm upset, too. Meredith jabbed her other arm into the sleeve and quickly buttoned her coat. At least she would be able to hitch up Sweetie. That was the only saving grace. She had prayed with all her might last night and still the dream remained in her heart. God had not taken it from her. She grasped the bag's straps, twisted the handle and opened the door. *Please, give me strength now, Father.*

Mama's footsteps shot like bullets on the hardwood floor. As Meredith seized the doorknob, she glanced over to see her mother throw up the dining-room window.

"You, there! Young man," Mama called across the yard. "You are not to hitch up any horse and buggy for my Meredith this morning. Do you understand? She is forbidden to drive to town."

Oh, Mama. Did she have to think of everything? Frustrated and hurting, she gritted her teeth, squished all the rising pain down where she couldn't feel it and stormed through the door. The steps pounded beneath her soles as she tumbled out into the yard. For such a stormy day on the inside, it was gorgeous outside. The sunlight washed the fresh green world with a gentle warmth. Birdsong rose from the fields and trees, and lilacs nodded pleasantly in the wind.

Forbidden to drive. Mama's commandment matched the angry beat of her shoes as she stomped down the walkway. Now what did she do? Did she defy her mother in this, too? Or was that the reason she heard the back door open with a squeak? Had Papa come out to ensure she could not disobey and use one of the family horses?

Well, no one had forbidden her to walk. She stared at the road ahead, her shoes crunching on gravel as she stepped into the light. Mama's orders to come back shattered the morning's stillness, but she did not turn around. Anger burned at the backs of her eyes and her throat. Soon all she could hear was her labored breathing and her shoes against the hard-packed earth. Birds fluttered from fence post to field and horses grazing in the pasture looking up curiously as she passed. She felt so bad over how things had gone back home; it diminished the beauty of the morning and the hope for her day.

How was she going to do well on her examination now? All the studying she'd done through the last month of evenings had flown right out of her head. She couldn't remember a single fact of the Revolutionary War to save her life. There was only an empty space in her brain where the information should be. She was more upset over disobeying her parents than she'd realized. She had not wanted to dishonor them, but in the end she could not dishonor herself.

Horse hooves clinking against the road were faint at first and then grew into a steady ringing *clip-clop.* A vehicle's wheels creaked and rolled on the rutted road behind her. Was it Papa coming to stop her? The last of her hopes plummeted to the ground.

Sure enough, she recognized the matched bay Clydesdales drawing alongside her. Papa. Her dreams melted away. She felt wrenched apart, bereft as the wagon rolled to a stop beside her. It was not wrong, this future she longed for. But it was her own. She did not want to lose it.

"You might as well climb up, Just Meredith. I don't want you to be late." A wonderfully warm, familiar, deeply welcome voice spoke into her despair. A hand shot out, waiting for hers. The sunshine, low in the sky, threw blinding rays across him, cloaking his identity, but he was no secret to her.

Shane. Hope and joy leaped through her, lifting her spirit as she laid her palm to his. Once again Shane Connelly helped her into the wagon, the last man she would have expected to come to her aid.

"I can't believe you're here." She settled on the seat, adjusting her skirts, more breathless now because she was at his side. "Mama forbade you to drive me to town."

"But not to fetch the day's order of grain from the feed store." With a casual flick of the reins, he sent the horses moving forward again. "And had the order not been waiting, I would have helped you anyway."

"Why? You will probably lose your job."

"True. I know what it feels like to have to make a tough decision. It's not easy to do what you know is right and leave your family behind." The sun threw playful shafts around him, hiding him from her sight, but she could read his voice, sensing the layers of regret, of sadness, of resolve.

"It was hard for you to leave them, wasn't it?"

"The hardest thing I've ever done." His confession ached with emotion and made him larger than life, larger than any one man could be.

"I may have left them behind, but I didn't stop loving them." He shrugged, as if he'd been torn apart, too. "I wish my parents could have helped me find a middle ground. It wasn't as if I was running around behind their backs causing trouble. I simply wanted to learn to train horses."

"And I to teach." They were so alike. Amazing that he had come into her life when she'd most needed someone to truly understand. She wondered about God's hand in this and dared to say the words troubling her most. "I don't want this to cost me my family, the way following your heart has cost you yours."

"I don't want that for you either." He stared at the road ahead, but he was honest and he did not offer her false comfort. "Your family has one thing mine never had. Love. Your folks aren't going to be happy with you. They may never understand, but I'm sure they will always love you."

"Thanks, Shane."

He turned away and said nothing more. A terrible stinging plagued her eyes, and she blinked hard to keep back the tears. It occurred to her how sad it truly was that she had found her soul mate, the one man she'd always hoped she would find, and she could not count him as a friend.

Chapter Thirteen

"How did you think you did?" Earlee asked as they walked down the street toward Main, leaving the schoolhouse behind them. "The exam was hard. My brain hurts from thinking so much."

"Mine, too." Meredith rubbed her forehead, wishing she could soothe away her other troubles as easily. The sun was past its zenith, the afternoon was halfway gone and she dreaded what lay ahead. Even thinking of going home made her stomach tangle up in impossibly hard knots. "There were several questions I completely missed. I just know it."

"Me, too." Earlee lifted her face to the sun and let the wind breeze over her, tangling her pure golden locks. "I'm hoping what I got wrong isn't nearly as much as what I got right."

"We'll find out in two more hours." She was aquiver at the thought. Pass or fail, she still had to face her mother. The sunlight seemed to drain a few notches in intensity as she fell silent, watching the grass blades shiver in the breeze ahead of her feet.

"Can I ask you something?" Earlee broke the silence

as they crossed the vacant lot at the end of the block. "I don't want to pry or anything, but I noticed something serious between you and your driver guy."

"Shane? There's nothing between us." This she knew for sure. She didn't even have to deny it. He'd made it perfectly clear—twice now. "He was helping me out this morning, that's all."

"But you like him. *Really* like him."

"I do not." There came the denial rushing like the updraft of a giant tornado. Heat blushed across her face like a sunburn. "Maybe that's a sign I do."

"I think so!" Earlee's good humor was a gentle one, laced with understanding. "Are you finding that it's complicated if you like someone? And that it's confusing?"

"I want to deny that, but I don't dare. I'm going to be honest with myself." She took a deep breath, hitched the strap of her book bag higher on her shoulder and stopped at the corner to check for traffic. "I like Shane in a way I've never liked anyone before and yes, it's confusing and complicated and horribly painful. I don't care for it."

"Me, neither." Earlee clapped her hand over her mouth, as if surprised she had revealed so much. "Oops. I was going to make this be a hypothetical discussion, but I let the cat out of the bag."

"I'll say." After a donkey and cart ambled by, she stepped into the road. "Who are you sweet on? I haven't noticed you talking with any boy at school."

"Oh. He's not in our school." Earlee blushed harder.

That explained it. Meredith searched through her

mind, thinking of suitably aged bachelors in town. "Let's see. There's Austin Hadly, the minister's son."

"No. He's cute, but not the one. Not that he has ever noticed me." Earlee had turned bright red, clearly uncomfortable. "And if you try guessing, it will take you an eternity. He no longer lives in town."

"But he used to?"

"Yes."

They'd reached the other side of the street where the boardwalk led them past the milliner's shop and the post office.

"I need to check for our mail." Earlee hesitated, gesturing toward the small shop bearing the United States flag.

"You are trying to get out of answering the question." Meredith wasn't fooled, but she thankfully didn't probe. "I know how it feels. I'm not ready to talk about what I feel for Shane, not even with my best friends."

"Thanks for understanding. Some things feel that if you talk about them out loud, then they will somehow vanish or change on you." She knew her face was still red because she could see the tip of her nose. Strawberry red. Completely embarrassing and far too telling. "Shane likes you. You know that, right?"

"What? Shane? No." She shook her head hard enough for curls to tumble down from beneath her bonnet. The silk ribbons of her hat bobbled and swayed. She blushed furiously. That was telling, too. "He doesn't. He's told me so."

"Then either he isn't being honest with you or he isn't being honest with himself." She took a step toward the post office, knowing how it felt to wonder if a guy liked you and fearing that he didn't. "You should see the look on Shane's face when he thinks no one is watching."

"What do you mean?"

"He gazes upon you as if you are his dream come true. As if you are his princess at the end of a fairy tale. Don't shake your head like that. I've seen him."

"You, my dear Earlee, have a romantic streak a mile wide." Meredith looked wistful for one brief moment before shaking her head, as if discounting her wish, and wrapped her arms around her middle. "This isn't a dime novel or one of the lovely stories you pen. There is going to be no happy ending for Shane and me."

"I've seen the way you look at him, too." It was simply the truth. "A change comes over you. You look softer and somehow more like yourself. I've never seen you so beautiful, Meredith."

"Now I'm really blushing. You and your imagination, Earlee." She swept at the curls always falling into her eyes, and it would have been simple as pie to put words to page and describe the love brightening the blue of her eyes and denial negating it. "Oh, I guess my ride home is here after all."

"She says, and *then* she turns around to see the handsome man in the fine buggy pull to a stop behind her." Earlee lowered her voice, buoyant with happiness for her friend. In her stories, love always found its match and that love was always true. Every now and then it was affirming to see the seeds of it in real life, the proof that true love could exist and even prosper. "Your Shane is here."

"Shh!" She blushed again. "He might hear you."

"I guess I'll head home on my own." She didn't

bother to disguise her gladness. "Have a very nice drive."

"Sure, considering the roads are much better these days. Just a little soupy in places." Meredith adjusted her bonnet bow beneath her chin. "And don't say it. I know what you're thinking. I can see it written all over your face."

"I wasn't talking about the roads."

"You couldn't be more wrong." She rolled her eyes, full of denial, turning just enough to spot Shane at the edge of her peripheral vision.

"The moment he is near, your spirit turns to him like he is the sun and you are the earth. Definitely like every romance I've ever read. Be honest with yourself. You're in love with him."

"I have to go." Love? That was a very powerful word and it hardly applied. It was ridiculous, that was what it was, but that was Earlee finding the beauty in anything—even if it didn't exist. She loved her friend, but she was sorry to say Earlee was exceptionally wrong in this instance. Somehow she scooted her feet forward toward the buggy where Shane waited, his face shaded by his Stetson and his unseen gaze a touch to her cheek, her mouth, her lips.

Now I'm *being fanciful,* she thought, waving good-bye to Earlee, who glowed happily, apparently sure she had things all figured out, before spinning around and hurrying down the street to the post office.

"How did it go?" Shane hopped down, not in the placid, doing-my-job way Eli Sims, her former driver, had done, but with a deliberate gentlemanliness that felt suspiciously like a courting man—although it could not be.

Whatever romantic fanciful tendencies Earlee had, perhaps they were as contagious as diphtheria. Meredith shook her head, hoping to scatter those thoughts right out of her mind, squared her shoulders and stepped into the buggy's shadow where Shane stood waiting for her.

"I have no idea if I passed or failed." She was talking about the test, but as he helped her into the buggy, dizziness swept over her, scrambling her senses.

"I'm sure you did very well." His words came as if from a great distance as the cushioned seat bounced slightly when he eased down beside her.

She gulped, surprised at the slight brush of his elbow against her sleeve as he took up the reins.

"There's no sense of you sitting in the back all by yourself and me being up here by my lonesome self." His baritone held a note she hadn't heard in it for a long time. Not since the first day they met. His combination of amusement and warmth and manliness could lull her into believing that Earlee was right. That he was attracted to her. Her heart fluttered, as if with wings.

"What are you going to do when you pass?"

"I suppose I will find that out in a little while. The superintendent said he will have the exams graded by three o'clock."

"We don't have to head straight back to the house." He knuckled back his hat like a Western hero. "We can wait her in town, if you like."

"Sure, but you are here to do a job, not to be friends."

She longed for him to argue the point. "Waiting with me certainly is not part of your job description."

"I figured I'm fired anyway, so why not?" There was a deeper nuance to his words, a layer of affection that he could not hide.

If only she did not feel it, she thought. It was hard not to care for him in return. Shane snapped Sweetie's reins and led them rambling down the road through town.

Earlee nearly died when she saw the letter in the small bundle the postmaster handed across the counter. Finn McKaslin, Deer Lodge Territorial Prison, was written in a clear script in the upper left-hand corner. She couldn't believe it. He'd actually written back. She ran her fingertips over the letters of his name, atremble with too many emotions to describe easily. She knew good and well what her parents would say if they knew she was corresponding with a man in prison, but hadn't Reverend Hadly preached on Sunday to see God's goodness in all those we met, and to wear a mantle of kindness?

That is not *the reason you're glad Finn to wrote you, Earlee Elizabeth Mills*. She pushed through the door, held it for elderly Mrs. Finch and headed straight for the bench situated next door in front of the bakery. Ignoring the hustle and bustle of the horse-and-buggy traffic, the rattling commotion of teamsters hauling their loads down the street and the clip-clip of shoes on the boardwalk behind her, she carefully tore open the envelope. The parchment crackled like dried leaves she shook so hard.

The same clear intelligent handwriting covered the page. She leaned over the words, to shield it from passersby, and began to read.

Dear Earlee,

I can't believe you actually wrote to me. I don't have a whole lot of spare time, being as this is a hard labor prison, but even here Sunday is a day of rest. I spent my free mornings in service and the afternoons writing to family and friends. Honestly, it's family. It doesn't matter how many letters I send out to friends, not a single one comes back. Not that I blame them. I messed my life up good, but I've never understood the meaning of friendship before or wished for it so much.

Poor Finn. Sympathy filled her. She glanced up from the letter, trying to imagine his life. Hard labor sounded awful, and so did his loneliness. She didn't know what she would do if something caused her to be parted from her friends. She felt so sorry for him, the young man she remembered as tall and broad-shouldered, muscled but not brawny. Before his trouble with the law, she'd had a crush on him with his bright blue eyes and dark fall of hair a little too long for fashion. The rumble of his deep voice could make a girl dream.

Now all his prospects in life and his chances were gone. It was good he saw the error of his ways and she felt the remorse in his words. She glanced across the street where sunlight reflected in the windows of the land office. Her throat ached from the lump of emotion settling there. She firmly believed there was good in everyone, and that everyone was worth a second chance. Maybe it was the dreamer in her or the writer wanting to pen a happier ending for him. She bowed her head and went back to reading.

Although your note was short, I was much obliged to hear about how you're doing and the town's news. Your letter was entertaining, I found myself smiling, and I thank you for that. I can't tell you what your gift of kindness means to me. How did the hunt for the calf turn out? Did you finish the dress for you sister in time for the Sunday service? I understand if you feel uncomfortable and decide not to write me, but I hope you do.

Hoping to be your pen friend,

Finn

She stared at his name, the confident swish of the letters and his vulnerable request on the page. He wanted to be pen pals. She thought of his friends who'd forsaken him and she pulled out a sheet of parchment, a bottle of ink and her pen. After loading the tip, she used the back of her slate for a lap desk and began to write.

Finn,

Yes, the calf story ended well. I didn't see the capture firsthand, but I heard about it from Scarlet Fisher, who lives next door to the Hoffsteaders. Late at night a clatter in the alley woke the Hoffsteaders from a sound sleep. The intruder in their backyard was threatened with a mop, since the family rifle was at the gunsmith's for repair, and the sheriff called. When the law arrived and one of the deputies lit a lamp, instead of the thief Mr. Hoffsteader had cornered on the porch, they found the runaway calf lounging on the swing. Mrs. Hoffsteader was beside herself because of the hoof prints in her flowerbeds and on the swing's cushion.

She lifted her pen from the paper, considering what to say next. She hoped Finn would smile at the tale, because it sounded as if he had little in his life that would make him do so. That was what she wanted to give him—a smile and a moment to forget his hardships. She bit her lip, gazed out at the street, watched an ox tied to a nearby hitching post attempt to eat a flower off a lady's hat, and let her pen guide the way.

I finished my sister's dress in time for Sunday school. That will teach her to daydream while she's ironing. I had to learn the hard way, too. I ruined two perfectly good dresses until I learned to keep my mind on the iron. The newest battle in my household is over who will do the barnyard chores. We have the cutest little batch of piglets born this spring, four dozen fluffy yellow chicks and twin calves that are too adorable for words. Add that to the new litter of kittens in the barn, and every morning the nine of us are squabbling over who gets to take care of what.

I won this morning and had the sweet privilege of feeding the calves. They have finally learned to drink from a bucket. Every time they spot a pail, their adorable brown heads rise up, their chocolate eyes glitter and they bawl in excitement. They run over on their spindly legs with knobby knees. They are so cute that it's no work at all to take care of them.

Well, I hope I haven't bored you. If I have, I'm sorry. If not, please write back and tell me about your life. What is it like to be so far away from home? What do you miss the most?

I'll save all my best prayers for you, Finn.

Your pen friend,

Earlee Mills

There. She screwed the cap on her ink bottle and stretched the kink out of her neck. The letter didn't feel like enough, so she bowed her head for a quick prayer. *Please, keep him safe, Father. Help him to find the better side of Finn McKaslin I know is there.*

When she opened her eyes, the sunshine appeared brighter. Maybe it was a sign. Encouraged, she folded the letter in careful thirds. She would get this addressed and posted so it could go out on the afternoon train. A warm, fizzy feeling filled her, the way soap bubbles floated weightlessly on the air. That was exactly how she felt as she dug in her bag in search of her spare pennies to pay for the stamp.

He had to be out of his mind. Shane watched Meredith take a sip of sarsaparilla, doing his best not to notice the delight that only endeared her to him more. The way she tilted her head to one side as she debated taking another sip. She had curly brown eyelashes and flecks of gold in her gray-blue irises. He'd never noticed that before. He hated that he noticed now.

"What will you do if you get fired?" She set the glass down, drawing his attention to her slender hands, hands that fit perfectly within his own.

He hated how empty his hand felt without hers tucked in it. There were few customers in the diner, which suited him fine. He took a swallow out of his glass, letting the sweet cool drink roll across his tongue. "I suspect Braden will let me stay on with him when he travels to Butte, since I haven't made a habit of rescuing pretty maidens in distress and costing us a job."

"Ha! That's not true." She licked custard off the tines of her fork, triumph lifting her delicate chin and sculpting her beautiful features. Her spirit sparkled through, captivating and endlessly drawing. She pointed her fork at him. "You rescue women all the time. Remember how we met?"

"Sure, Braden and I have helped others in our journeys. There was a young mother in a broken-down cart we hammered together enough to get her home. And an elderly woman whose horse lost a shoe."

"You're simply trying to sound noble."

"Not noble. Can't you see the only lady who has ever affected me like this is you?" His pulse screeched to a stop, and he winced, realizing he had said far too much. Could she see how he cared? He swallowed hard, doing his best not to retreat or to panic. Whatever tangled him up inside, it was a great deal more than simple *like*. The notion of never seeing her again ate at him. "If I have to pack up and ride out tomorrow and leave you behind, I'll regret it."

"You will?" Her fork dropped to the table in her surprise. Maybe he'd been afraid she would be dismayed by this piece of news, but she didn't look distressed. In the beat of silence between them, she drew in a shaky breath and he felt her answer because it was his.

The moment their gazes connected, it was like a spark to a can of kerosene. The explosion of brightness in his soul outshone the sun, making shadows of the world around him until there was only her beauty and color and life. Just Meredith and his love dawning.

"I don't want to be friends with you." His confession was whispered, so no one but she could hear. "Do you suppose the soon-to-be schoolteacher would let a simple horseman come beauing?"

"You will have to ask her and see." Her answer twinkled in her eyes as blue as his future, and they smiled together. He dared to reach across the small table and cradle the side of her cheek in his hand. Never had he felt anything softer, never had he touched anyone so dear to him.

"Shall we go back to the schoolhouse and see just how well you did on your test?" he asked, knowing full well he was ten times a fool.

When she nodded, gently leaning into his touch, he lost control of his feelings completely. There was no way to hold back the depth and strength of his love for her. It rose up of its own power and accord, against his better judgment and a list of reasons he shouldn't get involved.

When he pushed his chair away from the table, he felt like a new man.

*mental properties and a bit of lead-in... would float downriver to...

When he pushed the dark water from the... it felt like a silk slide.*

Chapter Fourteen

Banished to her room, Meredith plumped the pillow at her back, leaned against the window seat cushion and held her sewing hoop up to the lamplight. Tiny perfect stitches marched along the seam she'd finished sewing, bringing two more squares of her patchwork block together. Deciding the stitching was uniform and tiny enough, she smoothed the seam flat with her thumb and flipped the half-finished block over. The pretty cotton fabrics made her smile.

Fiona had talked her into buying the cheerful yellow sprigged, saying it was the perfect color to build a quilt around. She recalled how Lila had spotted the beautiful robin's-egg blue calico in a new shipment of fabrics in her parents' store and set it aside for her. Soft lovely emotions of friendship filled her whenever she gazed upon the pieces. Scarlet had helped her pick out the rose-pink calico and Kate, at one of their sewing circle gatherings, had pointed out she needed more contrast. So her father had driven them all to Lawson's mercantile after school one rainy day in February where she'd added the ivory, green and lavender calicos to the mix.

Earlee wasn't satisfied until she dug out a bold purple sprigged lost in the bolts of cotton. The laughter and happiness of that afternoon shopping trip rang through her, a dear memory she wanted to hold close forever.

She chose a purple cut square from her fabric pile, judging it against the other colors of the block. The merry brightness brought out the flowery yellow and the leaf green of the adjacent pieces. She carefully pinned it into place, eyeing the seam allowance. The end of the school year was almost upon them, and she would no longer see her best friends every day. School would end, they would graduate and all go their separate ways.

As she had tried to explain to Mama hours ago, that was a good thing. They were growing up and into the lives they had been dreaming of. But with the gain came losses. Sadness chased away the memories as she knotted her thread and stitched the raw edges of the fabric. Her thimble clicked as she worked, loud in the silent room.

A rap against the window cannoned like a bullet from a gun. The needle flew out of her grasp, she jumped in place and her pulse took off like a runaway freight train. She drew back the curtain. A face reflected in at her through the shadowed glass.

Shane. Night was falling, cloaking him in shades of darkness. He'd never been more handsome to her as she unlatched the window and opened it with care. The wood frame did not groan, the hinge did not squeak and a pleasant wind blew in the scent of lilacs. The maple's leaves shivered as Shane leaned closer to the sill.

"How's the new schoolteacher?" He presented her

a bouquet of fragrant flowers, the dainty little blooms the exact purple of the piece she'd been sewing.

"Fine enough." She accepted the blossoms and lifted them to her nose. The luxurious perfume filled her as if with hope. "It's the first big step on the road to my goals. I wish it felt more like an achievement instead of a source of unhappiness for my parents."

"They want what they think is best for you." He brushed the sensitive curve of her chin with his knuckle. "They will come to accept this."

"I hope so. And if not—" Because that thought made her sad, she cast it aside, focusing on the man before her. How rugged he looked with his hat slanted at a rakish angle and a day's growth rough on his jaw. Lamplight flicked in the wind, lashing at the slash of his high cheekbones and revealing the steady glow of affection in his eyes. Affection for her right there, revealed for her to see, tenderness that stretched without words from his soul to hers.

A like regard budded within her, as pure as the blossoms she held and as fragile. Caring deepened, and she could not stop it. The backs of her eyes stung and she carefully laid the handful of flowers on the edge of her nearby night table, leaning away from the window and away from him. But the distance between them made no difference. Somehow everything had changed.

"I have money set aside to buy land of my own when the time is right." Manly, quiet strength radiated from him like light from a flame. Unaware of his own brightness, he humbly shrugged one shoulder, his gaze intensifying, his seriousness arresting. "There's a meeting between Braden and your father tomorrow. If all does not go well, we will be leaving. Braden intends to head south to start our next job early."

"So soon." She expected it, but it hurt just the same. Everything within her stilled. The wind whipped her hair into her eyes again, and she moved to brush those curls aside, but it was his hand grazing her cheek, his fingertips caressing a sugar-sweet path from her forehead to her temple.

"Beauing a woman is much harder to do from a great distance." His words rumbled through her, layered with meaning and an affection he must have thought hidden in the dark.

"But I will not be staying either." Her fingers curled around his steely wrist, wishing she could hold him captive. "I have already inquired to several schools for the summer, and then I will be moving on to another permanent school in the fall."

"I could follow you." How certain he sounded, as if dreams were so easily set aside.

"But what about your apprenticeship?"

"I hate to end it, but I could." He winced, as if he were torn. "I've learned nearly all I have signed on to do."

"Then I think you should finish." She leaned into his touch. The wind stirred her golden locks against his knuckles. She unwound his fingers from her hair and cradled his hand in both of hers. "I am a very good letter writer."

"I'm sure you are." He stared at her smaller, paler hands clasped around his sun-browned, callused one, thinking how different they were and how like. Love enfolded his heart the same way her hands wrapped around his. "You would write to me?"

"I suppose I could be persuaded every once in a while to pen a note for you," she quipped, but she meant something more. He knew because he felt the same way.

"I'm glad to hear it." He lifted his hand, bringing her knuckles to his lips. "My understanding with Braden is done at the end of this year, and my traveling will come to an end."

"You want to train horses of your own?"

"I want to farm." He brushed a kiss to her fingertips, one by one. The tenderness taking over him was the sweetest thing he'd ever known.

Lord, she is the future I want. The prayer rose up with all the might in his soul. *Thank You for leading me to Meredith.* He was about to start the best adventure of his life.

"Farm?" Her forehead furrowed. "You mean to raise horses?"

"No, to rescue them." His kisses stopped, but he kept their hands linked. "I always meant to have my own stables, but then I've seen a lot of sad things in my travels. Hobo is a horse I rescued last year from a man beating him in the middle of the road."

"What? Why would anyone do such a thing?"

"I don't understand it. I don't know." Sorrow etched into the counters of his mouth. "The poor animal was covered in saddle sores, half-starved, and had collapsed on a lonely stretch of the Wyoming plains. His owner had taken a whip to him while he lay helpless in the January snow. Braden and I came upon them and I offered the man the contents of my billfold. He took the two hundred dollars. I got the better deal."

"You saved Hobo's life."

"He saved mine. Because of him, I knew what I wanted to do. Find a nice spread to buy, raise crops and give horses a second chance. Everyone deserves a safe place to prosper." Never had the man been bigger in her estimation. He towered before her, framed by the window, dominating her senses. He was all she could see, all she ever wanted to see.

"Are you surprised?" he asked.

"No. I approve." She squeezed her fingers entwined with his. As she let go of his hand, the bond between them remained as enduring as tempered steel, proof enough that she was right. They were kindred spirits. Souls so alike they felt as one.

Footsteps echoed in the hallway. A floorboard squeaked. Panic lurched through her, but the gait was not Mama's.

"I'd best go." He pushed away from the sill. The leaves rustled, and a branch groaned as he shifted his weight. "Tomorrow."

"Tomorrow." She reaffirmed his unspoken promise with a single nod. Something tore apart within her as they parted. She closed the window and he disappeared from her sight.

A tap rapped on her door. "Meredith?"

"Tilly." She jumped to her feet and her sewing tumbled from her lap. She caught the fabric by an edge. "Come in."

"I thought you might like some company." Tilly slipped into the room with her embroidery hoop in hand. "It gets lonely being sent to your room for the evening."

"Yes, it does. I'm glad you came. I was working on my quilt." She held up her partially finished block, doing her best to take her mind off Shane and enjoy this time with her sister. There would not be many evenings left to spend talking and sewing together.

"It's cheerful. I love the purple." Tilly inspected the squares. "It's a happy coincidence it matches the flowers Shane brought you."

"How did you know?"

"They weren't there when I brought up your supper tray." Tilly settled back on the window seat. "How did he get them to you?"

"He climbed the maple." Her fingers tingled from his gallant, sweet kisses.

"Wow, he must have really wanted to see you." Tilly stared hard at her hoop, where a pair of love birds were taking shape out of carefully stitched colors of floss. "I thought you didn't like Shane."

"Once I acted out of hurt feelings, but I was wrong." It was her turn to blush, her cheeks turning a furious red. Every time they were together, she found more to admire and more reason to care for him. But she didn't know how to admit it, so she fell to silence and straightened out the tangle her thread had become.

She was thankful for Tilly, who didn't say another word as she bent her head to her needlework, saying in understanding silence what could never be said with words. They stitched the evening away in sisterly solidarity. Every fiber of her being yearned for morning when she could look upon Shane again.

* * *

"Good girl." Shane praised from the back of the black filly, patting her neck. The morning sun was burning off the dew and mist from the pond, and larks sang gloriously celebrating the new day. Robins hopped through grasses searching for breakfast and a jackrabbit hid in the bushes near the fresh young sprouts in the garden.

The filly shook her head, jingling her bridle bits, as if proud of herself, too. The wind stirred her mane and brought the scent of lilacs and voices from the house. Braden's deeper voice mingled with the conversation. When Shane looked up, he spotted Mrs. Worthington at the end of the walkway looking like a general at war, directing her youngest daughter into the waiting buggy. Minnie skipped along ignoring her mother's request to walk like a lady.

He smiled. He was fond of the littlest sister. He would miss her. The oldest Worthington girl walked into sight and took the front seat. She would be driving to town this morning, which was fine by him. He had a lot of work to finish up. The filly sidestepped, as if anxious to go.

"Whoa there." He increased pressure on the reins until she stilled and made her wait. Her ears pricked, and she stood at attention waiting for the signal to go. He gave it before she could move again, touching his heels to her sides and lifting in the saddle. Her trot was disciplined as she circled the corral. Posting in the saddle, he felt something in the air change and in his soul.

Meredith. The morning brightened as she swept

down the front steps. Guarded by lilacs and accompanied by nodding daffodils, she was poetry in motion with her green bonnet ribbons trailing in the wind and her matching dress swishing at her ankles. He felt entranced, unable to look anywhere else.

"Meredith, you are to come straight home from school." Mrs. Worthington's command rose above the drum of the horse's hooves and scattered birds from the orchard trees. The jackrabbit ducked for cover. "Matilda will come fetch you. With our book club meeting this morning, that makes an unseemly amount of trips to town."

"We can always miss the meeting," Tilly answered from the buggy's front seat.

"That would be even worse. How else will I be able to keep up with the news in town?" A faint note of humor rang in the older woman's words, a hint she was not as hard as she seemed.

Still, Meredith dominated his vision. As if she felt his presence, she glanced directly across the driveway to where he stood in the middle of the corral. Time stopped. The world kept spinning, life kept moving forward but they—he and Meredith—did not. The distance of garden and yard and paddock between them vanished and it felt as it had when he'd kissed her every fingertip. She had agreed to wait for him. She had approved of his plans for his future; she knew he wanted to be a farmer. The smile that touched her lips let him know that her regard for him had not changed.

"Hurry up, Meredith!" Minnie hung out of the backseat, clinging to the frame. "We're gonna be tardy. I don't want to have to write lines."

"I'm coming." She tore her attention from him, and it ripped like a physical wound.

You are in so much trouble, Connelly. You are more in love with the girl than you think. The filly reached the end of the corral and he turned her smoothly, glancing over his shoulder to keep Meredith in sight. She clutched the side of the buggy and hopped up, settling her bag and her lunch pail, wholesome and golden in the pretty May morning. He could not gaze upon her enough.

Soon he would be leaving and all he would have were memories of her. His throat ached, growing tight beneath his Adam's apple. There would be letters and the hope of seeing her again, but the separation to come would not be easy.

"Connelly." Braden strolled into sight. "You've made fine progress with the filly."

"She's a great horse. It was a pleasure to work with her." The buggy rolled down the driveway, with Meredith hidden from his view. Minnie hung out the window, spotted him and waved her arms as if she were trying to scare cattle.

"Howdy, Shane!" she shouted.

"Think she's got a crush on you." Braden chuckled as he leaned his forearms on the top board of the fence.

"She's a good kid." He waved back, earning Minnie's wide grin. She disappeared inside the buggy as it bounced on the rutted roads and turned the corner. Trees hid the horse and vehicle, taking his heart with it.

"Minnie is not our problem."

"Don't even say it." Shane slowed the filly to a walk. "You were right. I shouldn't have gotten involved."

"I know you couldn't help yourself." Braden, tough as nails, was not a man to succumb to the charms of any woman, but neither was he unfeeling. "You gave your best attempt not to fall for her."

"It wasn't enough." He reined the filly to a stop. He couldn't help feeling he had made a mess of things, but on the other hand Meredith had been worth it. "Affection snuck up on me."

"That's how it happens. But I have to give you credit. It didn't affect your work. That's all I care about." Braden climbed between the boards and held out his hand to the filly. "You are a fine horseman, Connelly."

"Don't you mean I will make one someday?" He dismounted, his boots hitting the earth.

"Nope. I mean you are one." Braden smiled, a rare thing, and took the mare by the bits. "I'll take her in. I've got a little time before I meet with Robert."

"Do you think there's any chance we could stay on?" The road was empty, all sign of Meredith was gone, but he felt her like a sonnet in his heart, like a hymn in his soul. "There is still work to do here."

"We are at a good stopping place. The two-year-olds are saddle broke, the yearlings have most of the basics. We haven't finished what we've agreed to do, but I'm not sure I can take any more drama." Braden grinned over his shoulder. "The missus takes more work than the horses. We leave, and I won't have to worry about the smell of horse manure bothering her when she's gardening and the wind shifts."

"Or the sound of horse hooves interrupting her reading. You want to move on, regardless of what Robert says."

"That's an affirmative."

Shane knew it was coming, but the final answer hit like a blow. The idea of leaving Meredith behind was one thing, but the reality of it was another. The sun lost its warmth, the world its beauty and he felt alone in a way he'd never been before.

Meredith shifted in her seat, cradled her forehead in her hands and willed her mind on the open history book before her. But the facts of George Washington's presidency kept evaporating like smoke and refused to stick in her brain. What did occupy her mind? Shane astride the black horse, his face shaded by his Stetson, his wide shoulders straight and strong, her very own beau. She'd picked up a lilac blossom she'd pressed in her book and twirled it. The scent from the tiny petals launched her back in time. Instead of her history book, it was last night's history she reviewed—his story of Hobo, his dreams to farm and a sanctuary for abused horses.

Falling in love was not in her immediate plans, but she could no more stop her affections than keep time from ticking forward. She remembered the verse from Proverbs. *There are many plans in a man's heart, nevertheless the Lord's counsel—that will stand.* So much for her careful plans. She was not, in the end, in charge of them.

Something bumped her elbow. Scarlet nudged her

slate across the desktop with a one-word message scribbled in the corner. *Shane?*

Meredith nodded, ready to scribble back an answer, but Miss Lambert peered their way. Oops. She returned her eyes to her textbook as Scarlet hastily erased the message with her slate rag. The wall clock counted down the minutes until lunch break. Restless, Meredith leaned forward to glance past Scarlet across the aisle to Fiona and Lila, who shared a seat. They were bent in study, Fiona's curly black locks hiding her face, and Lila absently winding a stray tendril around one finger as she read.

Two rows over, Lorenzo Davis was staring openly at Fiona, lost in the look of her, affection poignant in his gaze. Poor Lorenzo. He had always carried a secret love for Fiona, who never had been interested in him. Proof enough that plans did not often work out because God was guiding them all. Perhaps there would be someone for Lorenzo when he was ready. She knew the rest of their circle would be thrilled to be beaued by the handsome man.

Miss Lambert's handbell chimed above the sound of pages being turned and the industrious scratch of pencils on slates. Lunchtime. Movement erupted as students slammed books, launched out of their seats and conversations boomed. Meredith carefully set the tiny purple blossom on her page and closed the book.

"I'm starving." Scarlet shot into the aisle. "I have a treat. I brought everyone cookies—"

"*Excuse* me." Narcissa Bell pushed her way by, nose in the air.

"Honestly. What an attitude." Lila rolled her eyes in response. "That girl bothers me."

"Aren't we suppose to find the good in everyone we meet?" Earlee said sweetly, book bag in hand.

"Yeah," Kate agreed. "I'm sure there's a speck there somewhere, but we might need a magnifying glass to see it."

"A really big one," Ruby agreed as she joined them in the aisle. "Has she always been like that?"

Narcissa was already out of sight, having pushed her way through the tussle of the crowd. Meredith followed Fiona's gingham skirt between the desks toward the door. Sunlight glinted on the windows as they approached. "Is it me, or is Narcissa worse than normal?"

"Worse," Lila agreed.

"Worse," Scarlet seconded.

"Much worse," Kate chimed in.

"Makes me miss her usual disposition. Almost." Earlee smiled her contagious smile, making them all do the same. "I wonder what bee has gotten under her bonnet?"

"Good question." Meredith took her lunch pail off the coat room's shelf. "Maybe she's jealous she's not the first of our grade to get married like Fee is."

"Oh, I don't think she's jealous of me." Fiona, the dear that she was, grabbed her battered lunch tin and waltzed through the sun-washed door. "Although I did manage to find the best man in the county."

"Probably the entire territory," Kate agreed as they tromped down the stairs.

"Your Ian is to die for," Scarlet added.

Her friends' voices faded, coming as if from far away. The moment her shoe landed on the top step, she knew why. She felt his presence like grace to her soul.

Shane. He sat stride his Appaloosa at the edge of the road, mighty and forthright, everything a man ought to be. He tipped his hat to her, and the surprise and thrill of seeing him lifted her feet from the ground. She might very well have floated down the steps, for the lightness of her being, for the greatness of her love.

"Girls, it looks like Meredith has a beau." Lila could not mask the delight in her words.

"A beau?" Kate sounded confused. "I thought she didn't like him."

"Shh," Earlee whispered. "That's the way love works sometimes."

"Love?" Fiona sounded stunned. "Really? Our Meredith is in love, too?"

"What about her plans to teach?" Scarlet wanted to know.

Meredith hardly noticed her friends had stayed back, to let her go ahead. She was being pulled to Shane with a force that was beyond her will. He dismounted like a man who had been brought up on horses, striding across the grass toward her with easy, confident strides that made every other man in existence pale by comparison.

"Hello, beautiful." He gathered her hands in his, gazing as if he could never get enough of her. "Hope you don't mind I stopped by. I was in town on errands."

"I'm so glad you're here. Come join us."

"Your friends won't mind?"

She glanced around, but her friends—her dear friends—were nowhere in sight. This time alone with Shane was a gift, because she knew without asking this was their last day together. Sadness lay behind his smile and in his manner as his fingers twined tight to hers.

She led him to the steps, where they could sit and talk like any young courting couple. For fifty wonderful minutes, they were.

Chapter Fifteen

The first peal of the school bell came far too soon. Shane climbed reluctantly to his feet, hating that their time together was done. He held out his hand, assisting Meredith from the step. Children streamed around them into the schoolhouse, but he had eyes for only her.

"Braden and I have a lot to finish up before we leave." His throat felt full and his chest tight. The weight of what he wanted to say was lodged in his throat. "I'll be busy, but somehow I'll figure out a way to see you."

"I'm sure you will." She nodded, scattering her golden mass of curls that bounced and sprang when she moved.

"There's always the maple tree as a last resort," he quipped, fighting to keep things light. He did not want to waste the moments they had left with inevitable sorrows.

Something touched his elbow—not something, someone. The haughty girl, the one Meredith didn't like, settled her hand on his arm, an unwelcome touch.

"Hi there, Shane." She preened up at him, eyelashes batting. "Have you heard from your mother lately?"

"What?" He pulled away, shocked by her forwardness. "Excuse me, but Meredith and I—"

"I hope she isn't getting too attached to you." Narcissa, honey sweetness and spite, turned to Meredith next. "My mother is friends with the Kellans."

"So what?" Meredith ignored her, turning away. The stream of kids broke around them, barreling up the steps, barring his way to her.

"For your information, the Kellans are close friends with the Connellys of Virginia." Narcissa smirked. "Don't you know your senators? We learned them last November. Senator Stuart Connelly?"

"My father." He broke through the trail of students to get to his beloved. He didn't know what the rude girl was up to, but he didn't like it. "I'm sorry, Meredith. I should have told you before this."

"I don't understand." Confusion hazed her clear eyes.

"Some say he'll go back home in time, after he's done having fun and sowing his wild oats. He's being groomed to take his father's seat when he retires. You know what that means. He will need a proper lady at his side, not a teacher." Narcissa, pleased to be the bearer of such news, smiled broadly as she tripped up the rest of the stairs. "I hope you didn't think his act was sincere."

"Act?" Meredith gripped the railing until her knuckles went white. "I don't understand."

"Don't believe her." Shane was at her side. The final clang of the bell resounded overhead. The sky remained as blue, the sun as cheerful, but everything had changed.

"She knew who you were all along." That explained a lot. Narcissa's attempts to get his attention and to get close to him. It all made sense now. Her anger when those efforts hadn't worked. And now the whole truth lay before her. His was no ordinary family. He was not the humble horseman he professed to be.

"There is no act, Meredith." The words rang with sincerity and might, a voice of an honest man. He squared his shoulders, back straight, iron jaw set. The only softness that remained was the plea in his loving eyes. "My intentions toward you are honorable. You know that."

"I apparently don't know anything about you."

"You know what matters. You know me." He laid a hand to his chest, as if to bare his soul. "I meant to tell you about my family, but—"

A handbell chimed furiously. The teacher glared at them. "Time to come in, Meredith. Girls."

Only then did she realize that her friends had held back, huddled together in the spill of sunshine, waiting and not wanting to interrupt. Their silent comfort and sympathy was a crutch she needed to lean on. She drew herself up, gathered her courage and faced the man who was full of apologies, almost as many of them as his unspoken truths.

"Let's go in," she told her friends. Turning away from Shane was like turning away from herself. Taking the first step toward the doorway was like ripping off a part of her soul. She left the real Shane Connelly behind as Miss Lambert shut the schoolhouse door.

"Maybe it isn't as bad as it sounds," Earlee soothed

gently, rubbing Meredith's shoulder. "Maybe there's a good explanation."

"For betrayal?" She'd believed in him. She'd thought they were kindred spirits, two halves of the same soul. But he was exactly everything she didn't want—someone with prominence, power and more money than compassion. She wanted an honest man, but the man she'd fallen in love with did not exist.

It was all a lie, and she was the fool. She followed Earlee through the schoolroom, aware of Narcissa in the back row laughing.

He hated having to ride away. Every step Hobo took on the road to the Worthingtons' ranch, the image of Meredith walking straight-backed, slow and shaken, tormented him. That wasn't the way he'd wanted her to learn about his family. He tugged his hat brim lower against the change in the sun as his horse rounded the corner and the manor house came into sight. If only Narcissa had spoken earlier, he would have had a chance to explain. Surely Meredith did not believe he had ever been anything less than one-hundred-percent sincere.

"There you are." Braden emerged from the barn's breezeway, his jaw set, a harness flung over his shoulder. "I just put up the missus's horse and vehicle."

"Sorry to leave you on barn duty."

"It was never your job to begin with. I told Robert and the missus that they had better find someone quick. After today, neither of us will be here to play barn boy." Braden shook his head as he hung the freshly cleaned harness on its proper wall hook. "There's more trouble afoot. The missus came home in a very happy mood. She asked about you twice."

"You're right. That does not sound good." Either she had figured out he was courting her daughter or—

"Mr. Connelly?" The auburn-haired housemaid cleared her throat, framed by the wide barn door, her simple calico skirts rustling as she waltzed closer. "Mrs. Worthington is waiting for you up at the main house. If you would be so good as to come along with me?"

"Up to the house?" That was surely the last thing he wanted to do. A bad feeling gripped his stomach and clenched tight.

"What did I tell you?" Braden called after him. "Trouble."

That was an understatement. Henrietta Worthington waited for him on the porch in what looked like her Sunday best. He might not know much about ladies gowns, but there was no missing the elaborate silks and adornments out of place in this country setting.

"Mr. Connelly, do come in." With great courtesy, she gestured toward the open front door as if she were greeting nobility.

She knows, too. Reluctantly, he took the stairs. "Good afternoon, ma'am. What can I do for you?"

"Oh, no, that is entirely wrong. It's what *I* can do for you." She waited until he was through the threshold before following him in, completely ignoring the maid who trailed them. "Please sit down, make yourself comfortable. I have to say I'm most embarrassed that I didn't recognize you first off."

"Why would you?" He swept off his hat while he glanced around the well-appointed parlor full of fine furniture and expensive knickknacks that looked exactly like the ones his mother collected. "My father is notable. I am not."

"You are too modest, sir." She gestured toward the sofa. "Your grandfather was senator before him and best friends with a former president of the United States."

"The rumors of me following my father into politics are not true." Might as well stop that notion in its tracks. He considered the comfortable-looking sofa the woman kept nodding him toward, but decided to stay standing. With hat in hand, he watched dismayed as she began pouring tea. Tension banded his chest, making it hard to breathe. "Not to be rude, ma'am, but I have work waiting."

"Nonsense. A man like you doesn't stoop to manual labor." She plunked a steaming cup of tea confidently on the polished coffee table. "That Braden person can put up the horses. I'm sure you are used to a few finer comforts. I've instructed the maid to make up a room in the north wing—"

"Mrs. Worthington, no." He had no time for this kind of nonsense and had long ago lost the stomach for it. "Thank you for your consideration, but I am the same person I was when I came here. Don't put your maid to the trouble. I'll stay the last night in the bunkhouse."

"Nonsense. I've completely changed my mind about you leaving."

And about seeing her daughter, he guessed. He plopped his hat on his head, his boots striking the floor as he retraced his steps. "My leaving is Braden's decision. I'm his apprentice. If I want to keep my job, I'd best get back to the corral."

"But—"

He seized the doorknob, yanked open the door and gave thanks for the blast of summery air. He breathed in the freedom of it and the tension released. Memories of growing up in a parlor full of rules and restrictions, his mother's endless list of criticism, his father's cool disdain and expectations, blew away like the dandelion fluff on the fragrant breeze. He followed the lilacs down the path, thinking of Meredith. Had she made the same assumptions her mother had? When she looked upon him next, would she see his father's son or the man he was striving to be?

Afraid he already knew the answer, he tucked his fears deep and took off for the stables where his work and his boss were waiting.

Late-afternoon sunlight slanted through the trees as the buggy jolted along the rutted driveway. Meredith rubbed at the pain behind her right temple, but the ache persisted right along with the one in her heart.

"Mrs. Bell was quite pleased to show up Mama at the book club meeting." Tilly reined Sweetie around the bend in the road and the stables and house came into sight. "After all, Narcissa recognized Shane when we did not. Apparently she had seen a picture of him when she'd visited relatives back east last summer. A friend of a friend sort of a thing. That's why she recognized him and knew his name."

"Everyone knows?"

"You know how rumors spread."

"Mama knows." That was the part she was dreading most.

"She's ready to burst with excitement. One of the Virginia Connellys right here on our land." Tilly didn't look happy either. "She's already planning the wedding."

"Then she may as well plan for disappointment." Meredith dreaded every step Sweetie took toward the stately looking home flanked by trees and surrounded by flowers. She wished she could slow time and prolong the inevitable from happening. She'd been broken apart enough today. Mama stepping in to take control would be akin to rubbing salt in a fatal wound.

"You must really be mad at him. I thought he might have told you but sworn you to secrecy."

"No. I wasn't important enough to him for the truth." There had been plenty of opportunity, like last night when he'd brought her the lilacs. He'd told her a sad story about his heroism and a fine tale about his supposed dreams, but as sincere as he'd seemed at the time she knew him now to be false. He'd told her his family had fallen upon hard times, but that could not be true. Not if he were both a senator's son and a senator's grandson.

"I'm so sorry, Meredith." Tilly hugged her tight. "Maybe you can work things out?"

"What is there to work out?" She set her chin with all the determination she could muster. "He's a liar."

"*I* still like him." Minnie in the backseat leaned forward to poke her head in between them. "And you're wrong. Shane wouldn't lie. Maybe it just seems that way. The truth can sometimes look bad because it's, well, it's the truth. A lie can look good every time."

"She has a point," Tilly agreed, but there was little hope in her tone.

Meredith didn't want hope, she wanted the hurt to stop. Everyone was quick to defend Shane, because he was from an impressive and influential family. But that man was a stranger to her. The buggy slowed as the driveway circled up to the house and Sweetie obediently stopped. They were home, but it was the last place she wanted to be. She lingered on the seat, unable to move. Minnie hopped to the ground and pounded up the walkway, her empty lunch pail jingling.

She couldn't delay the inevitable forever. Resolved, she curled one hand around the buggy's frame, lifted her skirt hem with the other, and scooted to the end of the seat. Shane was around here somewhere, so she was bound to run into him soon. Completely dreading that, she slid off the seat. She misjudged the distance to the ground and she hit it too hard. Her book bag slipped off her shoulder and crashed on the walkway. Her lunch tin rolled to a stop near the flowerbed.

"Here, let me," a deep baritone vibrated, a familiar voice, one she had once been so eager to hear. Shane knelt to retrieve her bag and scooped her pail by the metal handle. He strolled toward her looking like any horseman did, with a faint layer of dust on his muslin shirt and denims, his Stetson shading his face, a hint of stubble on his jaw.

It was a lie. She'd believed in him like a story in a book, something that was not real. She stared at his outstretched hands holding her things and remembered every time they had touched. He had made her believe.

Why did she still want the lie to be true? She could not stop wanting to see the goodness in the man when it was the lies that mattered more. She took a step back, her throat closing tight. She had fought all afternoon not to let Narcissa's words bother her, but they rang through her mind with the force of a rushing river dammed for too long. *He's having fun and sowing his wild oats. I hope you didn't think his act of love was sincere.*

"Meredith, don't look at me like that. Please." The quiet plea rang like a prayer, an honest request from his soul. He moved closer, bringing with him only pain. "Let me explain."

"Maybe I don't want to." Her hands fisted. She straightened her spine and stood her ground. If she gave in one inch, then the pain within her would crumble. The lunch hour they'd shared talking of little things, horses and her sewing and bits of stories about her friends seemed a lifetime ago, last night at her window two lifetimes.

"What does that mean?" His forehead furrowed. Agony touched his voice. "You don't believe what that girl said, do you? There's no going back for me. I don't want that world. I have you now—"

"You do not have me." She lifted her chin, defiance in her glare but it was not strong enough to hide the pain.

"Meredith, my family is far away across the country and that's where they will stay. I should have told you about them. I know that. I don't deny it. But they are not real to my life. I told you I've walked away. I'm disinherited. I am making my own way." All he saw was her hurt, and he wished he understood why. "As for what that girl said, you know my life here has not been about having fun. Your mother has seen to that."

"Don't try to lighten the discussion." She took a step back, holding herself tense and rigid, as if her self-control was all she had. The perfect May day surrounded her with colors and life, flowers nodding, the breeze whispering, birdsong serenading, and yet she looked as if there was no beauty left to her in the world. "I'm sure you are very sorry, but you lied to me."

"How? I showed you who I am." He wanted to smooth the crinkle of agony out of her forehead and to kiss away the sorrow on her rosebud lips. Turmoil roared through him, bringing with it the knowledge he was about to lose her. She, who mattered most to him, and he didn't understand the reason. "Why is this hurting you? What have I done?"

"You were so harsh with me when you discovered I was not the country girl you mistook me to be, when I did not lie to you. I was simply being myself. You have behaved so much worse." She wrapped her arms around her middle, so alone and vulnerable, with her broken affection in pieces at her feet. "How can I ever trust you again?"

"That's easy. You can always trust me—"

"No," she interrupted, her world already shattered, her unrealized dreams of him already crushed. "You have been pretending all along. You told me story after story to make me fall in love with you—"

"You're in love with me?"

"Not anymore. That's destroyed, too."

She broke away, hearing the shards of those stories in her mind, defining tales of his character that she had trusted. Tall tales now of being rejected by his wealthy friends, of humbly living with his grandmother, of long-lasting friendships and making a life for himself on his own. These were the keys that had opened her up, captured her affections and made her think they were soul mates, that only he could truly understand and love her.

She had been misled, and so much of it had been her own doing. Agony hammered through her as she tore up the steps, heaved open the front door. His remorse didn't stop her. She kept going, putting distance between them.

"Meredith! Why, you look positively wind-blown. Let's take a comb to your hair." Mama barreled over with the determination of a navy admiral, skirt snapping, the china figurines on the what-not shelves trembling. "It's nearly tea time and I thought this afternoon we would have a formal tea. I commissioned Cook to prepare a few refined desserts for the occasion."

"I'm not hungry." She had endured one battle. She did not have the energy for a second. "I'm going to my room."

"But I've invited a very special guest." Mama was delirious with happiness as she clasped her hands together, a woman who mistakenly thought an impossible prayer had been answered. "Someone I think you will be very happy to entertain."

"I am not going to marry Shane Connelly, so no matchmaking. Please." She circled around the couch to avoid her mother, and hurried straight to the banister.

"Meredith Henrietta Worthington! You come back here this instant." Mama's command echoed through the parlor and bounced against the walls of the stair-well, but Meredith kept going. Her eyes burned, her throat tightened and with every step she took up the stairs and down the hallway she left a piece of herself behind.

At least her room was private. She sank onto the edge of her bed, so hurt the tears would not come, the sobs would not escape. It was silly to hurt so much over a man. She was too independent for that, but she hurt all the same. She was not in control of her heart, not at all.

A light knock rapped at her door. Tilly slipped inside and held up her forgotten book bag. "You left this behind."

"Thanks." The word croaked out, heavy with pain. Surely Tilly had noticed.

Pity pinched her sister's face. Pity. Meredith bowed her face into her hands. Footsteps padded closer, the edge of the bed sank and Tilly's arm went around her shoulder.

"I know how it feels," Tilly confessed. "To fall so far in love, it's like you've both lost and found yourself at the same time. And then to discover you mean so little to him that he doesn't even look your way when he drives by on the street."

"You've been feeling like this all along?" Meredith choked out.

"Yes. Over Emmett Sims. For almost a year now."

"I'm so sorry, Tilly." No one deserved the sharp edges of a shattered love, edges that cut over and over again. "Does it ever end?"

"I don't know. I'll let you know if it does."

"That's what I'm afraid of." The injury reached into the deepest parts of her, places she didn't even know she had. Proof of how deep her love for Shane had gone, so quietly and lovely she hadn't even thought not to let him in. "I've changed my mind about love. It's bad. One should avoid it at all costs."

"If only we had known that from the start," Tilly agreed.

It was too late. Meredith took a steadying breath, wondering if Shane was devastated, too, or if he'd been able to go on with his work, his heart and his soul intact. She did not see the man with his head down, looking as if broken, standing at the end of the walkway where she'd left him, alone.

Chapter Sixteen

You have behaved so much worse. Meredith's accusations troubled him with every breath he took and every minute that ticked by through the worst afternoon of his life. While he'd been saddling one of the two-year-olds, her question filled his head. *How can I ever trust you again?*

He had his answer. She could not see beyond his family name to the man he was. He took a shallow breath, ignoring the squeeze of discomfort that had settled behind his sternum. The pain had made him numb, and perhaps he would stay that way. He had work to finish, which would give him time to figure out how to make this right. He had to get her to listen.

"Blow out your breath, Apollo." He gripped the cinch and splayed his hand on the gelding's ribs. "I know you don't like it, but we've got to get this nice and tight."

The big Arabian stomped one hoof and sidestepped, as if he didn't like the notion. Too bad he and Braden were leaving tomorrow. Not only did the horse need more training, but he was a kick to work with. Shane yanked a little harder on the cinch. "C'mon, big guy, let it out."

Footsteps tapped into his awareness, faintly echoing in the empty stalls. Shane knew who it was without turning around. He'd been expecting a visit from Meredith's father.

"Connelly." Robert's tone had changed, and he was home from work early. Still in his suit and tie, the consummate bank owner tipping his hat to an equal—and not to the horse trainer's apprentice. A barn swallow flew in through one of the stalls, wheeled around and flapped back out again. Robert cleared his throat. "I'm looking for Braden. My horse and surrey are waiting."

"Did you find someone to take over the barn work?" Shane buckled the cinch, checked the strap, unhooked the stirrup from the saddle horn.

"One of my teller's neighbors has a son looking for work. He's to start in the morning."

"Good." He didn't have to turn around to read the discomfort, perhaps embarrassment, in the father's voice. He patted Apollo's flank and walked him a few paces. "I'll take the kid through the morning routine here. Make sure he knows how things run before we leave."

"I appreciate it." Robert fell silent, but he clearly had more to say.

Shane stopped the gelding and checked the cinch. Still nice and tight, so he patted the horse's shoulder. "Good boy, buddy. That was a good job."

Apollo preened, pleased with the compliment.

"Connelly." Robert blew out a sigh, as if he finally

had figured out how to say what was on his mind. "About the way I treated you, told you to stay away from my daughter…"

"Said I wasn't good enough for her?" he finished helpfully, looping the ends of the reins through an iron ring in the wall. Leaving the horse secure, he turned his back. "I remember that talk very well."

"And I'm ashamed of it." Robert passed his hand over his face. "I probably looked like a fool, saying those things to you. You clearly are a better man than me."

"Sir, I've been the same man all along. I haven't changed." He headed down the aisle, where Robert had left his horse and vehicle standing in the hot sun without care. "I'm still the horseman's apprentice."

"Not *just* a horseman's apprentice." Robert relaxed now that his apology was past. He followed behind, his manner friendly. "You're Stuart Connelly's son, Aaron Connelly's grandson. I read a newspaper article about you long ago. Something about charity work."

"Today I'm the one taking care of your horse." He held out his hand to let the stately gelding scent him. "That's all I am."

"I hope now that this misunderstanding has been cleared up that you will stay on." Robert seized the bridle. "Of course, you won't be expected to shovel horse manure and unhitch the family horses."

"As I understand it, we're leaving tomorrow." Shane frowned. Robert had the horse by the bits. Annoyed, he patted the Arabian's neck and clicked his tongue. The powerful horse turned toward him, breaking Robert's grip. Shane led the horse deeper into the barn.

"Is there anything I can do to change your mind?" Robert sounded sincere. He wasn't a bad guy, not at all. "I want to make things right between us if I can."

"Believe me, I would like to stay. This is a pretty piece of Montana you live in. I can't say it doesn't make a man feel right at home." He unbuckled the traces one by one and led the horse out from between the bars. "It's Braden's decision, and he's had enough. He's moving on, and I go with him."

"I envy you, young man. Long ago was the day I had the longing to do something different than work in my father's bank. I loved horses and dreamed of my own stables one day with the most beautiful Arabians grazing in my fields. I was forty years old before I brought the first broodmare to these pastures, and the most I can do is watch from the sidelines." Robert shrugged, looking wistful. "Maybe you can stay in Montana?"

"No. Our next job is in Butte, then we move on to Boise." He unbuckled the cheek strap and removed the gelding's bridle. "Not sure where to after that, but I think it's Salt Lake City."

"What about Meredith?"

Meredith. He squeezed his eyes shut to hide the crash of emotion. He felt sucker punched, but he didn't want that to show either. His voice sounded strained, and he hoped it could be attributed to the act of lifting the heavy horse collar off the Arabian's neck. "I suppose Meredith will be teaching school over the summer like she plans to."

"I thought the two of you were close." Not a father's ambition that spoke, but a father's love.

"I thought so, too," he said, keeping his back to the

man while he slid the halter over the horse's nose and behind his ears. The coarse fetlock tickled the backs of his hands as he worked and the thought of Meredith angry and hurt destroyed him. He'd rather die than harm her, but that hadn't stopped it from happening.

"Perhaps I could talk to her," Robert suggested. "Maybe Braden could see reason to stay if more money was involved. If you would like to court my daughter, I would heartily give my permission—"

"Papa!" Meredith's dismay startled the horse and him. "I can't believe what I just heard."

The black's head came up and the powerful animal began to sidestep, nervously, about to bolt. Shane calmed him with a low murmur and a firm grip on his halter, drinking in the sight of his beloved. Like May itself, she swirled into the barn with a snap of her petunia pink dress and a sewing hoop clutching in one hand. Her hair a tumble, her bottom lip quivering with emotion.

"Meredith." A change came over Robert and his manner softened. The father's adoration of his daughter was unmistakable. "You surely have heard the good news. Your mother stopped by the bank on her way home from her meeting to let me know we have a very important person in our employ. I—"

"Papa, don't you dare try to distract me. You were trying to match me up with him." She held herself rigid, gesturing in his general direction as if she couldn't stand so much as to look at him.

Shane hung his head and led the horse away. The black went willingly and he left the father and daughter behind, their voices murmuring in the long stretch of the breezeway and bouncing off the empty walls of the stalls. Outside, horses grazed in summery fields and Braden's low mumble to one of the two-year-olds he was riding reminded him of what was at stake, more than his future and more than his heart.

He unhooked the stall gate, letting in the horse. Eyeing the paddock beyond and then his empty feed trough, the Arabian waited, giving Shane a look that clearly said, "I'm waiting."

"All right, buddy." He grabbed the grain bucket and upended it, the sound of cascading corn and oats drowning all sound of Meredith's voice.

I cannot lose her. He lowered the bucket to the ground. He would not admit defeat yet, not when there was still a chance. Latching the stall gate, he turned on his heel, determined to talk to her and explain, but she blocked his path.

"I'm sorry about my father." She faced him, jaw set and braced as if it took all her strength to meet him. "Papa should not have been saying those things to you."

"About encouraging a match between us?"

"Yes." A muscle ticked along her porcelain jaw, a sign of how hard it was for her to be with him. She stood stone-still. A slight breeze played with the lace edge of her hemline and teased the flyaway tendrils from her single braid.

"I know he was not speaking for you, Meredith." He wanted to make her smile. "You are far too independent for that."

"At least you know that much about me." No smile,

no softness, no hint that she intended to change her mind about him, or that she wanted to.

Please make her want to change her mind, he prayed. *Please, Lord, don't let me lose her.* He risked a step closer, the knell of his boots like a cannon strike in the tense silence between them. "I know a great deal about you."

"Is that so? Then you ought to know I am not going to believe your stories now."

"Stories. Fine, I'll admit it. I told you some stories." He fisted his hands, determined to take responsibility for his mistakes. He could be strong, too. "I wish now I had told you not parts but the whole of those stories. I'm sorry for that."

"All I wanted was the truth." Her blue-gray eyes shadowed and she spun away. "I can see that is not going to happen."

"Is that why you came?"

"No. I saw Papa arrive home and I knew what he was going to do the instant he went into the barn." She stared at the hoop she held, a colorful block of patchwork, and shook her head. She had obviously been in the parlor sewing. "You two didn't come to some kind of agreement, did you?"

"A betrothal agreement? No." He saw relief slumping her shoulders and the tension slipping from her jaw. He hurt to see how much she dreaded such an arrangement. She did not want him.

"Good. I caught him in time." She twisted away, her head down, an invisible barrier between them. Never had she been so distant. "My parents approve of you now."

"The only approval mattering to me is yours." There had to be a way to heal this breach between them. "I told you the truth and now I want to tell you the whole of it. The years we lived with my grandmother were the happiest of my childhood."

"I don't want to hear about them." She whirled at him, backing away. "I've had enough. There is no purpose in mending what is broken."

"I didn't mean to destroy your trust. My parents are not a part of my life, not anymore." He tugged off his hat, vulnerable, a man with nothing to hide. "Believe me. I have been honest about who I am and what I want."

"You have not. I am *not* some country girl easily fooled."

"I do not think you are." He stood resolute, like an innocent man. But how could he be? He looked so sad. "The day I walked away from my father's ultimatums and my mother's social scheming, I stopped being their son. I am my own man. Nothing is going to change that."

"It doesn't matter to me." He couldn't change the truth. She'd thought she had meant more to him than that. She'd been imagining that when he gazed upon her, the world vanished and all that remained was his infinite love for her. She'd thought that when he'd pledged his intentions, it was because she made him whole. That their love was the kind of a rare shining blessing bestowed sparingly in this world.

But she was not so special to him. Whatever caring he felt for her, it could not measure up to what she had imagined. He had been passing time, that was all, a rich man's harmless flirtations.

"My maternal grandmother was poor, but when we were in need she shared what she had with us." How sincere he looked, striving so hard to win back her regard. With another story, no less, one meant to tear down her defenses and overturn good sense. "What I told you was true. My father's investments improved and we moved back into our house, but I never forgot—"

"Please, not another tale," she interrupted. "You will say anything to salvage your self-opinion. When you leave tomorrow, you will not take my heart with you."

"But I love you."

"You love me?" She marched through the barn doors and into the yard, rocks crunching beneath her shoes, the cheerful shafts of sunlight threatening to steal her from his sight. His beautiful Meredith. Why couldn't she see his feelings?

"I think I fell in love the first moment I set eyes on you. You had a streak of mud on your cheek and you were standing in the middle of the road." *Please remember that moment,* he begged, the instant in time when their lives changed.

Her anger melted away, leaving a moment of pure longing that made her so sad that his soul could bleed. The wind gusted, bringing a few stray blossoms from the flowering apple trees. Soft pink petals rained down on her, clinging to her tendrils and the slope of her skirt. Being near to her brought more hidden places within him alive. Nothing could stop his love for her.

The future rolled out before him like the prairie

unspooling in every direction. He saw the year to come of courting the prettiest schoolteacher west of the Mississippi, his engagement ring shining on her slender hand. There would be a little wedding with wildflowers and Meredith radiant in any gown she wanted. He could picture their comfortable home and plenty of fertile land close to whichever town her teaching job had taken them. Horses grazing behind whiteboard fences, fruit ripening in the orchard and Meredith cradling their baby in her arms.

Never had he seen his future so clearly. Never had he wanted something so much.

"I remember thinking you were trouble on horseback." She stared down at her sewing hoop as if searching for a solution. Finding none there, she gave him one last appraisal. Her longing had vanished, but the sadness remained. She hiked up her skirts as if ready to flee. "I should have paid better attention to my first impressions."

"You loved me once. You said so. You can love me again." It was the only hope he had.

"No. I cannot. This is goodbye, Shane Connelly." She could not hide her sorrow as she hurried up the walkway, taking with her the best dream he'd ever had.

For what felt like the eight hundredth time, she blinked furiously until her vision cleared. It took a few attempts until the blurred colors of her quilt block took shape again. The purple stood out brighter than all the others, a reminder of everything she needed to forget.

Just put him behind you, Meredith. She willed every

thought, every image, every memory of Shane from her mind and concentrated on poking the needle through the fabric, feeling the contact of the tip against her thimble. She pulled the thread through in a muted rasp that echoed in every corner of her bedroom. She'd never felt empty like this, as if hollowed out of all feeling. She was as spent as if she'd run a hundred miles without rest.

Footsteps bounded down the hall, light and bouncy and cheerful. Minnie skidded to a stop in the open doorway, bits of leaves in her hair and shavings of bark on her dress.

"Whatcha doin'?" Minnie tromped in and bounced onto the edge of the bed.

"Stitching a block." She placed her needle again. "Have you been playing in your tree house?"

"Yes, but it wasn't any fun today, so I came in." Minnie sighed dramatically. "Aren't you going to ask why?"

"No, because it has to do with the man I refuse to think about, so you will just have to tell me about something else." She only had to hold her composure for a few more hours. Once the house was dark and she was in bed, she could cry if she wanted to. No one would know. She tugged her thread gently, tightening the stitch. "Judging by the delicious smells wafting up here from the kitchen, you succeeded in talking Cook into baking a chicken pie for supper."

"I asked her to make more molasses cookies for Shane, so he could take some with him." Her bottom lip wobbled. "I know you don't want to hear his name, but I'm sad he's leaving. He was so nice to me."

"He *was* nice to you." She couldn't refute that. Meredith pinned her needle into the fabric and set the hoop aside. The window seat creaked slightly as she stood. She brushed stray curls out of her sister's blue eyes filling with tears. "Who wouldn't be charmed by you, sweetheart?"

"There's no one like him. Just no one." Fourteen was a tough age, still so very much a child. Minnie swiped her eyes to keep the tears from falling. "I thought he was going to stay a long time and train all our horses."

"He was never going to stay for long, and I think Mama's interference made their stay much shorter." She eased onto the bed beside her sister and drew her close. "Sadie said that one day when we were at school, Mama went outside and told Braden and Shane all the qualities she expected to see in a Worthington horse. They were to be dignified in all respects. No biting or running away with their drivers. Sadie kept track of the clock. The lecture went on for over an hour."

"That's because Papa was really hurt by a horse once, remember?"

"Yes, I remember. God spared him, but Mama has never forgot it." She wanted Minnie to see this was for the best. Maybe it would bring back Minnie's smile. "I think it's easier for the horsemen if they move on to a quieter place."

"Do you think Shane will miss us?"

"It would be impossible not to miss you, dear one." She squeezed her sister tight, treasuring her like the precious gift she was. "Now shouldn't you be getting ready for supper? If Mama sees the leaves in your hair, she's not going to be happy."

"I have leaves in my hair?" This seemed to be news to Minnie.

"What do you expect when you climb around in trees like a monkey?" Meredith gave Minnie a final hug.

"I'm not a monkey. Tilly, did you hear what she called me?"

"I heard." A tray rattled as Tilly swept into the room. "Look what I brought. Supper. I talked Mama into letting us have a picnic up here. She's feeling under the weather."

"Disappointment, I expect." Meredith grabbed her comb off the bureau. "Knowing Mama, she already had the wedding planned and the invitations composed."

"She's taken it hard, it's true." Tilly set the tray on the bed, scooting it carefully into the center of the mattress. "Meredith, how are you doing?"

"It is not a mortal blow. It just feels like one." She took the comb to Minnie's hair. "I will survive, so there's no need to talk about it again. There, the leaves are out. Minnie, do you want to say grace?"

"I love saying it!" Minnie busily settled in front of the tray, crossed her legs, settled her skirts and steepled her hands. "Hurry. I've thought up a good one."

Over the top of her head, Meredith shared a smile with Tilly. Having them here was the best balm she could ask for. She settled onto the feather mattress, careful not to tip the tray and jostle the juice glasses, and settled beside Minnie on the duvet cover. Tilly did the same on the other side, and together they bowed their heads, folded their hands. Minnie cleared her throat.

"Dear God," she began primly. "Please bless this

food we are about to eat and especially please bless Shane because he's leaving and Meredith and me are gonna miss him. I think Meredith will miss him more, so please help her to be a teacher so she won't be so sad. Amen."

"Amen." Meredith opened her eyes only to find they were blurry again. "That was sweet, Minnie."

"You said a very good prayer." Tilly reached over to hug Minnie with one arm, Meredith with another, sisters not only by blood but of the heart.

Chapter Seventeen

It had been a rough and sleepless night as Shane halted Hobo and dismounted on the lawn outside the Worthington home. Dawn hinted at the horizon, turning the darkness to gradients of shadow, allowing him to make out the trunk of the maple and the branches beneath Meredith's window. His boots scraped against the bark and the leaves shivered as he pulled himself up limb by limb into the arms of the tree. His pulse drummed frantically against his rib cage, pounding in his throat and making him halfway dizzy.

"That's a female for you," Braden had said last night when they'd shared supper at the table in the bunkhouse. "Contrary. Not one of them make a lick of sense. They rip your heart out as easily as a basting seam in a dress they're sewin' on. It's why I'm a bachelor at thirty-five and proud of it."

He could see why permanent bachelorhood would be tempting. A lizard skittled out of his way and out of sight as he heaved onto the final limb and rose carefully to a standing position. The last thing he wanted was to wake the entire house with a crash and a boom and be caught in a crumpled heap on the ground outside Meredith's bedroom. Her parents weren't likely to be understanding. The bough beneath his soles groaned with his weight as he caught hold of the lip of the windowsill.

Being this near to her calmed him. The curtains were closed, but she was behind the glass, beyond the fall of muslin, close enough that he could wake her with a few words. The comfort of knowing she was close invited memories he could not stop—Meredith's laughter, Meredith's dimples, the fall of her hair in the sunlight. The way she filled him with love overflowing.

Please watch over her, Father. He set the small jewel box he'd bought in town. There. It was done. He ought to climb down and meet Braden outside the kitchen, because Sadie was packing them meals for the road, but he lingered. This would be the closest he would ever be to Meredith again.

"Psst. Connelly." Braden rode into sight below, saddle packs loaded. "Time to go."

The hardest step was the first. He tore himself away, ignoring the cruel pain. The next step down the tree was easier to stand. He swung off the lowest branch and hit the ground, leaves rustling, his heart bleeding. He could not endure looking back. The grass crunched beneath his feet, an owl gave the final hoot of the night, serenading him as he swung up into the saddle.

Goodbye, Meredith. He gathered Hobo's reins in wooden hands. Every bit of him went numb as he pressed his heels to the gelding's side and rode away from the only woman he would ever love.

Meredith woke with a start and the strangest sensation she was not alone. Dawn had yet to chase the darkness from her room as she threw back the covers, put her feet on the floor and followed the tides of her heart to the window. The muslin curtains whispered against her fingertips, soft cotton fluttering against her cheek as she drew them open. The faintest pre-dawn glow shone in the east, illuminating the underbellies of clouds and casting the view in silhouette. The maple shivered in the soft breezes and the faint *clip-clop* of steeled horse shoes chimed above the birdsong from the fields.

Shane. Her hand flew to the window, the glass cool against her palms as she searched the small section of the driveway visible from her room. Nothing moved in the shadows of the road and she waited, knees knocking. Need riveted her in place, and she could not move. She was driven by the need to see him one more time, the wish to memorize what she could of him and the longing to turn back time. If only she could relive the past knowing what she knew now. Maybe she could have kept her affections casual and her eyes wide open.

Maybe. Then again, perhaps she had been fated to fall in love with him. She feared God had led her to Shane for some reason she could not guess. She had made a mess of it. She couldn't have stopped herself from seeing the good in him—there was so much good. If only the man he had pretended to be was the real Shane Connelly. Maybe then their story would have had a different outcome.

A shadow moved on the distant driveway. Two riders on horseback! Her gaze fixed on the one nearest to her, his familiar wide shoulders set, tall in the saddle, and her feelings soared. For a single moment she forgot their differences. Affection rushed through her stronger than any force, diminishing her anger and betrayal. Love clung stubbornly, like roots to the earth, refusing to let go.

Time would do that, she told herself. There would come a day when he would be a vague memory. If time was kind, then she would forget every detail about him—his dimpled smile, his easy humor, the feel of his hand cradling hers, even his name. A lump rose in her throat as he rode out of her sight, disappearing down the road, gone to her forever. Still she yearned for him like winter missed spring and she almost didn't see the small jewel box glinting in the first light of dawn.

Heart pounding, she opened the window. The warm sun on her face felt out of place on this morning of loss, the scenery of the green grasses and trees and the merry splashes of purple and yellow flowers discordant. Those colors grew into blurs as she blinked hard to clear her vision and lifted the trinket from the sill.

What had he left her? Trembling, she opened the lid. Inside the exquisite box of ivory lay a piece of gold jewelry. The telltale ticking told her it was no locket, but a timepiece. Something every teacher needed.

She was not the sort of girl who cried over a man, but tears fell anyway, one by one, pieces of her soul she could not hold back.

"Meredith!" Minnie's voice came as if from a mile away instead of next to her on the buggy seat. "Meredith? We're here."

At school. She felt fuzzy, as if she were looking at

the world through a mirror, that it was only a reflection of little substance. She gathered her bag and lunch and didn't bother to wait for the new driver to help her down. He was a gangly boy from Angelina's grade who'd had to drop out of school to help earn a living for his family. Nice enough, but she could not stand to have him help her. It would only be another reminder of Shane.

"Meredith!" Kate called as she climbed out of her father's buggy. "Can you believe it? Two more days of school and then we're done. We're free."

"Unbelievable." It didn't seem real—not the morning, not the fact that Shane's departure was a rip in the fabric of her life that left everything in tatters, and surely not the fact that her school days would end. She'd been dreaming about the day, hoping and planning for it, yet now it struck her like a falling anvil. She would no longer see her dearest friends every day.

"Bye, Pa!" Kate called out cheerfully, waving as her father drove off, horse and buggy joining the busy traffic on the road. "I studied and studied last night and I'm ready for the tests today."

"Tests?" Her schoolwork had completely flown out of her mind.

"Arithmetic and history." Kate fell in stride beside her. A boy ran across their path, chasing a red ball. Little children's squeals of delight pealed until someone yelled, "Tag! You're it!"

"Meredith, are you all right? You seem distracted. It wouldn't have anything to do with a handsome black-haired, blue-eyed man?"

"I wish it didn't." Dimly she realized they were

climbing the stairs clomping into the vestibule. She plopped her lunch pail on the shelf along with all the others and her feet felt leaden as she continued on into the schoolroom.

"...Mama sent a telegram straightaway to our dear friends the Kellans..." Narcissa informed her group at the front of the room, talking loudly enough for her voice to carry. "They are very close friends to the senator and his wife, you know—"

"Ignore her," Kate advised on the way to their desks. "She's eaten up with jealousy because Shane wouldn't give her the time of day."

"He's gone." The statement came flat and, emotionally, as hollow-sounding as she felt.

"Who's gone?" Lila looked up from her history text. Concentration furrowed her brow and she tossed a lock of brown curls out of her eyes.

"Shane." The starch went out of her knees and she collapsed into her seat. His manly image silhouetted by the dawn tormented her. He'd ridden away and now there was no mending what had happened between them.

Not that she wanted it, not that it could be. Not after what he'd done. But she could not seem to help the tiny thread of wishing within her that would not break.

"You mean he left?" Kate slipped into her desk, her bag thudding against her desktop. "Just like that? After spending lunch with you yesterday?"

"Like a *courting* man?" Scarlet emphasized, walking up to their group. "Everyone saw it, Meredith. He's in love with you."

"It was not love." Love did not masquerade as

something else. She fumbled with her books. Her fingers did not seem to work properly. The texts tumbled and slid over the desk, falling onto Scarlet's side.

"How can you say that?" Scarlet gently pushed the books back.

"Even I saw it." Ruby, two desks behind, left her seat to join the discussion. "And I'm an official objective observer. I hardly know you all, but I recognize true affection when I see it. The way that man looked at you." Ruby paused and placed her hand to her throat. "It was like a dream come true. I would give anything to have a good man look at me like that."

"So would I," Earlee chimed in breathlessly, cheeks rosy from her long walk to school. "Perhaps you could write to him. He could court you through letters. It would be so romantic."

"It's not going to happen." She swallowed hard, determined to keep her feelings buried. She was perfectly able to manage a tiny disappointment in love. And if a voice inside her argued it was no small affection she felt, then she simply did not have to listen to it. She slipped out of her cardigan and draped it over the back of her seat. "Earlee, you're right, it would make a nice story, but Shane is gone. Please, let's not mention him again."

"I'm so sorry you were hurt," Ruby, as sweet as spun sugar, emphasized. "I've heard the best way to get over one beau is to find another. I noticed Lorenzo looking this way."

"He's wondering where Fiona is," Lila informed her. "He's always been sweet on her."

"And we've all been sweet on him," Kate spoke

up, earning a bit of light laughter. "Oh, there's Fiona now."

While her friends greeted the latecomer, who looked a bit windblown from her horse ride, Scarlet leaned close and squeezed Meredith's hand.

"I'm sorry, too," she whispered. "I prayed for the two of you."

"Some prayers are not meant to be answered." It didn't make her sad. Really. She was determined to control her feelings. She would make it true. Shane was gone and that was the way it should be.

Even if a little voice within her wanted to argue.

"...in spite of the fact he rode that awful horse, the one with all the scars—" Narcissa's words rose above the growing hubbub in the classroom "—*I* recognized him."

I never noticed Hobo's scars, she realized. She'd been so intent on the man, she'd been blind to the horse, the one beaten with a whip on a wintry road until Shane had come along and saved him.

Don't be a fool, Meredith. Keep control of your feelings.

She carefully removed her sewing from her book bag, doing her best to listen to Fiona's tale of her morning, of how close she was getting to Ian's grandmother and that it was hard to believe come Sunday she would finally be his wife.

"And he can move into the house and you won't miss him so much," Earlee said.

"I do. He's away so much, I hardly get to see him. He's lucky to have a job at the mill, but it's hard being apart. I didn't know it was possible to love someone so much there's no room to breathe. That's how full of love you are." Fiona blushed, a little shy.

"No one deserves it more." Meredith swallowed hard against overwhelming emotions—a mix of gratitude for her friend's happiness, a rush of loss of her own, the enduring bond of friendship that she treasured so much. She set down her sewing and twisted around to make eye contact with everyone, hoping they could read the meaning behind the question she asked. "On Saturday?"

"Yes," Lila agreed, catching her eye.

"Absolutely," Scarlet chimed in.

"I can have Pa swing by and pick her up," Kate volunteered.

"It's agreed?" Earlee asked.

"Agreed," Fiona finished as they all turned to Ruby, who looked confused by what was going on. "Would you like to join our sewing circle? We meet every week in the afternoon."

"I'm not a very good sewer." Ruby looked crushed.

"The friendship is the important part of the gathering." Meredith spoke from the heart, with love for the friends who had once welcomed her into their midst and with admiration for the young women they had all grown to be. "It's one of the greatest blessings of my life. Join us. We would love to have you."

"We could give you sewing tips," Lila encouraged.

"And you wouldn't have to sew. I often bring my embroidery," Kate offered.

"And I tat or crochet," Scarlet added. "I would teach you to do it. It's easy."

"And I am really good at sewing dresses," Earlee chimed in. "I'm always making something for one of my six little sisters. I could give you tips, too."

"Please say you will come," Fiona urged, her dark ringlet curls framing her face.

Ruby nodded, overwhelmed at being included.

Miss Lambert rang her handbell, calling for students to take their desks and quiet down. Because it was time to break apart, they settled back into their seats, opened their books and prepared for the day—one of the last days they would all be schoolgirls together. As Meredith gently placed her quilt blocks and squares back into her bag, she braced herself for the pain of seeing the purple color that reminded her of Shane. There were other colors, ones her friends had helped her choose in the mercantile. She heard again the conversations she'd shared with her friends and with her sisters as she'd sewed each square.

Life was like a patchwork quilt, she realized, seemingly haphazard pieces thrown together, but there was a great grand order to the colorful squares and a beauty that defied all, for it was stitched together with love.

"Meredith!" Scarlet's sharp whisper penetrated her thoughts. "Miss Lambert is calling us. Time for our arithmetic exam. The last one ever."

All things came to an end, she thought. It was the sweetness of the time that mattered for it made memories to cherish. She stowed her sewing into her bag, dropped it under her desk and trailed her friends to the front of the room where their teacher waited.

* * *

The sun was past its zenith before they stopped along the trail for lunch. The prairie rolled endless behind them, but the Rocky Mountains in the far distance flanked them. Up ahead hovered the promise of hills and, beyond, a mountain pass.

Shane dismounted, leading Hobo straight to the small creek gurgling beneath the shade of cottonwoods. The cool felt good, the breeze off the water better. While his horse drank he swept off his hat and stood a moment. Every mile behind them had been a torment, knowing it was taking him farther away from his Meredith.

She would have found the box by now. Was she wearing it, thinking of him? Or was she too proud? Too wounded? Judging by the sun, she might be chatting with her friends in the schoolyard, sewing away on her quilt patches. Simply from picturing her dappled with sun filled him with sweet agony, wanting the woman he could not have. She'd said goodbye, turned her back and walked away.

"Looks like pork loin sandwiches." Braden tossed him a wrapped bundle. "Whatever cons there were working for the Worthingtons, the meals were some of the best I've had anywhere."

"Are you sorry we left?" He unwrapped the sandwich and took a bite.

"I'm sorry I didn't leave sooner. I'd forgotten how controlling a woman can be." Braden shook his head, digging into his meal. "There's nothing like being a bachelor. It's a better option considering."

Shane unhooked his canteen from his saddle and twisted the cap. It wasn't that long ago he had agreed

with his boss. Getting out of an engagement that was
more duty than choice had left him with a bad taste
for marriage. That was before he knew what real love
felt like and how it could transform a man. He swigged
the lukewarm water, swallowing every last drop. His
love for her didn't stop like a match quickly blown out
but remained burning as if there were no force strong
enough to stop it.

If I'd had more time with her, he thought, taking
another bite of his sandwich. Maybe he could have
made her understand. Picturing how angry she had
been with him, how resolute, cast him in doubt. She
thought he'd deceived her with his tales, but it was not
true. There had been no lies, just the values he had
learned along the way.

"We'll fill up the canteens here and ride as far as
we can," Braden said around a mouthful. "Don't want
to waste any time. We'll stop and set up camp around
nightfall."

"Good plan." Going forward was the only sensible
solution. He'd come too far to quit on Braden and his
own ambition for the future. But nothing about his
future felt right without Meredith in it.

He wedged the last bite of the sandwich into his
mouth, knelt to fill his canteen in the fresh running
water, and offered Hobo a molasses cookie from his
pack. How could he go on? It was impossible, considering an unbreakable bond to Meredith held him back.

Chapter Eighteen

"See you tomorrow!" Fiona called from the saddled bay Clydesdale, who had been tied all day long with other horses on the shady side of the schoolhouse. Flannigan, eager to stretch his legs, tugged politely at his bit and Fiona laughed. "I'd like to stay and chat longer, but this guy has a mind of his own."

"Goodbye!" Meredith called out alongside her remaining friends. Kate had already taken off with her father, heading for their homestead far west of town. Ruby was expected home to help with the farm work, so she'd already taken off at a fast walk heading east.

"Meredith!" Minnie hung out of the buggy, waving wildly. "We're waiting for you!"

"Take Maisie home first and then come back for me." The last thing she wanted to do was to rush straight home. Too many reminders were there, aside from the fact that she wasn't sure she could face her mother's depression. Shane's leaving would be sure to hit her hard.

"Are you regretting sending him away?" Lila asked,

as they fell in step together. Scarlet joined them, followed by Earlee, catching up with them breathlessly.

Meredith didn't want to answer, but she felt the abiding affection of her friends and there was no safer place to admit the truth. "Regret? Yes. But I don't see any other solution. He's not right for me. He's not the man of my dreams."

"He seemed dreamy to me," Lila commented. "Really decent and solid. Not caught up in himself."

"I got the feeling he really cared about others," Scarlet agreed.

"And the way he looked upon you, Meredith," Earlee started.

"No! No more." She rolled her eyes. She loved her friends, but her heart could only take so much. "How about a change of subject?"

"I have one." Lila grinned. "There's someone waving at you. Isn't that the superintendent?"

Meredith stopped in her tracks. Sure enough, Mr. Olaff was crossing the street, an envelope in hand. She could think of only one reason why he would look her up.

"Ooh. Do you think he has a job for you?" Lila gripped her arm.

"Maybe it's the school you wanted." Scarlet grabbed her other arm.

"I've prayed so hard for you, Meredith." Earlee hopped up and down with excitement. "I have a feeling my prayers are about to be answered."

"Miss Worthington, good afternoon." Mr. Olaff tipped his hat cordially. He was a grandfatherly gentleman with a friendly smile and a likable manner. "Your letter of application has been at the top of our list for some time, and with your perfect score on the teaching exam, I am happy to offer you this."

"A school?" she croaked, not daring to hope but knowing it was true all along. She stared at the envelope he held out to her, importantly thick.

"It's a contract for three months' teaching at the Upriver School," Mr. Olaff said kindly. "June, July and August. I'm assuming you are interested?"

"Interested? I'm completely overcome." There was her dream, just like that, finally arrived. She took the thick packet gingerly, half expecting it to evaporate and disappear. "Thank you, Mr. Olaff. I would love that school."

"Then you take your contract home, read it carefully and bring it back to me by Friday. I'll let the folks know they have a fine teacher for the summer." With a tip of his hat and a wink, Mr. Olaff headed back to his office next to the bakery.

"Meredith!" Lila's grip tightened with bruising strength.

"You did it!" Scarlet squealed.

"Congratulations!" Earlee clapped with delight.

"You're officially a teacher!" Lila jumped with excitement, and suddenly they were all doing it, hopping as giddily as eight-year-olds. "But what about Earlee? Didn't you get a school?"

"I haven't put in my application yet," Earlee explained. "There's too much work at home with the animals and garden and the crops. I can't leave my sister Beatrice to handle it all. When the harvest is in, then I can think about teaching."

"And I'm not going to do anything," Scarlet bemoaned as they hesitated on the corner, about to go their separate ways. "I have no plans. Maybe I should get some."

"I'll be cutting fabric at the counter at my parents' store. Probably for eternity." Lila winked. "Unless Lorenzo changes his mind about me and sweeps me off my feet."

"I'm sure there are great romances ahead for all of us," Earlee declared, her sunshine hope infectious. "Lila, you need a handsome man of mystery to come new to town to sweep you off your feet."

"At least it would counter the endless boredom in the mercantile," Lila teased. "Speaking of which, my step-mother will be watching the clock and wondering why I'm not there to help out. See you all tomorrow!"

"Bye." Scarlet took a step in the opposite direction. "My ma is waiting, too. See you in the morning."

"See you." Meredith, alone with Earlee, wasn't surprised that her friend was gazing down the street where the flag was waving. "Are you hoping there's a letter at the post office?"

"You know I am." She squinted against the glare and adjusted her slouching sunbonnet's brim. "Did you want to talk about what really happened with Shane? You're obviously holding a lot inside."

"Talking about it won't help, but thanks." For a moment, she looked so sad it nearly brought tears to Earlee's eyes. She swallowed hard, wishing to high heaven her friend was not in too much pain. Meredith turned over the envelope in her hand. "This means I have to tell Mama and Papa."

"Do you think they will forbid you to teach?"

"It would crush me if they did." Meredith might have the prettiest dresses of any girl at school and she had the finest things, but she had sorrows, too.

"You know where I am if you need to talk." Earlee wrapped her arms around her friend, giving her a caring hug. "Come by any time. It's chaos at my house, but you will always be welcome. I'm here to listen."

"You are a treasure, Earlee."

"No, I'm no one special at all." She loved Meredith for thinking so. "Did you want to come with me to the post office?"

"Sure. I've got a few more minutes until Minnie swings back by for me."

"Great." It was nice to have company.

"So, are you going to tell me about him?" Meredith asked. "You haven't mentioned your interest in front of the others, so I haven't said anything. The curiosity is killing me."

"It's nothing like what you and Shane have." She blushed. "It's just a one-sided thing. I'm the one who cares."

"That can be rough. We've both agreed matters of the heart are confusing and complicated."

"And painful." The pain of not knowing, the pain of hoping against hope, the pain of being what she feared was too plain and too average for love. Then there were the constant demands of having a big family whose needs had to be met. What man wanted to put up with that? "Oh, look, there's Minnie. She's caught up to you."

"She can wait for me for a few minutes, if you need to talk."

"No, go on. You have to face your mother sometime. May as well get it over with." She gave Meredith another hug, this time for encouragement. She was grateful for the interruption because she was afraid Meredith would guess about her feelings for Finn. He'd been all she could think about all day, wondering if there would be a letter from him today and if he had been thinking of her.

Her stomach was a jumble of nerves when she stepped into the post office and asked for their mail.

"Nothing for your family," the postmaster commented across the counter.

Nothing? Again?

"Thank you anyway." She pushed away, feeling the first drop of disappointment fall and another. She had been waiting and waiting for a letter. She had to accept the fact none was coming.

It wasn't as if she were in love with him, just a harmless crush. She set her chin, blindly retracing her steps to the door. She knew full well Finn McKaslin did not feel that way for her. So why did the sun dim as she stepped onto the boardwalk? Why did her disappointment feel more like sorrow?

He's all wrong for you, she told herself. *He's four years older, he's in prison and even if he wasn't, he would not be the kind of man your parents would ever approve of.*

But he had so much goodness in him. She hated the possibility that all his goodness might be lost. She'd hoped she could make a difference. It was her Christian duty.

That was what she told herself. And it was all truth. But there was a deeper truth she could not hide from. She had secretly hoped he had been charmed by her letter and would fall in love with her. Foolish and unrealistic, she knew, but a tiny part of her had hoped anyway.

She hated to think that Meredith felt this way, too, crushed and hurting. It was what happened when the fairy tale did not come true. With a sigh, she hiked the strap of her book bag higher on her shoulder and set off down the boardwalk. She had better get moving. She still had Ma's medicine to fetch before heading home.

Every plod of Sweetie's hoofs on the road home reminded Meredith of the man who was missing. It wasn't Shane who sat silent in the seat in front of her, guiding the horse home. It wasn't Shane who drew to a halt in front of the house and held out his hand to help her down. The shadowed depths of the barn did not hide him from her sight. She could not listen for the pad of his step on the walkway or hope for a glimpse of him through the windows as she went about her afternoon. Not even the envelope she clutched in her hand could drag her thoughts from what she had lost.

He was false, she reminded herself. He was not what he'd seemed. But none of that could diminish her grief.

"I'm gonna see if Cook has any cookies to spare."

Minnie dropped her things with a plop on the entry table. "Want some?"

"Not today, cutie." She pushed the dark feelings down and set her things by the front door. "You go on."

"Molasses cookies are my new favorite." Minnie bounced away, skirts flouncing, china knickknacks tinkling on their glass shelves as she skipped by.

"Wilhelmina!" Mama's voice traveled through the reaches of the house. "How many times do I have to tell you? A lady does not run around like a herd of stampeding cattle."

"I'm not running." Minnie bounded through the dining room and out of sight. "I'm skipping."

Poor Mama, working so hard to make ladies out of them, but it was an uphill battle. Meredith eyed the path to the kitchen, where sanctuary awaited her along with a cup of milk and a plate of cookies, but she was a young woman and nearly a high-school graduate. She would behave as one. Clutching her contract, she went in search of her mother.

"Meredith, do come in." In the sun-filled library, Mama looked up from the pages of her book. "The ladies of the club chose Mark Twain for our next meeting, but he's entirely too outrageous. Hardly proper at all. I don't know what the world is coming to."

"It is a wonder," Meredith quipped, slipping into the overstuffed chair opposite her mother. Sunlight poured through the windows and winked in the pond outside, where ducks gathered and quacked, pleased that the trainers had gone from the nearby corral. Did everything have to remind her of Shane? She briefly squeezed her eyes shut, praying to forget him.

"Do you have a headache, my dear girl?" Mama slapped her book closed and dropped it with a thud onto an end table. "I'll have Sadie made a compress and some soothing tea."

"I'm troubled, Mama. That is all." No poultice was going to help with that. She toyed with the edge of the envelope, gathering her courage. "Mr. Olaff offered me a teaching position today."

"And I assume you did not turn him down on the spot?"

"No, this is the employment contract." She ignored the horror on her mother's face and tried to see the concern there. At least Shane had been right about that. She was blessed to have parents who fought so hard to protect her. "I'm asking for your blessing, Mama."

"I simply cannot give it. A daughter of mine working? It's nonsense. You have everything you need right here." She drew herself up, a general in charge of the battle she had resolved to win. "I forbid it. What will Leticia Bell say? Or the Wolfs? Or the Davises? It is not seemly. A young lady does not hire herself out like a teamster's horse for wages. I refuse to allow it."

"Mama, don't you see? I need your approval." She set the envelope aside and took her mother's hand. "I'm no longer a little girl. I'm all grown up. You've done your job."

"It's not done until you are suitably married, young lady." Mama's grip strengthened, holding on, her chin up, her tone nearly shrill, clinging so very tightly to what was past.

Falling in love with Shane had changed her. She could see that now. She understood something she'd never been able to fathom in her mother's overprotective, rigid ways. How very much Mama treasured being a mother, raising her little girls and all the happy times they'd shared. How hard it must be to let that go, as time demands by rolling forward, changing little girls to young women.

"You need to allow me to do this, Mama." She did not bother to hide the abiding affection she had and always would have for her mother. "It's time to let me take the love and the lessons you have given me and make my own way. I promise you, wherever I go it will always lead me back to you."

"I do not think I can bear it." Her mother's lower lip trembled, a rare show of emotion. "You will stay right here where I can take care of you. I demand it."

"I promise to come home for Sunday dinner as often as I can." Her vision blurred. Those pesky tears had returned. She blinked hard, but they fell anyway, one by one rolling down her cheek. "I love you, Mama."

"I love you, my precious Meredith." A single tear betrayed her. "Whatever will I do without you? We will need to get you a sensible horse, one that will not shy at the slightest thing. Perhaps you should take my Miss Bradshaw, she is a very respectable mare. We shall have your father order you your own buggy straight away."

"Thank you." Her throat closed, overwhelmed with gratitude and emotions too powerful to dare speak of.

"I just wish you had more traditional ambitions." Her mother sniffled, swiped at her eyes and sat up straight, in control again. "Are you sure there is no way you can forgive the Connelly boy?"

"You can't help yourself, can you?" Meredith ignored the cannon blast of grief at the sound of Shane's name, fighting not to let it show. "You only liked him when you found out about his family."

"Yes, because that's when I knew he was good enough for my girl."

"Because he is rich." She did not know *that* man—the wealthy senator's son from Virginia. Her gaze drifted to the window and the empty corral beyond. When she thought of Shane, she remembered his dependable goodness, the gentle notes of his baritone, the kind way he treated all manner of animals and people. She loved the country boy who'd won her heart. She missed him with all the depth of her being.

"You decided Mr. Connelly was *not* good enough because he was rich." Mama didn't bother to hide her smile as she reached for her book. "You might think I'm prejudiced, but you are, too, my dear."

"I am not," she denied, too fast and too vehemently.

"Then there's always Lorenzo Davis," her mother suggested.

What if Shane was more like her than she'd imagined, and his stories and his confessions were true? What if the pieces he had left out of the stories he'd told her had nothing to do with rebellion against his controlling family and everything to do with finding his own path? Just as he'd said. He may come from an influential family, but he did not rely on that influence.

It was his social position that had upset her. The

notion that he was a rich man, not a man who trained horses. That he would want a life in society and a wife to go with it, and not a girl who loved the country and wanted to teach small children to read. She had been the one. She had misjudged Shane, and there was no one to blame but herself. Ashamed, she opened the envelope and removed her contract. The carefully scribed pages offered her one dream, but she had lost another—the best one of all.

I have been honest about who I am and what I want. Shane's words came back to her, words she refused to believe were sincere at the time. *I am my own man. Nothing is going to change that.*

She could see the truth. She'd been so afraid of getting hurt, she had closed her heart to him. Now he was gone. There was no way to fix the mistake she'd made. Her grief darkened and deepened, as if to steal all the sunlight and warmth from the summery day—from every summer day to come.

She rose from the chair, clutching her contract and left the room. There was no spring in her step, no joy in her heart. She feared there would never be again.

Chapter Nineteen

"I hate that this party has to end." Meredith gave Fiona a final hug, looking so beautiful in her white muslin gown, simple but sweet. "It was such a beautiful wedding, I doubt any of us could top it."

"It was nothing fancy." Fiona's dark curls bounced as she shook her head, a vision of loveliness, lustrous with happiness. "Just Ian's grandmother and my best friends. Everyone who matters to me."

"It was our honor to have witnessed it." Meredith meant every word. Reverend Hadly had performed the ceremony after the Sunday service, and they'd had a small luncheon party at the little rental, where Ian and Fiona were to make their home together. It was simple to imagine the newlyweds' laughter filling the house like summer breezes.

"You are now a wife." It was Lila's turn to hug Fiona next. "Remember you used to tell us this day would never happen?"

"I do. I vowed never to marry and look at me, I'm the first one of us to be a bride." Fiona hugged Lila back. "Thank you all for being there with me today. As if marrying Ian wasn't enough, having my best friends with me made it a day I will cherish always."

"I wonder who will be the next of us to marry?" Scarlet asked, arms out. She drew Fiona into a quick hug.

"It will be Lila," Earlee guessed. It was her turn to embrace the new bride.

"Yes. Lila will be tallying up the purchases of all the men who come into the mercantile," Kate agreed. "She is bound to catch someone's eye."

"While I'm stuck on the farm all summer. There will be no romance for me." Earlee didn't seem to mind her fate in life, caring for her brothers and sisters and her ill mother. "I do, however, need to live vicariously through all of you."

"I need to do that, too," Ruby announced, hugging Fiona in turn. "I'll be out on the homestead all summer, just me, the pigs and the chickens."

"And I'll be up in the woods where there are no handsome men, just homely ones." Kate rolled her eyes. "Why can't lumberjacks be cute?"

"There must be a law against it," Meredith quipped, leading the way toward the awaiting horses and her new buggy. "Only horsemen seem to be handsome."

"And Lorenzo," Scarlet pointed out.

Lorenzo. Meredith untethered Miss Bradshaw from the hitching post. She could only pray that her mother would not start trying to fix her up with Lorenzo. There was only one man who could fill the void in her soul, only one who was her perfect match and her beloved in every way.

"Goodbye!" Ruby called out from the back of an old

bay gelding. The horse plodded off in the direction of the open prairie.

"I'll see you in church next week!" Kate slid onto the seat of a homemade cart and gathered her mustang's reins.

"Goodbye!" Meredith called out as she directed Miss Bradshaw down the driveway. On the seat beside her, Earlee, Lila and Scarlet leaned over the sides to wave at Fiona, arm in arm with her husband.

"She is a beautiful bride." Lila sighed wistfully. "Doesn't she look so happy?"

"Exultant." Meredith caught one last sight of the couple. What a picture they made. Ian brushed a curl from Fiona's eyes, carefully hooking it behind her ear. The act was more loving and tender than Meredith had ever seen. "They are going to live happily-ever-after beyond all doubt."

"I think so, too," Scarlet agreed.

"Me, too," Earlee chimed in.

"Me, three," Lila added.

Soon they were in town, Lila left in front of her family's store. Scarlet was next, dropped off in front of her home on Third Street. Earlee climbed out at the first crossroads south of town, leaving Meredith alone with a cheery wave. Miss Bradshaw kept her sensible pace as a runaway cow bolted into sight before dashing off into another field. A jackrabbit bursting out of the grasses did not so much as make the mare blink. Meredith wasn't sure when the musical clanking began to accompany the horse's gait until Miss Bradshaw drew up short and tossed her head, clearly deciding it was not prudent to go any farther.

"What's the matter, girl?" Meredith set the brake before clinging out to investigate. Puffs of dust rose up with each step. Temperate winds played with the hem of her skirt as she swished over to the mare.

Not one to withhold her opinion, Miss Bradshaw lifted her back left hoof and gave it a shake to emphasize the problem. A shoe had come quite loose and dangled by all but one little nail.

"Good afternoon, miss." A rumbling baritone startled her from behind. "Looks like you have a problem."

No, it couldn't be. She went icy-cold at the shocking idea. *I'm making it up,* she thought. *I want to see him so desperately, I'm imagining the sound of his voice.* She fisted her hands, doing her best to stay calm. It could not possibly be him. She had spurned him and sent him away. A man would not come back after such rejection.

"Looks like your horse threw a shoe. I can take care of that, miss. No problem." He strolled to her side. His shadow tumbled over her, tall and as substantial as the man.

Shane. She opened her mouth, but nothing happened. No words, not a sound, not even air. Her entire mind erased, as if she had forgotten the English language. She stared, captivated by him—his steadfastness, his determination, his love for her shining in the bluest eyes she had ever seen.

He towered beside her, mighty, rugged and trail-dusty. Her horseman with a black Stetson shading his face, as real as could be. What did this mean? All the terrible things she'd said, the way she'd spurned him and the assumptions she'd made horrified her now.

Surely he had not come back for her, could he? Everything inside her yearned for him to say those words.

She knew it could not be true. No doubt he had returned to Angel Falls for another reason. She had her chance, and she had failed him.

"It won't be the first time I've assisted a pretty country miss on this road." He knuckled back his hat, revealing the striking planes of his face. No dimples, no smile, no hint of softness gentled the hard unforgiving contours. Was he remembering, too, the moment they'd first met? Instant awareness had crashed through her hard enough to wobble her knees.

"This will only take a moment." As if he had no recollection of that day, as if she were a stranger he did not know, he approached the horse. The low notes of his baritone made the horse swivel her ears, eager to tune in. He laid a reassuring hand on the mare's flank. "Good to see you again, Miss Bradshaw. I hope you've been well."

The mare gave a very proper, distinguished nicker and shook her hind hoof impatiently. Clearly she did not appreciate having to wait for a solution to her problem.

"Shane, what are you doing here? Why have you come?" The words came out more strained than she intended. The wind caught them, stealing them away. She watched the impeccable line of his shoulders stiffen.

"Had a few loose ends to tie up." He sounded strained, too. He knelt, took a pair of pliers from his back denim pocket and gently cradled Miss Bradshaw's hoof.

"What loose ends? I wasn't aware you knew that many people in town."

"I don't." He gave the nail a twist and removed the horseshoe. "I got as far as Great Falls before I had to turn back."

"What about your job?"

"I quit." He lowered the mare's hoof gently to the ground. He rose to his full height and patted her on the neck. "There you go, Miss Bradshaw. You are a good girl."

As if that were irrefutable, the mare nodded with great dignity.

"You quit? The job you were so devoted to?" A gold curl tumbled from beneath her sunbonnet, bouncing along the edge of her face, making him remember all the times he'd used it as an excuse to touch her.

"It was time for me to move on." He braced his feet, steeled his resolve. It wasn't easy to face her. She hadn't given him one hint he had a chance with her. With the way she glared at him over this piece of news, it made him leery about offering his heart to her again.

"I suppose it's time to go back to your predetermined life." Her chin shot up a notch. All strength, his Meredith, and spirit. He saw her spirit as clearly as the road at his feet, as the grasses dancing in the wind, as the vulnerability in her gray-blue eyes.

"That's right. Back to you." He strolled toward her, palms sweating, pulse racing as if he'd been fighting a mountain lion. Oh, but it felt good to gaze upon her. To see again the roses in her cheeks, the dear little cleft in her chin, her beauty that sustained him. This was the moment of truth. He could not lose her. He did not know how to win her back. He'd come all this way, given up his apprenticeship, rehearsing what he would say to her with every passing mile.

None of it came to mind. Practiced phrases couldn't help him. Only one thing could.

"Meredith, please forgive me." He put aside his pride, because she was more important. He opened the door to the places within him he liked to keep under lock and key. "I was wrong. I should have told you the whole truth. My only excuse is that you bamboozle me."

"So, it's my fault?"

"Absolutely, darlin'." She had no notion the power she held over him. A man didn't stand a chance. "The first time I set eyes on you, it was like being kicked in the chest by a Clydesdale."

"It was?" Hope, silent but not mute, lit her eyes.

It touched his soul. Hope. She was hopeful. Maybe all was not lost after all. He swallowed hard, encouraged. "I wasn't looking for anything serious. I fought my feelings for you nearly the entire way. But something happened to me when I first gazed upon you. I've never been the same, Meredith. You've changed me, and I can't go on without you."

"But the things I said." She lifted her face to him, raw pain twisting her voice, out of place on this day of bright sunshine and beauty. She took a shaky breath, as if in the worst kind of pain. "I didn't realize until you were gone what I had done to you."

"You did nothing so bad." Everything within him ached to caress the furrow from her forehead, to kiss away her every sorrow. His feet pulled him forward, close enough to see the threads of green and gold in her stormy eyes, to see the silken texture of her creamy skin and the most precious gift he had ever been given—her love revealed.

"I sent you away. I wouldn't believe in you, the man you are." She hiked her chin higher, like a drowning woman going under for the last time. "I didn't forgive you when you asked me, and now it's too late."

"When we got to Great Falls, I told Braden that was as far as I could go. Not one more step. I had to go back." He reached out to brush an errant curl from her face. The caress of his fingertips against her forehead was the sweetest wish. "I had left my heart behind and I couldn't go on without it. Without you."

"Without me? Then it's not too late?" This had to be a dream too wonderful to be true. Her senses filled with him and only him—the scent of dust on his shirt, the warmth of his sun-browned hand, his loving kindness too incredible to believe.

"Too late? No, not as long as you take me back." He folded the lock of hair behind her ear and he did not move away. There in the middle of the road for any passersby to see, he cradled her face as if to cherish every detail, as if he could not look at her enough. "I owe you the truth. We can't go on if I don't."

"What truth?" Her mind had gone fuzzy again. Emotions more powerful than any she'd ever known lifted through her, as if to raise her feet from the ground.

"The things I didn't tell you." He had never seemed stronger than he did with his armor off, his defenses down, vulnerable. "I should have let you closer. I should have let you in. Then there would have been no doubt."

"Hearing the truth from Narcissa did come as a shock."

"I noticed," he drawled in his easygoing manner, but there was nothing easygoing about the steel in his voice, the certainty, the commitment. "The time I lived with my grandmother was the first I'd known of real love. When my father's fortunes reversed and we went back to our lives, I went back to loneliness and impossible expectations and family duty. I went back to friends who had rejected me years before and I could never really trust again. My parents' way of life of manipulation and self-interest left me unable to believe in anyone. Until I met you."

Beneath her palm, she felt his heart beating true.

If it is a dream, Father, please don't let me awaken. Let me stay right here with this man forever. She curled her fingers into his shirt. He was real beneath her fingertips, soft muslin and iron muscle and sun-hot warmth. She had missed him as if he'd been gone a century. She drank in the things she cherished most about him—his dependability, his integrity, his good character.

"I love you, Meredith." He'd said the words before, but this time with a force great enough to bind her to him forever. "I need to know if there is a chance you can ever love me again."

He had to ask? Couldn't he see it? Amazement swirled through her. His hand cradling her face trembled ever so slightly, a betrayal of his fear. She leaned into his touch, savoring the beauty of being held by him.

"There is a chance." She smiled, happiness rushing in. "A very good chance."

"How good?" A tinge of amusement hinted in the corners of his mouth. His heartbeat beneath her fingers slowed.

"One hundred percent." New dreams flashed into her mind, as perfect as could be. She saw a home full of cheer and laughter and calico curtains fluttering at the windows. Rescued horses grazed peacefully in green fields. Their children played happily in the front yard. Dreams only Shane could give her. Shane, towering before her like a gift from heaven, the greatest treasure of all.

"I love you," she confessed. "I love you with all I have."

"As I love you." He leaned closer, impossibly closer, until their breaths mingled. His gaze arrowed to her mouth and her lips tingled sweetly. He did not lean in for a kiss. "I was on my way to ask about a job."

"A job?"

"I hear someone by the name of Worthington is looking for a horse trainer. Figured he might give me a chance. I'd like to be gainfully employed when I ask for your hand in marriage."

"You're proposing to me?"

"Not yet, but I will when the time is right." His chuckle became a kiss, a tender brush of his lips to hers. His kiss was gentle and reverent and fairy-tale perfect.

Overwhelmed, she stepped back, but she could not let go of his shirt, let go of him. She was grateful to God for bringing them together. Love was an entirely new territory, but she had faith that God would see them through.

"C'mon." Shane took her hand. "Let's get you home."

"You know what this means, don't you?" She hardly needed his help into the buggy. Bliss filled her, made her lighter than air. "We have a chance to live happily-ever-after."

"A chance? No, darlin'. There's no chance. It's a certainty. I promise you that."

The sun chose that moment to brighten, as if they were not alone. Birdsong crescendoed, and their melodies carried on a loving wind. The green growing grasses, daisies blooming in the fields, the sky as blue as dreams. Never had the world been so beautiful. Never had she felt so whole. The pieces of her life were coming together, the pattern so beautiful that it hurt the eye to see. She remembered to take a moment to thank God for His gifts before she scooted over on the buggy seat to let Shane take the reins.

* * * * *

Don't miss Jillian Hart's
next Inspirational romance
HIS HOLIDAY BRIDE,
available October 2010 from Love Inspired.

Dear Reader,

Welcome back to Angel Falls. PATCHWORK BRIDE is the second book in my *Buttons & Bobbins* series. When you open these pages, you will revisit old friends from earlier books like the Worthington family from HOMESPUN BRIDE and Finn McKaslin from HIGH COUNTRY BRIDE. The *Buttons & Bobbins* girls are growing up, graduating from high school and adding a new member to their beloved sewing circle. I hope you enjoy revisiting old friends and meeting new ones as much as I have.

PATCHWORK BRIDE is a story I hated to end. Perhaps because I loved the bonds of family Meredith was blessed with and the circle of friends that reminded me of my high-school days. Most of all I loved the tender story of how true love comes to Meredith and Shane in God's time, a great blessing that is a complete surprise. It changes both of them into better people and transforms their lives forever in the most beautiful of ways. I hope you are touched by Meredith's journey, Shane's love for her and their discovery of their dreams for the future. Lila's story is next!

Thank you for choosing PATCHWORK BRIDE.

Wishing you the best of blessings,

Jillian Hart

QUESTIONS FOR DISCUSSION

1. Describe Meredith's first impression of Shane. How does she react? What are the reasons why she doesn't tell him her last name?

2. How would you describe Shane's first impression of Meredith? Why is he drawn to her? What role does his past play in regard to her?

3. What do you think of Henrietta Worthington? Is she a bad character? Is she good?

4. Meredith overhears Shane talking about her and reacts with anger. Why? What is behind her emotions? Has this ever happened to you? How did you handle it?

5. How would you describe Shane's character? The things he does in the book—for instance, the way he treats Minnie—what does this say about him? What are the deeper layers to his character?

7. What is the story's predominant imagery? How does it contribute to the meaning of the story? Of the romance?

8. Meredith looks to God to help her at her turning points and crossroads. When do you see Him in the story? How does He guide her? How does He guide Shane?

9. What role does Meredith's friendships play in the story and the romance?

10. What values do you find in this book? What are the most important ones to you?

11. How does Meredith resolve her conflicts with her mother? What meaning did you find in their conversation? How does it contribute to the larger story?

12. What do you think Meredith and Shane have each learned about love and about themselves? How has love changed them?

13. What role does the patchwork quilt play? What is its greater message?

14. There are many different kinds of love in this story. What are they? What role do they play in the meaning of the book? In Meredith and Shane's romance?

Love Inspired.
HISTORICAL

TITLES AVAILABLE NEXT MONTH

Available September 14, 2010

THE OUTLAW'S BRIDE
Catherine Palmer

DANGEROUS ALLIES
Renee Ryan

LIHCNM0810

REQUEST YOUR FREE BOOKS!

2 FREE INSPIRATIONAL NOVELS
PLUS 2
FREE
MYSTERY GIFTS

Love Inspired

HISTORICAL
INSPIRATIONAL HISTORICAL ROMANCE

YES! Please send me 2 FREE Love Inspired® Historical novels and my 2 FREE mystery gifts (gifts are worth about $10). After receiving them, if I don't wish to receive any more books, I can return the shipping statement marked "cancel". If I don't cancel, I will receive 4 brand-new novels every other month and be billed just $4.24 per book in the U.S. or $4.74 per book in Canada. That's a saving of over 20% off the cover price. It's quite a bargain! Shipping and handling is just 50¢ per book.* I understand that accepting the 2 free books and gifts places me under no obligation to buy anything. I can always return a shipment and cancel at any time. Even if I never buy another book, the two free books and gifts are mine to keep forever.

102/302 IDN E7QD

Name	(PLEASE PRINT)	

Address		Apt. #

City	State/Prov.	Zip/Postal Code

Signature (if under 18, a parent or guardian must sign)

Mail to Steeple Hill Reader Service:
IN U.S.A.: P.O. Box 1867, Buffalo, NY 14240-1867
IN CANADA: P.O. Box 609, Fort Erie, Ontario L2A 5X3

Not valid for current subscribers to Love Inspired Historical books.

Want to try two free books from another series?
Call 1-800-873-8635 or visit www.morefreebooks.com.

* Terms and prices subject to change without notice. Prices do not include applicable taxes. Sales tax applicable in N.Y. Canadian residents will be charged applicable provincial taxes and GST. Offer not valid in Quebec. This offer is limited to one order per household. All orders subject to approval. Credit or debit balances in a customer's account(s) may be offset by any other outstanding balance owed by or to the customer. Please allow 4 to 6 weeks for delivery. Offer available while quantities last.

Your Privacy: Steeple Hill Books is committed to protecting your privacy. Our Privacy Policy is available online at www.SteepleHill.com or upon request from the Reader Service. From time to time we make our lists of customers available to reputable third parties who may have a product or service of interest to you. If you would prefer we not share your name and address, please check here. ☐

Help us get it right—We strive for accurate, respectful and relevant communications. To clarify or modify your communication preferences, visit us at www.ReaderService.com/consumerschoice.

LIH10R

HARLEQUIN®

A Romance

FOR EVERY MOOD™

Spotlight on
Heart & Home

Heartwarming romances
where love can happen
right when you least expect it.

See the next page to enjoy a sneak peek
from Harlequin Superromance®,
a Heart and Home series.

Enjoy a sneak peek at fan favorite Molly O'Keefe's
Harlequin Superromance miniseries,
THE NOTORIOUS O'NEILLS, *with*
TYLER O'NEILL'S REDEMPTION,
available September 2010
only from Harlequin Superromance.

Police chief Juliette Tremblant recognized the shape of the man strolling down the street—in as calm and leisurely fashion as if it were the middle of the day rather than midnight. She slowed her car, convinced her eyes were playing tricks on her. It had been a long time since Tyler O'Neill had been seen in this town.

As she pulled to a stop at the curb, he turned toward her, and her heart about stopped.

"What the hell are you doing here, Tyler?"

"Well, if it isn't Juliette Tremblant." He made his way over to her, then leaned down so he could look her in the eye. He was close enough to touch.

Juliette was not, repeat, *not* going to touch Tyler O'Neill. Not with her fingers. Not with a ten-foot pole. There would be no touching. Which was too bad, since it was the only way she was ever going to convince herself the man standing in front of her—as rumpled and heart-stoppingly handsome now as he'd been at sixteen—was real.

And not a figment of all her furious revenge dreams.

"What are you doing back in Bonne Terre?" she asked.

"The manor is sitting empty," Tyler said and shrugged, as though his arriving out of the blue after ten years was casual. "Seems like someone should be watching over the family home."

"You?" She laughed at the very notion of him being here for any unselfish reason. "Please."

He stared at her for a second, then smiled. Her heart fluttered against her chest—a small mechanical bird powered by that smile.

"You're right." But that cryptic comment was all he offered.

Juliette bit her lip against the other questions.

Why did you go?

Why didn't you write? Call?

What did I do?

But what would be the point? Ten years of silence were all the answer she really needed.

She had sworn off feeling anything for this man long ago. Yet one look at him and all the old hurt and rage resurfaced as though they'd been waiting for the chance. That made her mad.

She put the car in gear, determined not to waste another minute thinking about Tyler O'Neill. "Have a good night, Tyler," she said, liking all the cool "go screw yourself" she managed to fit into those words.

It seems Juliette has an old score to settle with Tyler.
Pick up TYLER O'NEILL'S REDEMPTION
to see how he makes it up to her.
Available September 2010,
only from Harlequin Superromance.

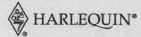

Love Inspired®

Fan Favorite

Janet Tronstad

brings readers a heartwarming story
of love and hope with

Dr. Right

Treasure Creek, Alaska, has only one pediatrician:
the very handsome, very eligible Dr. Alex Haven.
With his contract coming to an end, he plans
to return home to Los Angeles. But Nurse
Maryann Jenner is determined to keep Alex
in Alaska, and when a little boy's life—and
Maryann's hope—is jeopardized, Alex may
find a reason to stay forever.

ALASKAN *Bride* RUSH

Available September wherever books are sold.

Steeple
Hill®

LI87620